THE SUBMARINE EFFECT

An Original Novel

By Norman Ray Fitts

Copyright © 2008

Dedicated to my wife Sally

Whose thoughts and suggestions helped in the telling of this story

Table of Contents

"The world will be...
...what we make of it"

The Submarine Effect

Norman Ray Fitts

ISBN: 978-1438240480

Chapter One: In our not too distant future

The year is Twenty Seventy-three and the world has become an incredibly dangerous place if you happened to be an American. We, as a nation, exerted little influence over what happened outside of our own borders.

If not for the development of a number of renewable energy sources our loss of imported oil would have destroyed our economy years ago. If not for the changes made to our corporate infrastructure the loss of our ability to outsource much of our manufacturing would have ended with the total collapse of our industrial framework. Trade agreements with the Canadians, the establishment of a common currency and the opening of our borders to citizens of both countries actually formed a single community and raised the standard of living for everyone.

In a palatial hall, part of a grand complex located high in the Swiss Alps, plans were finalized and put into motion. The Zealots, who now controlled and dictated to most of humanity, had been patient. When it became clear that no amount of external pressure would bring us into the fold we were placed on a back burner and they went about assimilating the rest of the planet. It had now reached a point where we, and the Canadians, were the only remaining bastions of free thought left in the world.

The beginning of the end began on September eleventh, twenty seventy-three at three a.m. Zulu, military time. The date was definitely symbolic. Two satellites, in orbit two hundred miles up, passed over the North American continent and delivered a massive electromagnetic pulse leaving the Canadians and us deaf and blind to what was coming.

Because of the fear of discovery none of our countermeasures were ever shared with our friends to the north. When the attack came they were left to their own devices. The hope was they had put in place the things needed to preserve their own way of life.

Thirty minutes later the missiles struck. Not a nuclear strike, but a biological one. Every major population area, in the continental United States, Alaska, Hawaii, Canada and the Caribbean was hit with an airborne virus so deadly death came within minutes of breathing it in. The virus was programmed to attack human DNA only leaving the wildlife unaffected. Twenty-four hours later it mutated into a harmless microbe.

Ultra low frequency military broadcast stations, located in Maine and Oregon, were left virtually unaffected due to a contingency plan put in place twenty-five years earlier. No one knew then when the attack would come, or in what form, only that it would.

The air filtration systems, built into the military broadcast stations, the Blue Ridge Mountain complex, and underground sites in Houston, Sioux City, Atlanta and nine other locations held it off.

Keys were turned and buttons were pushed. That sequence of events did not directly launch a retaliatory strike. What it did do was send a flash message to our submarine Commanders at sea. A message that began, "The Submarine Effect has been activated."

Twenty-five Years Earlier
The beginning of the end

The year was twenty forty-eight. The direction the world was taking had become very clear to some.

Jake Taylor, six feet tall, thirty-five years old, with steel gray eyes that looked straight into your soul was about to embark on a journey that would span the next two and a half decades. He was a man with secrets, some of which had to be kept.

Six months earlier Jake was working for a civilian contractor licensed covertly by the U. S. government to conduct search and destroy missions where the government had to remain disassociated.

His current assignment was to seek out, and do whatever was necessary to plug an information leak. It was detected during a random wiretap placed on the private phone lines belonging to Gregory Gleason an information coordinator for a project the government could not afford to have show up in the headlines of the New York Times.

Jake operated with a level eight authorization. Everything above a five sanctioned the use of deadly force. At level eight the use of deadly force was left to the discretion of the operative.

Having listened to the recordings and after reviewing Mr. Gleason's recent financial history it was obvious he was selling us out, but it also indicated why. He had incurred medical expenses involving one of his children and was in danger of losing the treatments required to keep his youngest daughter alive.

Unfortunately the information being leaked to our enemies could result in the deaths of thousands of innocent people. Picking him up was not an option. His arrest could expose a number of enterprises that would endanger, if not destroy, our national security.

Jake sat in his car parked just up the street from the Gleason residence. He was dressed as a utility company service technician. He had observed the family's routine over the past two weeks. This was the morning Gregory's wife would take their other two children to school and their youngest to the medical center for her treatment.

He watched while they said their goodbyes at the door. The wife loaded up her car, pulled out of the driveway and drove out of sight.

Jake slipped on a pair of latex gloves. What he was about to do left a bad taste in his mouth. He left his car and walked up to, and through, the wooden gate leading into the Gleason's back yard. He picked the lock on the back door and entered the house.

Pausing for a moment in the kitchen, he could hear activity up stairs, and then the sound of someone descending the staircase.

He had been in the house once before to decide how to handle what was about to happen next. He watched from the kitchen as Gregory left the staircase and moved toward the front door. He was dressed for work. Jake moved up behind him and popped him with a hand held TASER. Gregory dropped to the floor unconscious in front of the exterior door.

Good, it would look like he was trying to escape, thought Jake.

He went to the kitchen phone, removed the cover and attached a very small sparking device to the ring tone generator and then replaced the cover. The home used gas for cooking and heating. He then went to the oven and extinguished the pilot light. With that, he left the house and returned to his parked car. As far as he could tell no one had taken any notice of him.

Ten minutes later he pulled away from the curb and drove past the house. He used a disposable cell phone to place a call. The resulting explosion blew out the front of the house and set fire to it.

The explosion immediately brought people out of their homes. Several were already on their cell phones calling for help. .

Gregory's wife and children were innocent victims in all of this. Jake had used his influence, and personal resources, to insure the ailing child would be taken care of.

*   *   *

Jake's next assignment took him to an office in a high-rise building. The room had no furnishings other than the chair he occupied. He sat for, what seemed to him to be an inordinate amount of time; too much time. As he stood to leave, the door opened and two men entered. The man on the right carried a portfolio.

7

The man on the right said, "Sorry for the wait. Would you please sit down?" He closed the door.

Jake glanced around. "There doesn't seem to be enough chairs."

The man on the right motioned to the chair. Jake considered the two men for another moment and then returned to his seat.

The other man stood off to the left. Jake addressed the man on the right. "What's the assignment?"

Without saying anything, the man on the right handed Jake the portfolio.

Jake opened it and began to read through the contents. After the first couple of pages he looked up. "Are you kidding?"

"I assure you, we are anything but kidding. Please finish. If you have any questions you may ask them then."

Jake read through the rest of the documents. When he finished he closed the portfolio. "Assuming this is for real, why me?"

The man on the right reached out and Jake handed him back the portfolio. He then turned and took a step away. "Mr. Taylor you have quite a resume. You work in the shadows and maintain a very private lifestyle. You have proven time and time again that you will do whatever is necessary to complete the job at hand. We assume your success stems from the fact that you truly believe in what you're fighting for. We have also seen you show compassion to those who deserve it." He held the portfolio away from him. "The mission contained in here may well be the most important assignment ever entrusted to a living human being. What I have to know right now is, are you interested?"

Jake had long depended on his ability to read other people. To know when they were sincere and believed in what they were saying. He didn't hesitate. "I'm in," was Jake's answer.

"Very good." The man on the right turned to face Jake. "Then let's go. There's a lot to do."

Jake stood and glanced at the man on the left. "He doesn't say much. What's his part in all this?"

The man on the right moved toward the door. "His part was to handle the situation, had you said no."

Jake smiled. He could try, Jake thought.

Over the next six months Jake found himself involved in what could only be deemed, pure science fiction.

*   *   *

When it all finally came together it brought Jake back to another nondescript hallway leading to an unmarked door in a high-rise office building. A card reader, located on the right side, controlled the lock. He swiped the card in his hand. The lock, securing the door, released. The pneumatic system that sealed the room opened the door.

He entered and the door resealed itself. Jake stood and took in the room. Five people sat around an oblong, stainless steel table.

Janet Crowley, twenty-eight years old, with short-cropped auburn hair, bright emerald green eyes and lashes most women would kill for carried a PhD in Psychology. She specialized in the effects of long-term confinement on the human ability to function as a team. She had designed most of the protocols in use by both the Space Program and the US Submarine Service. She had authored half a dozen books on the subject.

Next to her sat Christopher Wincrest, thirty-seven years old. His six-foot tanned physique said *beach volleyball* when in fact he had graduated in the top two percent of MIT's school of engineering. For most of his career he had specialized in robotics and containments designed to handle the long-term effects of deep-sea exposure and pressure. His designs were already in wide spread use throughout the oil and gas industry and on occasion had found their way into some shadowy U.S. military projects.

Next to him, leaning back in his chair, sat Jonathan Chambers, forty-two years old. His salt and pepper, close-cropped hair added detail to his weathered facial features. The oldest of the group he'd spent most of his professional life outdoors. He was a logistical engineer specializing in supply chains and the long term planning required to keep a large population fed and functioning. It was his strategic use of both staging, and coordinated surface and aerial delivery systems that kept a town of over one hundred thousand from starving after a massive earthquake had isolated it from the rest of the world.

Next to him sat Peter Arnest, twenty-seven, one hundred and thirty pounds soaking wet, and the youngest of the group. Peter, half African-American and half Korean, was at the other end of the physical spectrum from Jonathan. His soft features reflected a career spent indoors. He was an environmentalist specializing in the long-term effects of nuclear contamination on the ecosystem. He had also published a number of widely read articles on the long-term effects of global warming. It wasn't until environmentalists, and researchers from around the world had settled on one message, Peter's message, and delivered it in one loud voice, that the industrialized nations of the world finally stepped back and took a long, revealing look at themselves.

Rounding out the group was Clinton Potts, thirty-five years old, with shoulder length blond hair. His distinctive one blue eye and one brown eye gave him a face that was hard to forget. He possessed a level of nervous energy noticeable even when he was sitting still. A nuclear engineer specializing in clean, nuclear power applications, it was his research and development that had produced the current generation of nuclear propulsion systems used by both the maritime service and the military.

Peter had taken the stand that the phrase "clean nuclear" was an oxymoron, and looked at Clinton as another reason he was along for the ride.

These five people were the best in the world, in their chosen fields. Each had been contacted. Having shown an interest, they had survived a highly detailed interview process, background check, and security scan that went back several generations.

The final question that required a *yes* was put to each of them individually. Knowing what's at stake, can you commit to a time line that could extend for years? Their presence at the table indicated their answer.

Janet glanced around the table and then at Jake, "Well, I'm guessing from the way we were extracted from our everyday lives, it's a go."

Everyone around the table waited for Jake's response. "For the next three years we answer to no one but the President," he said. "And even he doesn't have enough clearance to get some of the answers."

Janet stood up. "Well then, lead on McDuff."

Jake wasn't a scientist. He was a facilitator. It had been his job to put this team together and then make sure any obstacle they might encounter went away. If the world he knew stood any chance of survival it was with the five people in this room with him today. He swiped his card again. The door reopened. Everyone else got up and left the room past Jake who then followed them out.

*   *   *

The Gulf of Mexico was calm today. Five large, sea-going commercial tugs pushed, and pulled, a massive oil well platform toward a predetermined set of coordinates. Jake was on the bridge of one of the two tugs up front. He stood and looked out across the bow while the tug's captain used GPS equipment to confirm their location.

"We're here," the Captain announced.

Jake didn't answer, but continued to gaze out the bridge port.

The Captain picked up a mike and keyed it. "Back 'em down and hold this position."

The tugs, pushing the rig, backed off. The slack came out of the steel cables attached to the bow. The water behind the tugs began to churn as the forward motion of the rig began to slow. The two tugs up front swung around and added their power in an effort to overcome the forward momentum of a hundred thousand tons of floating hotel.

Janet and the others were having a late breakfast around the galley table. With the change in motion and direction Janet got up and left the room. A couple of minutes later she returned. "Come on guys we're here."

They all got up as one and left the galley.

The team moved toward the bow and watched as the tugs maneuvered to bring the platform into position.

"It messes with your mind, just imagining something that big could float," said Clinton.

"It's just a matter of displacement," answered Chris. "As long as..."

"I know what makes it float."

"Then why the question," asked Chris?

"It wasn't a question. It was an observation."

Over the past few weeks Chris and Clinton had become friendly adversaries, which had taken on the form of frequent verbal sparring.

Clinton and Chris faced off. "It sounded like a question," Chris insisted.

Clinton countered. "And how would you know what a question sounds like when *your* opinion is the only one that counts?"

Janet stepped in "It floats, okay... Jesus, you two are worse than an old married couple."

Clinton started to respond. Janet put up a finger. He glanced at Chris, grinned and turned away to watch the platform.

Chris started to reinforce his position. Janet cut him off as well. "You too." She then took up a position between them while Peter and Jonathan quietly laughed at the whole thing.

The little flotilla rose and fell with the gulf waters thirteen thousand feet above the Sigsbee Abyssal plain, the deepest part of the Gulf. Securing the platform at this depth was not a problem. Existing technology could handle greater depths. The tricky part was yet to come.

The tugs kept the platform in place while the technicians went about securing it to the bottom using a modified retractable gravity base system combined with dynamic positioning. Several days later the people and supplies were transferred over from the tugs.

*　　*　　*

The specially modified rig was three hundred feet square and nine stories tall. Jake, and the rest of the group, moved over to the railing. The steel deck they stood on was ninety feet above the water.

Chris chanced a look over the edge. His knuckles were white as he griped the railing. "Whew, that's a long way down." He pushed himself back. His quick breathing gave notice to his slight feeling of panic inside.

Clinton grinned. "A little green around the gills, are you?"

Chris cut his eyes at Clinton. "We'll see who grows gills when you're two and a half miles down and the only thing between you and a billion tons of water, is my little creation."

"Well," Clinton mused. "By the time that happens I'll know if it works, or I'll be comforting your girlfriend for her loss."

Janet was fed up. "Now look you two, in case it's escaped you both we have a single purpose here, and that's to make sure all of mankind has a future. When we're done with that, you two can tear each other's heads off for all I care. But until then, just *stuff* it."

Chris and Clinton just stared, neither one wanted to challenge the look in her eye.

She turned away, and then looked back. "Well?"

The two men quickly moved up, one on each side of her. They all three walked back toward the hatch leading inside. Behind her back, Chris offered up his thumb. Clinton accepted the challenge and the thumb fight was on.

Chris was losing the thumb war and said, "I agree with you, she's kinda cute when she's pissed."

She punched at Clinton causing him to break contact with Chris's thumb thus forfeiting the match. They both stopped and suppressed a laugh into a tight grin. Janet finally realized they had been having fun at her expense and stormed inside.

Jake had watched the proceedings from the railing. The next three years were going to be anything but dull, he thought.

*   *   *

The living quarters were very Spartan. This cabin had an attached bathroom. Jake sat at a desk and flipped through a lot of paperwork compiling the information he would need for the next day. There came a knock on the door.

"Yes, come in."

The door opened and Janet stood in the doorway with a clipboard in her hand, taking in the room. "Well I guess rank really does have its privileges."

He glanced over. "What?"

She stepped in. "The bathroom. I have to share the one down the hall with fourteen guys, oh yeah, I forgot, we're at sea. It's a *Head* and it's down the *passageway*." She closed the door behind her.

He grinned. "Well, isn't that what you do? Figure out ways to co-exist in small, confined spaces."

"I guess *raise the toilet seat and then put it back down* is as good a place to start as any."

He grinned again and pointed to a chair.

She sat. "I looked at the roster a few minutes ago." She flipped through the top couple of pages on her clipboard. "Counting construction, engineering, support personnel and the members making up our team we're looking at two hundred and fifty people."

"Logistics?"

"It's in place. Jonathan said the first of the barges are due on site tomorrow afternoon. There're loaded with provisions and equipment. After that, the people." She fidgeted in her seat for a moment and then asked? "Are we really gonna be able to keep this a secret?"

"The future of our way of life, hell, the future of mankind could depend on it."

"With real time satellite surveillance I just don't see how they won't..."

14

"...Spot an oil platform anchored on top of the single larg-est oil reserve that exist in the Gulf of Mexico. You could say we're hiding it in plain sight if they don't look too close."

She flashed a quick smile and got up. "Guess I'll see you at breakfast."

"I guess," he said as he watched her walk to the door. "Hey..." She looked back. "If you want, you can use the shower in here."

She smiled an easy smile. "Thanks..." She opened the door and left.

He watched the door for a moment. In the weeks that pre-ceded this moment he had become quite fond of Janet. As pleasant as the thought might have been, he would never allow himself to become involved with anyone working for him. He knew full well, in his line of work, there might come a time when he'd have to make a choice between the good of the project and her. He went back to his paperwork.

*   *   *

The next day Jake and Chris stood on an elevated deck and watched the last of the supplies and equipment being off loaded onto the platform from a flotilla of barges.

Chris was still a little uneasy with the height. He took a deep breath. "The submersibles are coming on the next trip."

"How deep have you taken them?"

"For security reasons, we weren't able to test them any-where near the construction site. The field test took them down to eight thousand feet and kept them there for ten hours. The equip-ment isn't what concerns me."

"What then?"

"The construction teams will be breathing a special oxy-gen-nitrogen compound mixed with an enzyme that will raise their internal body temperature several degrees. It's the only way we can combat the cold long enough to have any hope of completing this on time."

"These guys are Navy SeaBees," Jake said. "They've worked under extreme conditions before."

"Not this extreme. No one has ever done this before. We have to allow enough time with the assent, for the atmospheric change to flush out the enzyme."

Jake sensed this was going somewhere. "What else?"

"Well, the tests were clean, but ten hours at eight thousand feet is not ten hours at thirteen thousand feet."

"Okay?"

Chris hesitated thinking about what he wanted to say next.

Jake was tired of the bush Chris was beating around. "Come on. Spit it out."

"I wanna take one down for a field test here, before we put all of our eggs in this one particular basket."

Jake considered the request for a moment, and then answered. "I'll agree to the test but not with you."

"I helped designed it. If something goes wrong no one understands the systems better than I do."

"That's exactly why I can't let you go. This isn't an experiment we can abandon if something doesn't work. You were picked because you're the best at what you do. There's no replacing you. If something goes wrong, I need you up here not trapped down there. Set up the test. Teach someone whatever they need to know to pilot it down and back up."

Chris knew there was no arguing the point and slowly turned away toward the hatch. Making decisions about who lived, and who might die, wasn't part of his resume. But then constructing a city almost two and a half miles under water wasn't part of anyone's.

Chapter two: Will they work

The glow of the morning sun had begun to lighten the eastern horizon when the barges arrived carrying the construction mules, twelve in all. Each side of the platform had a crane that was used to lift and place the mules onto a deck that spanned all four sides of the structure.

These one-of-a-kind, thirty-foot long submersibles were a marvel of engineering. Each were fitted with two sets of manipulator arms one set forward and one set aft. These arms would be used to maneuver and fit together the components that would become New Atlantis. Their hulls were made of a new alloy, Tiridium the same alloy that would form the dome for this city under the sea. Capable of withstanding pressures up to five million pounds per square inch and being one-third the weight of aluminum, Tiridium made this whole project possible.

Because of the down time and extreme pressures, any type of view port was subject to failure. There was no room for error. Even external cameras or lights could implode at that depth. To solve this problem a completely new technology had been developed.

ViewScan came into being. This highly evolved sonar system sent sound pulses through the pressure hull and into the sea three hundred and sixty degrees in all directions. Those impulses were then returned and received by special sensors located just under the pressure hull. A very sophisticated piece of software converted those impulses into a color representation of everything within a hundred yards of the sub. Six external maneuvering thrusters provided propulsion. The housings were made from the same alloy as the hull and commands were radioed to them from inside thus eliminating the need for hull penetrations. The four grasping arms were also radio controlled.

Chris had no problem finding a volunteer to make the dive.

Andrew Morehead, twenty-six, was part of Damage Control Services for the platform. Everything from firefighting to a leaky toilet fell under their jurisdiction. He was also an experienced diver and loved to wind surf.

Chris spent two days teaching Andy to handle the mule in a series of shallow water dives.

*   *   *

The morning of the test brought everyone out. It was apparent that Chris was nervous and it showed in his body language. Jake and the rest of the team, and forty odd others, filled the platform railings. The only one who appeared perfectly calm was Andy.

Chris gave a last briefing. "You really shouldn't have to do much."

"Piece-a-cake," came the answer.

"Any questions?"

"No sir, this thing pretty much drives itself. I'm just along for the ride."

"Okay..."

Andy climbed aboard, dropped through the hatch and pulled it shut. The diver on top made sure the hatch was secured and signaled the crane. Everyone watched as the mule was lifted and swung out over the water. A few moments later it entered the sea. The lifting cable went slack and the diver disconnected it. The crane brought the diver back on board. The thrusters came to life and the mule began to circle.

Chris, Jake and the other team members entered the heart of the command center. From here they would coordinate every move of the monumental task that lay ahead. At any one time six

18

of the mules would be down. Each would have a crew of three, a pilot and one forward and one aft to manipulate the arms. For safeties sake everyone was qualified as a pilot.

Six consoles were set up to mimic exactly, the control centers on the mules. From here they could monitor what the crews were seeing, the interior, the vessel's systems and the bio-signs of the crew. Piloting could also be transferred, and the mule could be remotely operated from the command center.

Chris sat at the console. "Check list complete?"

A filtered response came back. "Yes sir. Waiting for permission to proceed."

Chris took a deep breath, glanced around at everyone.

Jake broke the silence. "Take it down."

Chris spoke into his headset. "Proceed, maintain an open mike."

"Understood," came the response.

The water around the mule erupted as the ballast tanks were opened and seawater replaced the air. The submersible slipped below the surface. In a few moments it was gone into the crystal blue depths of the Gulf.

*   *   *

The ten-hour shifts did not include the trip down and back up. That would extend the time in the vessel to closer to seventeen hours. The crew would then be given a seventy-two hour down time to recover.

After the launch the others began to drift away. There were still preparations to complete before the arrival of the construction personnel who would populate this manmade island for the next three years.

Chris remained to monitor the mule and its lone occupant. There wasn't much to see during most of the descent. As the light faded, the ViewScan system began to do what it was designed to do. A joystick allowed for a three hundred and sixty degree view in every direction around the small sub. A digital representation of the occasional inhabitant of this watery world passed in and out of view.

The Sigsbee Abyssal Plain is a deep, flat portion of the Gulf bottom located northwest of Campeche Bank. In this relatively uniform area of the Gulf bottom, the Sigsbee Knolls and other small salt domes represented the only major topographical features. This made it the perfect place to locate what might be the only surviving members of the human race. In many minds the only outcome would be a thermonuclear exchange that would lay waste to the entire surface of the planet. This complex was designed to keep its population alive, and virtually unapproachable until it was safe to return to the surface.

At first the cold penetrating the mule had its effect on the pilot. Then the enzyme took hold and the effects of the cold began to subside. It would take two hours to reach the bottom. With higher concentrations of oxygen being used it was decided that a heating system would just add to the possibility of fire and the electronics preferred the colder environment anyway.

Janet popped in with a sandwich on a plate and a canned Drink. "How's it goin? Thought you could use something about now."

He took the plate. "Thanks, does *watching grass grow* have any meaning for you?"

She laughed. "That's good, I guess."

He looked in the sandwich. "Peanut butter and grape jelly. My favorite."

He sat the plate and the drink aside and picked up a case and opened it. Inside was a chessboard and the pieces. "I found out he likes to play chess. I sent his board down with him. It'll keep us both from going stir crazy." He began to set it up.

"Okay, I'll leave you two to your game. If you need anything just buzz me."

"If you don't mind, come back in about three hours and let me stretch my legs."

"You got it." With that she left.

Chris ate his peanut butter and jelly sandwich while Andy sampled the rations that would be served on the subs for the duration of the construction project.

Chess occupied them for the next few hours. Chris had to admit his opponent was quite good. The game was being used for more than just entertainment. It was also a test to see how prolonged exposure to this hostile environment would affect someone's ability to concentrate on the task at hand. The fact that Chris was down three games to five answered that question.

Janet was as good as her word and showed up to relieve him for a few minutes. He took a turn outside. The sea breeze and warmth from the sun felt good.

The next step in this test would tell the tale. Returning to the surface was the key. The concentration level of the enzyme used at eight thousand feet was lighter than that used at thirteen thousand feet.

Chris looked at the chronometer. It was moving up on ten hours on the bottom. In addition to the chess games Andy had performed several maneuvers not only to test the equipment at that depth, but also to allow for a level of activity on his part. Everything had performed according to specs.

Jake and Jonathan entered the command center. Chris was writing some things down.

Jake spoke up. "About time to bring him up?"

Chris looked around. "Yeah, just making a few notes."

The screen showed the inside of the sub, but not Andy. "Where's our pilot?" Injected Jonathan.

Chris put away his clipboard. "When you gotta go, you gotta go."

When you're down for eighteen hours nature can come calling so a small-enclosed chemical toilet was provided.

The three men watched as Andy stepped into view. The image jerked once, and then all hell broke loose.

The interior view flipped over and over. All telemetry was momentarily lost. As quickly as the screens blacked out they were back. From the view on the monitor it was obvious the sub was

21

upside down. Andy lay on his back against the top of the cabin. He wasn't moving but the telemetry showed he was alive.

Chris quickly transferred control of the mule over to him and tried to get a response from the ship. "What the hell was that?"

Jake was right behind him. "Can you bring it up?"

"It's not responding!" There was panic in his voice.

Jonathan reached for a place on the control panel. "Just blow the ballast."

Chris pushed his hand away just in time. "No!"

Jonathan started to protest. Chris cut him off. "If we blow the ballast it might not even work, but if it did..."

Jake interrupted. "It would bring him up too fast."

"Yes," Chris continued. "The enzyme in his system would burn him up from the inside."

Jonathan was at a loss. "Then, what do we do?"

Chris looked at Jake and then switched to the intercom. "Prep another mule." Before Jake could say anything. "He's my responsibility. Even if the sub's intact the re-oxygenating system won't last long enough to train anyone else." Chris started for the hatch, paused and glanced back. "And if you need another reason. We can't afford to lose the mule." With that he was gone.

Jonathan and Jake stared at the open hatch. Jonathan broke the silence. "The Seabee's could recover the mule."

Jake started out. "Yes, they could."

*　　*　　*

It took a couple of hours to get the mule ready to launch. A harness had to be attached to the aft arms. Everyone was on deck and doing what they could to speed up the process. Even Peter, who had kept pretty much to himself, helped do what he could. The time was here. A diver stood next to the hatch ready to lock it down from the outside.

Chris keyed the walkie in his hand. "How's it look?"

"Everything's in the green," came the response.

Chris was ready to climb aboard when Clinton walked up. "I'm coming with you."

"Like hell."

"Like hell, you can't fly this thing and use those arms at the same time."

Chris looked up at the deck above. Jake was talking with others. "Jake will never let us both go."

"Jake's busy." Clinton climbed to the hatch and slipped in.

Chris stopped him when he asked, "Who's gonna comfort my girlfriend?"

"You actually have one," said Clinton with raised eyebrows?

Chris took a step up, onto the mule. "You talk to your sister lately?"

Clinton grinned; he'd give that one to Chris, and ducked inside.

Chris smiled, and then glanced up at Jake still too busy to notice. If this little stunt, Chris thought, doesn't kill us, he will.

Chris climbed up and lowered himself into the hatch. He paused and looked up at Jake. "Hey," he shouted.

Jake looked down. Chris gave him a thumbs-up. Jake returned it. Chris slipped inside and closed the hatch.

Jake, and the others moved back inside. The diver checked the hatch cover, made a circling motion with his index finger and the crane took the slack out of the cable.

Inside Chris stepped off the ladder and looked around. The pilot sat on an elevated deck above the forward arm handler's position. Most of the interior was covered with instrumentation that monitored every aspect of the mule. At thirteen thousand feet, if you couldn't find and solve the problem roadside assistance could be a long time coming.

Clinton was wrong about one thing. The control center on the platform could have maneuvered the mule while Chris used the arms.

Chris quickly glanced around. "Clinton, where the hell are you"?

The door to the Head pushed open. Clinton sat on the toilet, grinning, showing a thumbs-up.

"Idiot," Chris said and closed the door.

Chris hadn't put up much of an argument about Clinton coming along. He much preferred piloting the ship himself while someone *onboard* used the arms.

* * *

Inside the control center Jake, Peter, Janet, Jonathan and several others stood behind the Console Operator and watched Chris settle into the pilot's seat.

The crane picked up the mule and swung it out over the Gulf. The diver gave the hand signal and the mule was lowered into the water.

The sea was running one to two feet and the interior of the mule moved with the water. Chris ran through a checklist and brought everything on line.

"Cable is clear, free to submerge," came across his headset.

Chris responded. "Check list complete all systems in the green."

"Transferring control. Good luck," came the Console Operator's voice.

"Thanks."

Jake's face appeared on the screen in front of him. "Hey buddy, everybody's here. It's gonna take you several hours to make the descent. Andy's vitals are still good. He hasn't moved. We're gonna analyze the data and the video and try and figure out what happened. I'll let *you* know as soon as *we* know."

"Thanks," Chris responded.

Janet's face appeared on the screen. "This stuff is all state-of-the-art. Even the contingencies have contingencies. We'll have you both back in no time."

"I'm not worried." He lied.

She glanced around, and then back. "Now I'm gonna go find Clinton and give him a piece of my mind. He could have at least hung around long enough to see you off."

Chris offered a quick smile. "See you in about ten hours." I hope, he thought.

They were still receiving the locator beacon from the disabled mule. Chris set the autopilot to home in on the beacon and sound an alarm when they were two hundred yards away. He then left the command seat to retrieve the stowaway on the pot. Clinton had to master the use of the arms.

*   *   *

Peter had gone back to his cabin to work on his scenarios. It wasn't that he wasn't worried about Chris it was just his way of dealing with stress. Jake and the others gathered around the console monitor in the control center reviewing the images recorded by ViewScan just before whatever happened; happened.

Jake sat at the console and used the joystick to slowly move the view in a three hundred and sixty degree circle. At about two hundred and seventy degrees everyone took a quick breath.

Approaching the sub was a giant, translucent worm-like creature. At a guess, it was ten feet in diameter and at least one hundred feet long. The image consumed the screen, and then crossed over the sub. For the next few moments the scene was one of green slime and bottom debris, and then the image cleared. Jake moved the joystick. ViewScan was still functioning. One of the thrusters lay a few feet away obviously torn loose by the encounter. He moved the stick again and the image shifted until it picked up the creature moving away, out of range.

Janet was the first to comment. "I don't think it attacked the mule. I think it was in its path, and it crawled over it."

Jake answered. "I think you're right, but we can't have those things crawling back and forth through the construction site."

"Maybe," Jonathan suggested. "We can fit a couple of the mules with a way to deliver an electrostatic discharge. That might discourage them."

Jake flipped his display over to the rescue mule. "Maybe, but Chris needs to know about this."

The seat in front of the flight center came into view. It was empty. Jake began to scan the cabin. He settled on Chris and Clinton working with the arm controls.

25

"No wonder I couldn't find him," Janet said. "I thought he was hiding in the John or something."

Chris and Clinton worked with the controls unaware they were being watched until Jake broke the silence in Chris's headset. "You're both grounded when you get back."

Chris jumped and looked at the screen in front of the flight center. Jake's face was looking back.

"Don't blame me," Chris came back. "I found him hiding in the head."

He could hear Janet laughing in the background. "What's so funny?"

"I'll tell you when I see you," came her reply.

Chris justified Clinton's presence, and then listened and watched as Jake passed along the details, and the video, of the encounter.

Along with its imaging capability, ViewScan functioned as a state-of-the-art conventional sonar receiver using both sound and water displacement. Chris set it to issue a warning if it picked up movement within a quarter of a mile of its location. He went back to teaching Clinton to use the arms. The rest of the decent was uneventful.

*   *   *

Chris had already returned to the seat in front of the flight center before the beacon alarm went off. The monitor showed the damaged mule directly in front of them about fifty yards away. It was upside down but appeared to be intact except for the severed thruster pod.

Andy would have died instantly if the pod had been attached directly to the cabin and had ripped a hole in its pressure hull. These attachments were designed to break away in case of a collision, or in this case an encounter with a really big worm.

Chris called the command center. "We're here, how's he doin' in there?"

Janet came back. "His vitals are still good but he hasn't moved. All of this is tied to medical. They're concerned that he's been out so long. What's *your* next move?"

"Well, first we've gotta flip the mule over. Once that's done we've gotta secure the harness around it and then lighten it. That's the tricky part."

Janet broke in. "Here's Jake."

Jake took her place in front of the monitor. "I take it you haven't detected any large creepy-crawly inhabitants of the deep?"

"No," came Chris's response. "Can we determine what is, and isn't, working over there?"

Jake looked to his right for a few moments, and then back. "Best we can tell the only thing that *isn't* working is propulsion."

"Okay, I need you to use the emergency override to transfer systems control over to you. I'm gonna have to flip it over. After that, whatever happens next will decide the ending we're gonna have."

"We're standing by," came the response.

Using ViewScan to guide him, Chris eased his mule in close. Looking back over his shoulder. "Okay, we have to use the harness to roll it over. We'll take it slow. There's no tellin' what condition the hull is in. If it fails, and implodes, the atmosphere inside could vent with enough force to take us with it."

Clinton, to himself, "Now he tells me."

"What?"

"Nothing. Just get me closer."

The rescue mule moved in. The thruster pod on the far side was intact. The mule moved over the damaged vessel. The arms were used to attach the harness to the intact propulsion pod. The trick was to slowly lift the mule, and hope the pod's breakaway struts could handle the maneuver. Then, using the harness, bring it over and let it slowly back down. There was a collective sigh of relieve when the damaged mule rocked into an upright position.

Andy had rolled over and now a wound on the left side of his head was visible. His vital signs were weak, but stable.

Clinton detached the harness and Chris pulled the mule back. He then moved them back into position so Clinton could attach the harness to the lifting eyelets on the nose of the mule.

Jake watched the monitor. Chris reappeared and said, "There's no way this mule can lift the other one with its ballast tanks full. Under normal conditions the computer controls the assent, but with the engines offline the program has shut down."

"I see. We have to release enough ballast to make the mule buoyant."

"Yes," but here's the trick," answered Chris. "Because of the weight of the water on top of it you'll have to release a lot of it. And then as we start up you will have to keep adjusting the ballast to allow us to provide the power."

"Don't worry," Jake said. "We'll handle it on this end."

Chris continued. "You won't have to worry about the enzyme mix. Fortunately the program that controls that runs independent of the other one. It's controlled by the amount of water sensed above the mule, the duration clock and the water temperature. Okay, on the control console you'll see a section labeled assent. The tanks should be reading one hundred percent. Above the readouts you'll see a three-position switch. Move it to the center. That will let you drain both tanks at the same time."

Jake took a deep breath. "Here goes."

He moved over to the console controlling the damaged mule. The override had taken control from the pilot's console on the damaged mule and moved it to an identical set of controls in the command center. One section was labeled ASSENT. There were two ballast tanks. Both were reading one hundred percent. Jake found the switch and moved it. Above that switch was a button labeled DRAIN and another button labeled BLOW.

Jake moved back to the monitor. "Okay it's done."

"Okay, above the switch is a button labeled drain. When you press it the tanks will drain, I hope. The readout will change by percent. When the mule starts to rise I'll tell you to stop."

Everything paused for a moment. The silence was deafening. Then Jake said, "Here goes."

He pressed the button. Both percentages began to drop, ninety-nine, ninety-eight and so on. Jake stared at the gages. They kept going down into the seventies and then the sixties and then the fifties.

Chris's voice broke his concentration. "Okay, it's moving."

Jake let off the button. The tanks were reading forty-six percent. He moved back to the monitor. Chris was there. "Bring her up. I'll stay with the ballast controls."

"Here we go," came Chris's response.

Inside the rescue mule ViewScan showed it all. Chris had to override the assent system in his mule in order to control the assent of the other one. At this point they were all headed home. The journey back took eight uneventful hours.

Chapter three: Construction begins

When both mules broke the surface the divers attached the lifting cables. The harness was released and the damaged mule was brought aboard first. As soon as it touched the deck, the hatched was released and Andy, unconscious, was removed and taken to the infirmary.

When the second mule was recovered the hatch was released and Chris pulled himself out. The entire roster of personnel was manning the railings. Jake, Janet, Peter and Jonathan stood on the platform outside the command center. Jake started clapping his hands. A moment later all hell broke loose with clapping, shouts, cheers and whistles. It was a moment that Chris would relive in his mind for the rest of his life.

* * *

The arriving SeaBees had a long and glorious history with the naval military. It stood for Construction Battalion or "C" "B". Their insignia was a worker bee with wings and a sailor's hat. They came into being at the beginning of World War Two. Formed from civilian contractors, they were given military training so they could defend what they built and if captured would be treated as prisoners of war. They were used extensively to repair, or construct airfields on the Pacific islands to support our march to Japan. Since that time they've been an integral part of military operations all over the world.

The SeaBee Commander was Commander Edward Willingham. If Jake had been expecting a spit and polish Naval Commander the man who stepped aboard the platform was anything but. At six-two, two hundred and twenty pounds with kaki pants and a plaid shirt he *looked like* what he was, a construction foreman. Jake liked the man the moment he met him.

Commander Willingham was career military. His father and grandfather had enjoyed long and illustrious careers extending back past the turn of the century. They had both attained the rank of Master Chief Petty Officer the highest of the enlisted ranks.

At the age of nineteen Commander Willingham had begun his career as a seaman on the deck force of a destroyer and then went on to complete the educational requirements to apply to Officer Candidate School. With the help of his father he got the sponsorship he needed and became the first in his family to make the jump to the commissioned officer ranks.

The day he graduated the first words from his father were, "So you're tired of working for a living." He followed that with a salute and a grin.

In the case of Commander Willingham nothing could have been farther from the truth. He had gone on to get his degree in structural engineering and then applied that to the path he wanted to follow, commanding a Construction Battalion.

When it came time for this assignment his name was one of only three that came under consideration. With a record of getting things done in the face of any odds, and the solid ties his family had to the service, the choice was easy and he hadn't hesitated a moment in accepting the command. After all, they were going to build something the likes of which the world had never seen and in fact never would.

The first time the Commander, Jake and Jake's team sat down in what served as a conference room, Jake filled him in on the encounter with the worm. This contingency had already been considered and he planned to arm all the mules with an experimental electronic pulse weapon designed to use the water itself as a projectile.

His maintenance crews had been supplied with an onboard state-of-the-art repair facility to maintain the mules and every other piece of equipment on the platform. The first order of business was to repair the one they had already managed to break.

The Commander placed a case on the table. He removed and passed out folders to each of Jake's team.

"In those folders are the project requirements for each of your specialties," said the Commander. "Solutions have to be found and policies and procedures have to be written."

Each member of Jake's team had come aboard with an idea of what was needed. Now, everything to the smallest detail was laid out in black and white.

Janet glanced through hers and said, "Well, I've already put together several different protocols. I wasn't sure which direction this was going to take. Nothing I've done to date is too far off the mark."

Everyone, after inspecting theirs, agreed the original specs were still basically in place.

The Commander then got down to business. He unfolded and spread out construction plans for a domed facility three thousand feet in diameter and four hundred feet high at the center. A vertical wall rose up one hundred feet and the dome capped it off.

Everyone got up and gathered around. Each took their turn and discussed their part in the largest and most dangerous construction project ever conceived by man.

This first meeting solidified the bond of cooperation required; if there were to be any hope of completing it.

The last thing the Commander did, as he left the room, was to shake the hands of Chris and Clinton congratulating them on the level of courage and professionalism displayed during the rescue mission.

* * *

Andy had sustained a severe blow to the head. This had caused some internal swelling and a small pocket of fluid to form.

Because of the level of secrecy surrounding this project they weren't allowed to evacuate him to the mainland.

The medical staff drained off the fluid. After that all they could do was watch and wait. He remained in a coma for five days before coming around. The first person he wanted to see was Chris to thank him for saving his life. Chris said it was purely a matter of pride. No way was it going to be left at three games to five.

*   *   *

While life settled in on the construction site a meeting was held at a very secure location. The large oval, stainless steel, conference table had seating for eight. This complex had been under construction for two years. The finances set aside for its completion, did not show up on any fiscal budget anywhere. The five-story complex was located two hundred feet below the surface.

The doors opened and four men and one woman entered. They took their seats and the room was sealed.

Philip Antar, seated at the head of the table began. "Well, *lady* and gentlemen project Aquarius is officially underway. All elements are in place."

The only female in the group, Susan Stanton ask. "How do we explain two carrier groups on station in the Gulf for the next three years?"

Kirk Leber, to her left provided the answer. "We're currently supplying a carrier group to the French and Spanish alliance to protect the Mediterranean Sea lanes from terrorist attacks. They've been using small private aircraft laden with explosives. We've notified the Mexican government that we're conducting long-term training exercises in a twenty-mile section of the Gulf and they've agreed to route all commercial air traffic around that area. It has also been posted as a *No Incursion Zone* for private aircraft and surface vessels."

Philip asks. "Posting a marker is one thing, but how do we guarantee the integrity of the zone?"

Kirk looked from face to face. "The military will destroy anything that slips through, without question. For the benefit of the satellites we will actually conduct those exercises around the platform. It's hoped that all the activity will be a distraction from the real objective."

Susan took a deep breath and then let it out slowly. "And what about operation Arc Angel?"

Philip answered that one. "We have at least three years before we condemn our souls to hell with that one."

*   *   *

A year had passed and the construction of New Atlantis was well under way. They had weathered a near miss by a category three hurricane four months earlier. About a week of construction time was lost, but this floating hotel barely noticed the twenty-five foot seas and ninety-knot winds.

Jake's team was a long way toward developing the strategies required to populate and maintain life for an extended period of time within the structure. Except for Jake's team and the Seabee Commander, no one knew its true purpose. The story circulated around the platform wasn't far from the truth. The word was; it was to support a large, secret government research and development group geared to tap into the sea's vast resources.

Then on one clear, sunny day something happened. It was during one of the barge deliveries. Material and supplies were being transferred to the platform. Several people heard it at the same time. Jake and Janet were in the command center. They both stepped out by the railing and watched the clear blue sky. Both were sporting a very nice tan. The faint engine sound from a small plane droned in the distance. Janet shaded her eyes and searched the sky.

You saw the distant explosion before you heard it. A small ball of fire formed in the air, and then dropped into the sea. Janet and Jake looked at one another.

The Commander's voice came over the PA system. "Relax everyone. We were just informed by the Navy they're conducting aerial warfare exercises to the north of us. What you just saw was a target drone taken out by a long range missile defense system."

Janet and Jake both knew better. No radio communication of any kind was allowed on or off the site. Everything that came and went was encrypted and arrived sealed in a dispatch case.

Jake could tell it was upsetting to Janet. "Maybe it *was* a drone. They are conducting exercises around us."

She looked at him. "Or a man with his wife and kids out for a spin." With that, she went back inside. Jake watched the horizon for a moment, and then joined her. The whole incident had brought things back into perspective.

*　　*　　*

The construction project was carried out in two phases the elevated platform, and then the dome itself. The first phase was nearing completion. For security reasons the prefabricated components had been outsourced to several companies. No single contractor was given a complete picture.

All of the components were delivered to the Navy Yards at Norfolk Virginia. From there they were loaded onto what appeared to be civilian transports and taken to the blockade. The packaged components were labeled as drilling equipment. They were transferred to the barges and taken to the site. It was the long way around, but it kept suspicions to a minimum.

These barge deliveries were made on what appeared to be a sporadic timetable in hopes of not attracting too much attention.

From the beginning of the project the one security concern centered on the crews manning the tugs delivering the barges. They alone had contact with both sides.

A deck hand on one of the tugs had managed to make friends with a female sailor aboard one of the transports. The deck hand had taken some pictures. Between them they hatched a plot to sell their story to the wire services. He planned to slip the photos, along with some voice notes, to her the next time the rotation brought her back.

The only thing that saved the project from exposure was the heighten level of paranoia surrounding this particular endeavor.

The two conspirators had no way of knowing how closely monitored the ships were. Unbeknown to the crews, there was *no place* aboard the transports or the tugs that weren't being recorded for both sight and sound.

At two in the morning Seaman-Striker Shelly Brinkman was rousted from her bunk. Without being allowed to change, the twenty year old was taken, under protest, several decks down and locked in a cabin that contained only a chair.

She looked around the room and finally went to the chair and sat down. She had fought against being pulled below decks and verbally protested all the way, but that had been mostly for show. Inside she was terrified.

A half an hour passed before the cabin door opened and three men entered. The middle one carried another chair.

She got up and moved away. "What do you want? What have I done?" Her voice quaked a little.

The man with the chair placed it in front of the other chair and sat down. "Please Miss Brinkman, sit down."

"What have I done?" Her voice now reflected the fear she felt inside. "I don't understand."

"Sit." Was the reply from the man in the chair.

She slowly walked to the chair and sat.

"Thank you. Now, we need to talk about Arnold Colar. I believe you know him."

Her heart sank. "I don't believe I do."

The man in the chair watched her for a moment, and then stood up. He nodded to the man on his right, and then turned and left the room.

She watched as the door was closed and locked. She stood up and backed away. Her eyes were beginning to tear up. "Stay away from me."

There was nowhere to go. One of men walked up and backhanded her hard enough to take her off her feet. Blood from her mouth splattered him. Before she could react, her shoulders were pinned to the floor and her clothing stripped away.

A half and hour had passed. The interrogator approached the cabin door, opened it, and entered the room.

36

Shelly was again in the chair. She was naked. Her hands were secured behind the chair back and her legs were secured, at the ankles and just below the knees, to the front legs of the chair.

This placed her in a very revealing and compromising position. Her head was hanging down and she was sobbing. The man again took to the chair in front of her.

"Now Miss Brinkman let's try this again. Do you know Arnold Colar?"

She raised her head. Her eyes were red and her face was wet. Her mouth was swollen and her right cheek had been cut by the man's ring. "Please don't let him hurt me again." Her voice was tiny and the words trembled from her lips.

"Just answer the questions truthfully and no one has to get hurt. Now, do you know Arnold Colar?"

She nodded.

"Very good. Now I want you to tell me about the conversations the two of you have had over the past few weeks, and Miss Brinkman, we've recorded most of it so think very carefully about what you say."

The interrogation lasted for more than two hours. Afterwards she was given something to put on, and then taken to a small cell in a secure holding area.

Two days later Arnold was picked up waiting for Shelly. He was also interrogated but they weren't so nice. When the interrogator was sure he had told them everything and that all the photos and recorded accounts had been recovered they took his bruised and battered body and dumped him in the cell next to the girl.

When they were absolutely sure the project had not been compromised, Shelly and Arnold were hooded and taken to an outside hatch. There they were weighted and dropped into the Gulf. If they were lucky they both drown before the water pressure crushed them out of existence.

The only thing left to do was to notify the relatives of the freak accident and assure them that everything had been done to recover the bodies.

* * *

Another year passed and apparently not a word about the project had leaked to the public.

Everyone on the platform, civilian and military alike, had formed a bond of trust and respect. Between the sexes, another type of bonding had occurred.

On September fifteenth, 2050 Elizabeth Jennet Campbell was born. That day was set aside to celebrate a new life. It was somehow symbolic considering this whole project was designed to return life to a dead and lifeless planet. Everyone had pitched in to make it a very special day for mother and child.

One of the sidebar projects assigned to Jake's team was cataloging and classifying the many forms of sea life encountered during the construction process. Like migrating herds on the surface, once the domed enclosure got in the way. The giant worms, and other forms of life, simply altered their beaten path to avoid the obstacle. The pulse weapon was never used. No doubt the military would find other uses for it.

Jake and his team were invited by the Seabees to witness first hand, the setting in place of the last piece of the dome. Once the seal was made the real test would come. The dome would be drained and the full force of two and a half miles of salt water would come to bear on it.

What stood before them was an absolute marvel of engineering. The simple fact that it could exist at all broke all the rules. The platform that would support this underground city was a special blend of reinforced concrete and epoxy grout. Even that would succumb, sooner or later, to the long-term effects of current and pressure. To combat those effects a watertight external shell made of Tiridium would isolate it from the elements and, at least in theory, it would last forever.

The key to making it livable was the docking points located every one hundred and fifty feet all the way around the perimeter. Each docking point was one hundred feet in diameter. An airlock was fitted in the vertical dome wall directly in front of these docking points. These airlocks would allow entry into the dome. Over time large containers, designed to lock into place on the platform at these points, would contain what was needed to bring all of this to life. Until then, they would be scattered all over the Gulf. They would sit there on the bottom, to be retrieved when the time came.

It took several days to set up the pumps needed to drain the structure. On paper it would work, however all it would take is a single failure in any one of a million seams to bring it all down. The implosion would be catastrophic. All unnecessary personnel, that included Jake and his team, would watch this moment of truth from a safe distance.

The day came to see if the design would hold up. A select few would witness this moment in the command center. The rest would wait for confirmation, good or bad, to come over the PA system.

Andy had received his invite personally from Chris. Over the last two and a half years, and so many chess games no one kept score anymore; they had become close personal friends. Because he had literally been the first one on site, it seemed only fitting that he stand with the others to be part of this culmination of all the effort.

All of the chitchat stopped when the Commander keyed the mike. "Final check."

"We have a green panel," Came the response.

The Commander looked around the room and keyed the mike again. "Light 'em up."

"Yes sir."

The console had readouts for each pump showing the volume of air being transferred from the surface. That translated into the volume of water being forced out. As they each came on line the readouts began to change. When all five pumps were running a slight drone filled the air and a barely noticeable vibration set up in the platform.

"How long," Jake asked?

"Let's see," said the Commander. "We have five pumps each displacing five thousand cubic feet of water per minute. We're looking at about two billion cubic feet. Probably two months to completely empty it. That is if we can keep all the pumps up and running, but we'll know if it's gonna work long before that."

"Okay." Jake glanced around the room. "Everything is up and running folks. Everyone has things to do."

The audience began to drift out as the Commander made the announcement across the PA system.

Chapter four: Arc Angel

A dispatch was delivered to the Commanding officer of the two carrier fleets that had enforced the no-intrusion order. After almost three years, everyone was avoiding this patch of water. They had to intercede less and less now to the point of almost never.

The Commander was handed the dispatch on the bridge. He retired to his cabin. He knew what it was before he opened it.

It read, "Arc Angel has been approved. Stand by for further orders."

He stared at the words for a few moments and then said, to himself. "May God have mercy on us all"

* * *

Like the Astro Dome, the first enclosed sports stadium constructed almost a hundred years before, when the supports came out, in this case 2 billion cubic feet of seawater, the dome settled into place exactly the way it was designed to.

The date was August the third, twenty fifty-one. Everyone was anxiously awaiting the arrival of a new submersible. This one was much larger and was equipped with a universal fitting capable of attaching itself to the airlocks leading into the dome.

The pressure required to empty the dome would have been fatal to anyone inside. The dome did not require the air pressure to withstand the force of the sea outside so the atmospheric pressure was brought back to sea level.

Everyone, not required to be doing something, watched from the railings when the mini-sub broke the surface a few yards off the north side of the platform.

Peter, whose contribution to all of this resided in volumes of text relating to hundreds of scenarios of what might happen, asked, "How many will it hold?"

Jake replied, "A crew of three and twenty-five passengers or a ton of cargo."

"When do we get our turn?" Asked Jonathan.

"We're on the list for next week. That's when Clinton will bring the nuclear power plant on line."

"How big is this, power plant?" Asked Janet.

Clinton answered, "About what you'd find on West Virginia class attack sub."

That brought a chorus of blank stares.

"It'll supply about 250 mega watts of electrical power.

Again, came the stares.

"It can supply the needs of a city of about thirty thousand, virtually forever. It's designed as a module that can be delivered and plugged in."

The sub finally docked with the platform and the crew transferred over.

At dinner that night there was electricity in the air. Not only would tomorrow mark the first time anyone would set foot inside of New Atlantis, but the beginning of the end of three years of isolation. Very soon everyone would be going home.

*   *   *

The airlock system worked perfectly. Commander Willingham entered New Atlantis followed by his men. Inside the air was fresh with a hint of sea salt. It was pitch black. His crew had been equipped with a miniaturized version of ViewScan. What they saw through their visors was a digital representation of a very large and empty void.

Several trips were made down to deliver the propane-powered generators and the equipment and lighting to use them. There were tests to run and integrity inspections to complete before allowing a nuclear powered, turbine generator to be installed and brought on line.

Their day arrived. Jake and the rest of his team assembled next to the docked submarine. Aside from Clinton, there was really nothing for the rest of them to do. More than anything, it was the feeling of accomplishment that each of them would experience. They would step into what had become an almost living entity they had helped to create.

The seating was located along the sides of the cabin allowing space down the center for freight. Jake, Clinton and the rest strapped themselves in and waited.

Peter broke the silence. "Sort of reminds me of a ride they have at Sea World near where I live."

Clinton was holding onto his laptop. "Once I supply power to the complex there won't be much left for us to do here. What are the chances of catching a ride outta here on one of the tugs?"

Chris jumped in. "yeah, Andy plans to set me up with his sister when we get back. And I'm gonna teach him to fly fish."

Janet added hers. "Yeah boss, when can we fly this coop?"

The sub rocked as it left its moorings. Several grabbed their seats.

"I'll speak to the Commander when we get back. Now everyone, lets go visit the city under the sea."

Jonathan reached into a pocket and produced an action character of the Little Mermaid. Everyone just looked at him. "Seems appropriate, some how," he said.

Clinton just shook his head. Janet smiled at him. "I think it's cute," she said.

He slipped it back into his pocket.

The sub maneuvered away from the platform. The tanks were filled and it dropped below the surface. The trip down passed quickly. The sub had internal heating. A couple of them napped. Clinton reviewed the protocols on his laptop. Janet had brought a book. Jake knew things he had never shared with the others. After three years of rehearsals, nothing he'd come up with made them sound any better.

The two sleeping members of his team were jarred awake when the docking clamps sealed the sub to the airlock. The energy levels building in the passenger compartment could have powered the complex.

The seal was broken and the hatch opened. A rush of fresh air, and the glare from the construction lighting greeted everyone.

For most of Jake's team the realization of it all didn't hit them until they stepped out of the sub and into the dome. Until now it had existed in the form of construction drawings and ViewScan's interpretation of what was real. Now it was solid, under their feet. It could be touched.

The Commander and several of his men, greeted them. The construction lighting only revealed the area in front of the airlock and lighted the path to the control room.

The control room had been assembled on the surface and fitted to the skin segment before it was lowered and sealed to the dome. This segment had required several mules to move it into place. The first thing the Seabees did was to remove the protective shell and make the connections to the module that contained the nuclear reactor.

The reactor itself had been no easy piece of deep-sea manipulation. It had come prepackaged with its own propulsion system and had been piloted into position. At that point a special air lock allowed the reactor to be moved from the shell that protected it from the sea into a specially prefabricated compartment attached to the inside of the dome wall.

What Clinton had said was exactly true. His design simply plugged in like a power cord into a socket. The construction teams then completed the connection to the steam-turbine generator that would one day supply power to the dome's human population. Right now it would power the lighting along the top of the dome. Ultra violet was also provided to simulate sunlight.

A cracking system to break down seawater into its basic elements would be used to eventually supply some of the raw material required to produce other things. For now it would be used to keep the oxygen/nitrogen levels high enough to support life. Large hydroponic gardens would supply food and help to recycle carbon dioxide. All of this was part of a highly sophisticated atmospheric regeneration system that worked on paper, but until now had never been field-tested.

The others stood around while Clinton went about bringing the reactor on line. The faint whine of the generator, and the overhead lighting system coming on, measured his success. It was only then that the enormity of this project came to light, so to speak.

The next couple of hours were spent just wandering around this vast empty floor, each one trying to imagine what it would look like with several thousand people, working and living out their lives inside this man-made time capsule. In what he determined to be the exact center of the dome, Jonathan sat his Little Mermaid on the floor thus christening this place New Atlantis, the city under the sea. Their work here was done. During the trip back each talked about what they would do next.

*   *   *

It had been several days with no barge deliveries. The job was completed officially on September the tenth, twenty fifty-one with the placement of the traditional tree on top of the platform. In this case it was an artificial tree but the symbolism was the same, but still no barges. The population voiced their impatience with the delay.

That night a movie was shown in the dining hall. Most of the personnel were there, including young Elizabeth's parents. The infirmary was just off the hall and was used as sort of a day care center for the baby.

All of Jake's team had been summoned to the Commander's quarters. Each thought it was to set up the groups and the time frame for the evacuation of the platform. Evacuation *was* the order of business, but only two groups were leaving.

When they entered his quarters the Commander was just signing off on a radio communication. He stood and faced them.

Clinton pointed to the equipment. "How long has that been here?"

The Commander glanced around. "Since a week after I arrived. It's a secure uplink to a satellite."

Janet broke in. "And why weren't we informed about this?"

The Commander took a deep breath and looked at his watch. "In exactly ninety minutes, about half way through the movie everyone is watching, two cruise missiles will home in on this location and erase it and everyone on it, from the face of the Earth."

The words hung in the air for several moments.

"You're full-a-shit," came Chris's reply.

Everyone spoke at once, but Janet was heard above all the rest. "The mules and the sub, we can get some of them off on those." She turned and jerked open the door to be met by two armed guards. She turned to the Commander. "Get them out of my way!"

Peter was next. "What about all the research, all the data collected over the last three years?"

The Commander addressed Janet first. "The mules have been disabled," he then said to Peter. "All accumulated data has been uploaded to a secure satellite and downloaded to the Blue Ridge Mountain complex," to Jake, "The sub will take you and your group to the mainland."

Janet was furious. "What makes us so special?"

The Commander went eye to eye with her. "I don't know but somebody thinks you are, or believe me we would not be having this conversation."

She turned to Jake. "Did you know about this?"

"No". He lied.

Chris suddenly jumped in. "Andy, he comes with us or I'm not going."

"I have my orders," said the Commander.

Everybody had run out of things to say. Jake stepped in. "What about you?"

The Commander hesitated. "Myself, and six of my men, will be dropped off at the dome. We and a few others will be the guinea pigs to see if life can actually survive down there."

Peter asked. "How long could you last down there?"

The Commander answered. "Quite a while. According to the readings the ambient temperature has risen to sixty-eight degrees and is still going up. We've transferred enough supplies and equipment to last us for years."

Peter wasn't finished. "If this place is such a damned secret how is anyone going to know?"

"You'll know when you break the seal. You'll step into an established eco system or hopefully what's left will give you a hint about how to fix it."

"You've got room for one more," Jake added and then looked at Chris. "Go find Andy and meet us at the docking area." Jake was face to face with the Commander who voiced no objection.

"But Jake," pleaded Chris.

"Chris, he lives or he dies tonight."

Chris moved to the door to be stopped by the guard. The Commander added. "If you're not to the sub in fifteen minutes you'll spend the rest of eternity here with your friend."

Janet spoke up. "There's something I need to get."

"All of your personal belongings have been moved to the sub," said the Commander.

"Not this," she said. "I'll get there"

The Commander addressed them both. "If either of you try and warn anyone. If you start a panic my men have orders to shoot to kill. You can't prevent this. When it happens it'll be quick. Let 'em enjoy the movie."

Janet watched him for a moment. Every ounce of human decency in her was screaming for her to do something, but he was right. Nothing could be done for those in the mess hall. There was something she needed to get. She and Chris turned toward the door. The Commander allowed them both to leave and then he and the others left.

*　　*　　*

The sub was ready to launch. The Commander, four armed soldiers, Jake, Chris and Andy were there. The only one missing was Janet.

The Commander looked at his watch.

Jake saw Janet running toward them carrying something in her arms. "Here she comes."

Janet stopped out of breath in front of them. She carried the baby wrapped in a blanket.

Before anyone could comment she said, "She had the misfortune to be born in the wrong place at the wrong time. She can't give away any state secrets. She's coming with us."

"Can she survive the dive," asked Jake?

Janet looked at the baby. "I don't know, but her death is certain here."

She handed the baby to Jake and stepped aboard and reached back for Elizabeth. Jake handed her back and everyone boarded the submarine.

What happened on the surface, twenty minutes into the dive, was horrific. The first of two cruise missiles struck the center of the platform. The ensuing blast consumed everything. Five minutes later the second missile detonated on the surface to ensure anyone who might have been thrown clear, died in the water.

*　　*　　*

The fleet commander stood on the port wing of the bridge and watched the nighttime horizon. The faint glow to the north began to fade. He stood for another moment and went back inside. Two weeks later he would commit suicide at his home in Portsmouth.

*　　*　　*

Baby Elizabeth had no problem with the descent. The airlock seal was acquired and everyone left the sub.

Andy was at a loss for words. He gave Chris his sister's phone number and address. Maybe someday she, and rest of his family, could be told the truth.

The Commander was right. The air temperature had reached the mid seventies. Several small structures had been assembled and a huge stockpile of supplies and equipment stood in the distance.

Clinton took the time to check on the reactor, and the rest of the equipment that would sustain their lives for as long as they would last. One of the men the Commander brought with him had a degree in nuclear engineering and another was a doctor. The Commander had not just included men. There were six women already in the dome along with two other men. Six men and six women had been paired up. Part of this experiment was not about the survival of mankind, but the continuation of it.

Jake and the Commander stood away from everyone else. Jake asked, "Do you have a family?"

"Yes a wife and three kids."

"Does your wife know you're doing this?"

The Commander took a moment to answer. "No, they're the *reason* I'm doing it."

"I don't..."

"You think it was easy to know all these years that the men under me, and all those others up there, were going to have to die to keep this secret?"

"If it makes you feel any better you weren't the only one."

The Commander watched him for a moment. "Yes, well, at least those who came with you are leaving with you. I'm doing this to make sure my family survives what's coming. Their names are on a list. Jake, I have one favor to ask. Make sure that promise is kept." He handed Jake two envelopes. "One is for you. It has names and addresses and phone numbers. The other one's for my wife for when that day comes. She's gonna think I died on the platform. I hope she finds it in her heart to forgive me."

Jake looked at the envelopes and then put them in his jacket pocket. "You have my word." Jake extended his hand and the Commander shook it.

Goodbyes were said all around and Jake's team, and little Elizabeth, boarded the sub.

Jake had his own crosses to bear. The people he'd worked with, and laughed with, and celebrated with for three years had just paid for the salvation of mankind with their lives. Not by their choice, but by his. He would carry their faces and the sound of their voices inside of him for the rest of his life.

Twenty hours later Jake and his team were picked up by the U. S. Coast Guard and carried back to the mainland.

Ten minutes after the transfer a missile fired from a jet ten miles away destroyed the submarine and its crew. The first phase of Operation Aquarius was complete. Phase two would take decades.

Chapter five: In the face of death, life goes on

The civilians who had volunteered for the New Atlantis project had been carefully selected. They all had no immediate family. The military was made up of volunteers, all single.

The story released to the public stated that a joint civilian and military research project studying global warming effects on marine life in the Gulf had suffered a catastrophic accident with a total loss of life. The water depth made a recovery of any kind virtually impossible.

All of the barge operators and crews disappeared leaving no unessential personnel alive to compromise security.

Jake's team broke up, each fading into the larger scheme of things. Janet adopted little Elizabeth to raise as her own. Jake was taken into the inter-circle. Chris, Jonathan, Peter and Clinton all had their part to play and left in as many different directions.

Janet and her daughter lived very close to a research site set up for her to literally test out the theories she had developed while she was on the platform.

* * *

Three years had passed without any contact with the others. One day she read where the relatives of those lost on the platform were holding a memorial service in remembrance of their loved ones. Lately she had been thinking a lot about those who died that night and she decided to attend.

It was an outdoor gathering of about one hundred people on the seaward side of Galveston Island. Janet stood to one side holding little Elizabeth's hand while the names of the lost were read one by one. Faces came and went in her mind as they read down the list.

The crowd had broken up when she spotted Chris. She hurried after him.

They were almost to the parking area when she called out. "Chris, wait."

It wasn't his name as much as the voice that stopped him. He turned and broke into a smile as Janet, leading Elizabeth, came to a stop in front of him.

They just stared at each other for a moment. He looked down. "Is this...?"

"Yes," kneeling down. "Say hi to uncle Chris."

"Uncle is it." Kneeling in front of the little girl.

"Hi uncle Chris," came the child's voice.

"I don't think you remember me."

"Yes I do, mommy has a picture."

Standing. "Really..."

"An older one, off the internet." She stepped behind the child. "Do you ever see the others?"

Chris looked around. "Let's find some place less public."

Janet took Elizabeth's hand. The little girl held out her other one to Chris.

"I know just the spot," said Janet.

He took Elizabeth's hand, and the three of them moved on into the parking area.

* * *

The small coffee shop had just survived its noontime rush and the place was all but empty. Janet, Chris and Elizabeth occupied a booth in the back, away from the traffic area.

Janet helped Elizabeth with her chocolate milk.

Chris sipped on his coffee. "Are you still connected?"

Janet glanced up. "Yes, I'm doing research not too far from here. How about you?"

"I'm in the middle of something that's pure science fiction, or it would be if I weren't touching it every day."

"How did you hear about the gathering," she asked?

"I kept up with the news stories. Andy's family was one of the organizers. They were here today. He gave me their pictures. You have no idea how hard it was not to tell them that he's probably still alive two and a half miles under the Gulf of Mexico."

Janet watched Elizabeth, and sipped her coffee. "You think they still are?"

"Unless cabin fever drove 'em crazy and they killed each other."

"What about the others?"

He smiled at Elizabeth and she smiled back. "I was hoping you knew."

"Every time I bring it up I get the feeling I shouldn't. What kind of science fiction?" She asked.

"If I talk about this, and you talk in your sleep, we're both dead, literally."

"The only one in bed with me these days is her, when it thunders."

"I wouldn't be to sure about that. Paranoia is running pretty high."

She laughed at that. Chris went on to talk about submarines designed to carry people not missiles, submarines that can be reconfigured under water to serve other purposes and nuclear power plants that are smaller and more powerful than anything available before. He was sure Clinton had something to do with that.

She talked about developing indoctrination procedures to precondition a population to exist, and function, for a long time in a confined space, and not just on paper. Her lab was on top of a vast underground complex completely isolated from the world above. Men, women and children lived and worked, attended school and worshiped for a year at a time in this fully functional underground city.

They had been talking for a couple of hours when Chris looked at his watch. "I gotta go. I've got a plane to catch. It's been real nice seein' you and Elizabeth again." Of course Elizabeth was asleep on the seat next to her mother.

Chris got up. Janet eased out and they both stood looking at each other.

Janet hugged him. "You have no idea how nice it's been to see you again."

He kissed her on the forehead, and then picked up the check. "This one's on me," he said. "If we get a chance to do this again it'll be your turn. Say goodbye to Elizabeth for me."

"I will."

They both hesitated for another moment, and then Chris turned and left.

It would be the last time she would ever see him. She attended the memorial gatherings for the next two years. He never showed up. Maybe the thoughts of his friend were too troubling.

* * *

Operation Aquarius had never stopped evolving. Jake's primary mission had been perhaps the most critical, the completion of New Atlantis. There were four others like him overseeing various other clandestine operations around the country.

Janet's project was in its tenth year when he came to visit. It was a Saturday. The doorbell rang and Elizabeth, now eleven, answered the door.

There stood Jake. Not much had changed about him, maybe a little graying at the temples. "Hello, you must be Elizabeth, I'm..."

"I know who you are." Shouting, "Mom, it's another one of my uncles!"

She swung open the door and stepped aside.

Jake gave her a curious look and stepped in. Elizabeth shut the door and left him standing. She passed her mother and rolled her eyes. Janet patted her on the back of the head.

Janet smiled, walked up to Jake and hugged him. He hugged her back.

"She's really grown up," he said.

"Yes she has. Let's sit in the living room."

He followed her into a very comfortable looking room furnished in hardwood and crystal. He sat on the couch. "Another uncle?"

"It's a long story. I bumped into Chris several years ago. Would you like something to drink," she asked?

"No, I can only stay a minute."

"It's been what ten years, and you can only spare a minute?"

He smiled. "Okay, a soda if you have it?"

"That's better. Don't move." She left for the kitchen.

Jake looked around the room. There were pictures of Elizabeth and Elizabeth with her friends, all over. His eyes fell on a gold-framed photo sitting on a table by the window. He got up, walked over and picked it up. It was a photo of the platform.

"Here," came her voice from behind him.

He turned and handed the photo to her. "Where did you get this?"

She handed him the drink and took the picture. "From a deckhand on one of the tugs. He offered it to me when I caught him snooping around."

"And you didn't tell anyone."

"Yes, I told the Commander. He said he'd take care of it. He didn't ask for the photo. I guess he assumed I destroyed it" She sat in a chair across from the couch. "Why are you here Jake? Obviously not a social call."

Jake sat on the couch. "We're going to shut you down as of the tenth of next month."

She sat straight up. "Shut us down, why? The data we're finally getting is giving us a true picture of what life will be like on New Atlantis."

"Don't get me wrong. What you've accomplished here will assure our way of life will continue."

"Then why?"

"Hear me out. We're going to expand and refit the site. Several more are under construction. You and I both know that New Atlantis was designed to be a failsafe system. When it comes, and between you and me it'll be sometime in the next ten years, we need to make sure there'll be survivors here, on the surface.

He took a drink. He had her attention. "There's no way of knowing how much advanced notice we'll have. It could be weeks, or days or only hours."

"But who lives and who dies?"

"Leave that up to us. I just want to make sure that you and Elizabeth are among those who do."

"What do you want me to do?"

He finished his soda, sat the glass on a coaster on the table next to him and stood up. She did the same.

"Right now, take a vacation. Go see family or friends. Just get out of here for a while. Don't worry; you're still on the payroll. Oh, and get rid of that photo. I mean that, it could get you both killed."

She walked him to the door and opened it. "How's everyone else doing? If anyone knows, you do."

He hesitated for a moment. She knew that wasn't good. "Clinton died two years ago, an explosion in his lab. Everyone else is fine."

She reached up and kissed him on the cheek and stepped back. "See you when I see you, I guess."

"You take care of yourself and that little girl."

"You know I will."

With that he left and she closed the door. Her eyes began to tear as a picture of Clinton, grinning and sitting in the john on the mule, coursed through her mind.

For the next three months she and Elizabeth toured the country seeing family and friends. She couldn't bring herself to destroy the photo. She needed it as a reminder of what was lost. But it bothered her enough to take it with her, a good thing.

Upon their return she found their entire household had been moved into living quarters prepared for them above the underground site.

*   *   *

The time was getting near. The insertion of two satellites into an orbit that brought them northwest to southeast across our continent had not gone unnoticed. With the International Space Station in hands not friendly to us and with the older shuttle system shut down decades ago, we had no way to get a closer look. What it did do was set in motion operation "Faint of Heart".

Lists of names had been compiled from the areas surrounding the underground sites. Most of these people were in some way connected to various federally funded research projects. In-depth background and security checks were initiated.

The developers insisted that they needed to involve some of those on the list with the sites. The security protocols prevented that from happening. The only live site was the one in Houston where Janet was testing her theories.

*   *   *

For five years Janet and Elizabeth had been living at the facility above the underground site. She was still conducting research on various follow up projects. Elizabeth, now sixteen, was finding it difficult living under the restrictions posed on them by the people her mother worked for.

Having been home schooled, and at five foot five, one hundred and fifteen pounds, hazel eyes, sandy blond hair, and a disarming smile it was no surprise when she was noticed by one of the young maintenance workers, Daniel Lieberman. It didn't take much to build on the relationship.

One afternoon Janet went looking for her. She was nowhere to be found. Liz would normally ask if she wanted to leave. No one had seen her for several hours. In a panic Janet began going through the security video's flash memory. She stopped when she caught Elizabeth talking with a young man she had never met. She watched as Elizabeth and her friend left the complex, got into the young man's truck and drove off.

After passing the photo around, and threatening to call the police, one of Daniel's friends gave them up.

Janet drove her car north on Interstate sixty-four toward Cleveland, Texas. Daniel's family owned a piece of land about twenty minutes north of Houston and on this land was a pond. According to what she was told, Daniel and his friends had used it for an East Texas version of a pool party on several occasions.

The directions led to a red and white gate leading off the highway. Janet approached a stand of trees. She could see Daniel's parked truck. She pulled in beside it and stopped.

She hadn't moved very far into the trees, when the sound of Elizabeth's laugh came from somewhere just ahead. She eased closer until she was standing just inside the tree line overlooking the pond.

Elizabeth and Daniel were frolicking in the water. From the piles of clothes on the bank she was sure they were planning to take it a step farther, if they hadn't already.

Elizabeth glanced away from Daniel and screamed, "Mom," and stood up. Then realizing she was naked dropped back down.

Daniel started to say something and was cut off. "Not a word. Both of you out of the water," Janet said in no uncertain terms.

"We're naked," Elizabeth said in a panicked voice.

Janet, looked at her daughter, "I've seen you naked before."

Elizabeth glanced toward Daniel. "Mom!"

Janet looked at Daniel, who was trying not to go eye to eye with her, "You ought to be ashamed of yourself."

She then turned around to the sound of both of them clamoring out of the water.

After a few minutes of chaos behind her she turned to face the two of them standing holding shoes and boots with their clothes stuck to their wet bodies.

Janet began, her eyes burning a hole through Daniel. "You're old enough to know better. She's only sixteen. Tomorrow morning I want *you* standing in my office at nine a.m.

58

Elizabeth tried to defend them. "It's not what you think."

Janet wasn't in the mood for explanations. "I don't want to hear it." Back to Daniel, "If you decide not to show up, well, I know people that dark allies run away from. Get my drift?"

Daniel, still not wanting to make eye contact, "Yes ma'am."

With that the two of them, followed by Janet, walked back to the cars. She actually felt a small amount of self-satisfaction every time they stepped on something.

On the drive back, Elizabeth had lost the urge to talk. Janet had only one question. "Did the two of you?"

Elizabeth, still looking down, "Almost."

Nothing else was said. Elizabeth took a shower and went to her room. Tomorrow morning would prove interesting.

* * *

Janet had the resources and used them. Before she went to bed that night she knew everything there was to know about Daniel Lieberman. The part that struck close to home was that he was an orphan. His family had been killed in an auto accident when he was six. His aunt and uncle had raised him.

The next morning Daniel was outside of Janet's office when she walked up at 8:30.

Daniel was desperate. "Ms Crowley, I want you to know..."

She stepped past him and swiped her card unlocking her office. She walked in. Daniel hadn't moved. She looked back, "Don't just stand there." She kept going. He followed her in.

The conversation started about him. He was nineteen and a freshman at the University Houston at Galveston studying marine biology. The summer job with the contractor was to earn spending money.

Her background check had substantiated everything he said. She also knew the extent of the background check run on anyone having anything to do, with any part of this project.

Finally they got around to the reason she had him there in the first place, her daughter.

"How long have you been seeing Elizabeth?" She asked.

"Ms Crowley, I really think Liz should be here. We care a lot about each other and I don't think it's right you stopping us from seeing each other without both of us being here."

She liked the way he stood up for the two of them. "First of all, you don't have anything to say about any of this. If I were ready to separate the two of you, you'd be in jail and we wouldn't be having this conversation. You understand what I'm saying?"

"Yes ma'am."

"Okay, now answer my question."

"About six months."

"And this was your first trip upstate together?"

Daniel wasn't sure what to say.

"I talked with your buddies," she continued, "to hear them tell it, you've done a lot of partying up there."

"Well, I guess we've had a bar-b-que or two that maybe got a little outta hand, but nothing to do with Liz. It wasn't my idea to go. I'm not saying this was her fault in any way. She'd heard us talking about it and wanted to go somewhere away from here... I guess I let things get a little outta hand."

"I'd say."

"Look you gotta believe me. I would never do anything to hurt Liz, not anything." He was beginning to fear the outcome of all of this, and it showed in his voice.

When she removed Elizabeth from that platform, in her mind, she gave life to her. Just because it wasn't a biological birth didn't diminish her instincts about what's right or wrong for her child. She knew the effects raging hormones could have if they go unchecked. On top of all of it, she liked this kid.

"This is the way it is," she began. "She's sixteen. I want to know where she is and what's she's doing especially when it comes to you."

He jumped in. "You mean it's okay if we..."

"We what?"

"See each other."

She let him hang there for a moment. "That's all you do." She could see the muscles in his body relax. "She's sitting at home waiting for the sky to fall. I'm sure you know the way. Why don't you go tell her it's not, not today anyway."

Daniel was up and to the door.

"And Daniel…"

He stopped and looked back at her.

"I wasn't kidding about those dark allies."

He took a long moment to think about that, "Yes ma'am," and then he left.

Chapter six: Time was getting close

Jake, and other members of the Blue Ridge Mountain project, sat across a large conference table from the President of the United States and senior members of his Cabinet.

Jake acted as spokesman for his group. "Mr. President, we're completing work on twelve underground sites. When the time comes, and you notice I said *when*, select groups of researchers, technicians, and professionals with their families will be moved into the sites."

"How many people are we talking about," the President asked?

"About a thousand for each site."

The President's group began to talk amongst themselves. The President again addressed Jake. "Out of a population of almost five hundred million we can only save twelve thousand?"

"That, plus the twenty-five hundred or so that will occupy New Atlantis."

The Secretary of State, sitting next to the President spoke up. "I've seen the specifications and the inventories for these sites. They can handle a lot more than a thousand."

"Yes sir," Jake replied, "They could at first, but you have to remember we're not talking about a few months or even a year or two. We could be looking at a hundred years underground. Each of these sites will have areas that will support hydroponic farms and livestock as a renewable food source. Ten million gallons of fresh water is storied in huge Porcelain lined stainless steel tanks under the site. Everything has to be recycled from sewage, to what they breathe, to the moisture in the air."

The Secretary of Defense was next. "How can human beings possibly function underground for that long a time?"

"A colleague of mine heading up the research group outside of Houston, has developed and tested the profiles that will become their way of life. They will adapt and survive. Now, if you'll hold your questions until the end I'm going to go through, in detail, everything we've accomplished in the last fifteen years. Basically a step by step break down of what is about to happen in our very near future."

Everyone listened while Jake painted a very bleak picture of the future of mankind.

*   *   *

Six years had passed. Life, in and out of the underground site had become routine for Janet and Elizabeth and Elizabeth's family.

Daniel had not gone away. He and Elizabeth developed their relationship over time and in the end the bond between them became unbreakable. Two years ago they were married. A year later Mary Louise was born.

Daniel had completed his degree in marine biology. Elizabeth had been trained by her mother to assist her.

Daniel had applied for and got a spot on a marine research vessel, the SS Endeavor, leaving out of Galveston. Elizabeth had ridden down with him to see him off. Janet was left to baby-sit.

We were not totally without intelligence sources. That same day the alert went out. Janet was working in her office when the alarm sounded. Fixtures, resembling the fire strobes you see in most public buildings, were flashing all over the complex.

Janet had made it to the door when the phone lit up on her desk. She looked back. The flashing button was the red one.

She grabbed the receiver. "Yes?"

Jake was on the other end. "Janet, it's a go. Notifications just went out. We don't have the lag time we'd hoped for."

It suddenly occurred to her, "Oh my God!"

"What?"

"Daniel, Elizabeth's husband, is going offshore. She drove him down this morning. How much time do we actually have?"

He answered. "At 5:00 a.m. your time tomorrow morning, the site will hermetically seal itself for at least the next one hundred years. If you're not in it by then, you never will be."

"Tomorrow morning? I have to go." She hung up, punched another line and spoke Elizabeth's name. "Come on, Come on, answer."

Elizabeth picked up. "Hi Mom."

"Elizabeth, where are you?"

Elizabeth was on her way back, nearing Old Clearlake. She could hear the panic in her mother's voice. "What's wrong?"

"He's gone isn't he?"

"Yes, what's wrong?"

Trying to control her panic, "The alert. We've received the alert.

Elizabeth's car screeched to a stop on the side of the road. "I'm going back. How long?"

"Five o'clock tomorrow morning. What are you gonna do?"

Elizabeth's car sped back toward Galveston. "I'll think of something. Mom, don't let 'em lock us out."

"Just hurry baby, hurry," she pleaded. She was being paged. She killed the call. There were things she had to do. She was trembling when she left the office.

*   *   *

Elizabeth knew exactly what she was going to say when she stepped into the harbormaster's office. The story was simple. On her drive home her mother had called. Her little girl had been hurt in an accident. She had to get in touch with her husband on the

SS Endeavor. The research ship had sailed a few hours ago headed for The Bay of Campeche.

A call went out immediately to the ship. Daniel came on the radio. "What's happened?"

It took every ounce of determination she had to lie to him, but she had to get him back. "Mom called. Mary fell. She hit her head. She's at the hospital." She began to cry. "Her skull's fractured. They need us both with her now."

"Oh God, how am I...?"

"They're sending a helicopter to take you off."

"Okay, stay in touch with the hospital. Let me know if..." The words hung in his throat. "Let me know."

Faking an emotional moment of silence. "Just get back. I'm waiting."

After that, in private, she called her mother and filled her in.

*   *   *

All over the country, those chosen to populate the underground sites went about their everyday lives. In Janet's case it was a little different. This site was smaller than the rest slotted to handle about six hundred. Over the years she'd cycled the members on her list in and out of the site running through one scenario or another. As far as anyone knew they were helping develop procedures for survival underground in the event of a manmade or natural disaster. That was not far from the truth.

At the moment of the alert about half of them were already on site. The call that went out to the others was in the form of a drill, not an order, so as not to cause a panic. They managed to contact most of them. Most of those responded. This wasn't the first time Janet had used a drill to determine how long it would take to pull everyone in. They were used to it. Those already there simply sat back and waited. No one had commented on the strobes, the one difference that signaled this was the real thing.

The only two that had a ways to travel were Daniel's aunt and uncle. These two had been added without going through channels or getting the necessary clearances and over the years they had kept it to themselves. They were also the only two who knew exactly what the site was for. For the love of her daughter and son-in-law Janet had taken a real chance.

The other sites were not so lucky. The developers had been right. There should have been at least some involvement. No one was in a hurry or they ignored it altogether. It became obvious that many of them would be abandoned to their fate above ground.

*   *   *

It was two in the morning when the helicopter touched down in the parking lot. Elizabeth stood next to their car shielding her face from the debris cast up by the rotors.

Daniel stood in the doorway shouting something to her. She couldn't make it out. She frantically waved to him to join her.

He said something to someone in the helicopter, and then jumped down and ran to her.

When he was sure she could hear him he began shouting. "Come on, they're giving us a lift to the hospital." He couldn't understand why she didn't move.

When he stood in front of her she said, "Mary's fine. They've issued the alert. She looked at her watch. "In two hours and twenty-one minutes they're locking down the site. If we aren't there it'll be too late. We won't get in and Mary will never get out."

Daniel stared at her for a moment, and then turned and waved the helicopter off. The guy in the door gave them a questioning palm's up. Daniel and Elizabeth were already in the car headed north.

Daniel drove. "I hope you know you scared the hell outta me."

"I'm sorry. It was all I could come up with. I didn't have time for them to *think* about bringing you back."

He reached over and took her hand and squeezed it. That was the sign they used to let the other know they understood. She

66

squeezed it back and put her head on his shoulder. He put his arm around her. The car sped through the early morning.

Two thirds of the way back doing ninety in a sixty-five did not go unnoticed.

Elizabeth's head came up when the car slowed down. "What, why are we...?" The flashing lights behind them caused her to look back.

The car came to a stop on the side of the road. The police cruiser pulled in behind them.

Elizabeth looked at her watch. "We don't have time for this."

The officer sat in his car. Elizabeth kept looking back. "What's he doin'?"

"Running the plate".

The Officer waited for his computer to bring back anything that might be filed against the plate. The screen lit up. "Daniel Lieberman, 2337 Linquest, Houston, Texas, 77015." "Wants and warrants, bench warrant issued on July 5, 2073" "Unpaid traffic fine."

His shift had been uneventful until now. This would give him a reason to cut it short. By the time he hauled this guy in and filled out the paperwork it would be too late to go back out. The officer got out of his car and approached the other car's driver's side window.

Daniel lowered it half way. "Officer we were going a little fast but our baby's been hurt. We have to get to the hospital."

The officer shinned his flashlight into the back seat, then at Elizabeth, and then back into Daniel's face. "I'm sorry, but I don't see any baby. May I see your I.D. please?"

Daniel fished out his wallet. Elizabeth, sounding as panicked as she really was said, "My mother called. Our daughter was hurt at her home. She's been taken to the hospital."

Daniel passed him his I.D. The officer looked at it. "Which hospital?"

Elizabeth's mind went blank.

"That's what I thought." He stepped back from the door. "Mister Lieberman, a warrant's been issued for you on an unpaid traffic fine. I need you step out of the car, please."

Elizabeth took his arm. "We've got less than an hour."

"I know."

The officer touched his sidearm. "Out of the car, now!" This time it was a command.

Daniel opened the car door, got out and shut it. Elizabeth pressed a button on the steering wheel and a heads up display popped up on the windshield. It was a phonebook. The fourth line down read "MOM."

The officer motioned to Daniel. "Turn around and place your hands on the car."

Daniel turned and did as he was told. The officer moved up behind him and began to pat him down.

Elizabeth leaned over. "Mom!"

A second later she came back. "Where the hell are you, time's running out."

The sound of the third voice caused the officer to push Daniel aside with one hand and lean inside the window.

Elizabeth's intension was to try and get her mother to somehow intercede. What happened next was a reflex action. She pushed the window button. The window came up under the officer's chin, catching his head. That was Daniel's que to grab the sidearm. Elizabeth lowered the window.

The officer moved away. "Alright, give me the gun. Don't make it worse than it is."

Daniel waved him away from the car with the gun. "Just back off. Don't make me use this."

The officer took a step closer. "Right now it's assault and resisting arrest. You use that, and it becomes at least attempted capital murder."

Elizabeth couldn't see much from inside the car. "Daniel, what are you doing?"

Daniel glanced toward her voice. The officer lunged forward. The weapon discharged.

The bullet caught the officer where his leg joined his hip and he went down.

Daniel tossed the gun, jerked the door open, climbed in and slammed it

Elizabeth just stared. "You shot him?"

He turned the key and slammed down the accelerator. The wheels broke loose for a moment and then caught. "The leg. He's alright, besides in a little while it's not gonna matter anyway."

The officer managed to drag himself to his sidearm. He got off one shot at the fleeing vehicle.

The bullet entered the back of the car, passed through the back of the passenger seat and into Elizabeth below her shoulder.

She lunged forward. The bullet passed through her and slammed into the dash. Blood splattered the windshield. Her eyes were wide in disbelieve.

Daniel reacted. "You're shot. God Liz."

She leaned back. The seat began to collect the blood from the wound. "Just get us home."

Janet's voice came back. "What's wrong? Where are you?"

He looked at his watch. "Ten minutes. Liz has been shot."

"Shot! I don't understand. Who shot her," came the panicked reply?

"When we see you. Get a medical team to the gate."

The wounded officer called in a ten one hundred, officer down. The alert was out. Every car within ten miles was converging on the path taken by Daniel and Elizabeth.

She was losing consciousness from lose of blood. Daniel screamed at her. "Don't you quit on me."

Her eyes opened wide again and she griped his leg.

His heart was in his throat. "You've never quit on anything in your life." He pleaded, "I can't raise Mary alone."

Through a weak smile she answered him. "You're gonna be a great dad."

With that her grip relaxed, the light left her eyes and she died.

He knew instantly she was gone. Tears filled his eyes and flashing lights filled his rear view mirror. Now the only thing on his mind was to get to his daughter.

He swung off the highway and accelerated toward the entrance to the site.

Janet, a medical team and five armed Marines were waiting at the gate. Daniel hit the breaks and let the car slide to a stop inside. The Marines closed the gate.

Janet jerked open the passenger side door. The moment she saw her, she knew Elizabeth was gone. Everything left her and she went to one knee.

Daniel stood behind her crying. "I'm sorry. I tried."

A siren inside the site brought her back to reality. The police cars screeched to a halt at the gate. They emptied out and were pressing the Marines to get in.

Janet stood and looked back toward everyone. "Forget everything. We have to get inside, now!"

The medical team broke and ran for the building.

She took Daniel's arm. He looked at her. "I can't just leave her here like this."

"You're not leaving her, I am." She shoved him. "Go, see to your daughter while you still can."

Daniel took one last look at Liz and ran.

Janet and the Marines pulled back. The police were trying to force the gate. The last two Marines through the door fired a burst into the ground in front of the gate. The police ducked for cover and returned fire. There was nothing to hit.

* * *

When the elevator doors opened, two hundred feet down, nothing on the surface mattered any longer. Nothing short of a tactical nuclear weapon could breach the underground site.

The Marines and the med staff moved off to join the others. Daniel and Janet stood together. Neither had any idea what to say to the other. Janet put her arms around him. Their sense of loss was over powering. She could feel him trembling in her arms.

Daniel said it for both of them. "She was the best thing that ever happened to me, and I will love her and miss her for the rest of my life."

She pushed back and looked at him. "We still have a little piece of her, and right now I think we both need to go see her."

"Did they make it?"

"Your aunt and uncle, Yes."

He hugged her again. "Thank you."

With that, Daniel and Janet and several hundred others began a journey that would take a very, very long time to complete.

*   *   *

On the surface, the police had used a car to breach the gate. Most of the officers closed in on the building, weapons drawn. A couple had stayed with the cars and called for backup. One checked on Elizabeth's body. The siren wailed in the background.

Inside, the top of the elevator bank descended into the floor. The entire complex had thermite explosives imbedded in the walls and roof.

The police were trying to force the doors when the siren stopped. Everyone paused for a second. The blast generated a fireball that consumed everyone and everything for three hundred feet in all directions. When the air cleared all that remained was smoldering debris and the scattered, burning wreckage of hundreds of vehicles.

Chapter seven: Everything was set in motion

Four days earlier. The USS Georgana, a research and development submarine belonging to the Blue Ridge Mountain group, had set sail out of Norfolk, Virginia. On the crew manifest was Christopher Wincrest.

For the last twenty years a submarine taskforce numbering eight subs, controlled by the Blue Ridge Mountain group, had at least half of their number at sea at any given moment. These submarines were armed with torpedoes only, and were fitted with special grappling equipment. Four of them contained wards to sleep the two hundred Seabees required to bring New Atlantis on line when the time came. The other four carried time sensitive supplies such as medicines, plasma and anything else with an expiration date. Every two months the subs rotated in, and then back out.

All of these submarines were constructed of Tiridium and had pressure hulls capable of surviving the trip down to New Atlantis. They all had new generation power plants safer and more powerful than anything in current use anywhere else in the world. They, and the rest of the US submarine fleet, were fitted with a new stealth technology that made them invisible to all known underwater tracking and detection systems.

In a secure, covered dry-dock at the Portsmouth shipyards containers were constructed year in and year out. As these containers were completed they were filled with nonperishable supplies and components needed to build a city under the sea.

This secret flotilla then deposited them deep at various locations all over the Gulf. To date not one had been disturbed. The other unique feature was the crew; at least fifty percent were females of childbearing age.

The Georgana was something very special. She was one of two submarines capable of transforming itself into a deep-sea construction crane. If deep-sea emergency repairs were required large amounts of supplies and material could be moved very quickly. The purpose of this mission was to field test some refinements.

This entire fleet had been Chris's brainchild twenty-five years earlier, but now younger minds were advancing his original designs. The old man still came up with an original thought from time to time so he kept his hand in.

On the same day Jake contacted Janet The Georgana was three thousand feet below the surface of the Caribbean.

The only boats at sea to get the alert were the Blue Ridge Mountain submarines. What this meant to them was stay put and observe complete radio silence. Back at Norfolk emergency crew recalls went out and the measures required to put the other four subs to sea, began.

*   *   *

On the Georgana, Chris was summoned to the Captain's cabin. Chris knocked on the bulkhead.

A voice came from inside. "Come."

Chris entered.

The Captain motioned with his hand. "Please, close the door and sit down."

Captain Michael O'Donnel was younger than most of his peers. At six foot two inches he was also a little taller than most. Most submariners were shorter for obvious reasons.

He had graduated at the top of his class from everywhere. What made the difference was not what he knew, but how he used it. After two years of sea duty he had exhibited a special ability to make the right decision at the right time.

This had not gone unnoticed and he was recruited for the Blue Ridge Mountain mission. Youth and ability were two of the attributes sought after the most. Three years later he was given his first command. The Georgana.

Chris took the seat. Michael got right to it. He handed Chris a communication. "Is this the real thing?"

Chris looked at it and took a deep breath. "This came in thirteen hours ago. Why are you asking me now?"

The Captain took the paper back. "This was marked eyes only. You're technically just a passenger, but I also know *who* you are so I'm breaking protocol"

Chris sized up the man in front of him. He knew very well what it meant. His life, and the lives of everyone on board, was now in the hands of an untested captain. "Most of the alerts are to put everyone on notice that something is in the air, but this one. This one is level one. It went out to the sites on the mainland." He paused.

"And?"

"And, I'm afraid life as we know it, is about to change."

"Captain to the bridge," came across the speaker in the Captain's cabin.

Chris and Captain O'Donnel both stood up. "Stay on me," said the Captain and they both left the cabin.

The Captain and Chris stepped onto the bridge. A seaman shouted. "Captain on the bridge."

Everyone snapped to. "As you were," came the Captain's response.

The Executive Officer, Lieutenant Commander James McReynolds, informed the Captain before he asked. "We floated a surface antenna to receive our daily ops reports. There's nothing but dead air. I ran a diagnostic on the antenna. It's working. I tried all the commercial bands. Nothing". We're under orders to maintain radio silence. Should we try and raise them anyway?"

"No". The Captain looked at Chris. "Thermonuclear attack?"

"Have the seismic sensors detected anything," asked Chris? The Executive officer shook his head.

Chris thought for a moment, "Maybe electromagnetic pulse." He turned to the Executive Officer. "Retract the antenna just in case."

The Executive Officer moved over to communications. "Bring it in."

"An electromagnetic pulse is lethal to electrical circuits not people ," said the Captain.

Chris replied, "My guess would be biological," he glanced around the bridge and then back to the Captain, "It's begun."

Captain O'Donnel didn't say anything, but in his heart he knew his family and the families of his crew were gone.

*   *   *

It was September the eleventh, twenty seventy-three. The time was three a.m. Zulu, military time. Every piece of unprotected electrical and electronic circuitry in the free world died. Planes fell out of the sky. Cars, and every other form of transportation, stopped. Every home, business, school and hospital went dead forever.

Those who orchestrated the end of our way of life didn't let us suffer for long. Half an hour later the missiles struck. Thousands of air burst occurred over every populated area, not nuclear but biological, a virus so lethal a single breath proved fatal. Within an hour, ninety-nine percent of the population was dead. The virus was designed to mutate into a harmless microbe within a few hours thus leaving the country's intra-structure intact. It was also programmed to recognize human DNA and leave the wildlife unaffected.

The underground sites could still communicate with each other but would never know exactly what happened. Where *their* equipment remained working, there was no one left on the surface to talk to.

The evil that now ruled the world would find their reign, short lived.

Deep inside the two shielded military broadcast stations keys were turned and buttons were pushed. A flash message was sent.

Every Attack Submarine Commander, cruising the depths of the world, received their orders. Those orders began with "The Submarine Effect has been activated."

*　　*　　*

Satellites confirmed the success of the attack. Our enemies knew we had submarines positioned to strike back. To date they had not been able to circumvent the cloaking system, but with nowhere to go, and without a chain of command, most of the Sub Commanders would be looking for a safe haven for their crews. Besides Americans had proven, on many occasions, they had no stomach to finish a fight.

There was always the chance one or two would launch their payloads. Because of this, fortified bunkers shielded against radioactive contamination, were burrowed into the mountain below their stronghold. These new World Leaders felt safe in their nest.

History had taught them nothing. They had failed to understand what the Germans and Japanese learned over a hundred and fifty years ago. When our country, our way of life, is attacked without provocation our desire to finish that fight knows no bounds.

They were absolutely sure this long-range strike would safely eliminate the last bastion of resistance to their rule; they never really attempted any serious intelligence gathering. Between *their* over confidence and *our* level of paranoia the biggest secret in the history of all mankind, had remained a secret. Consequently, they had no clue to what was about to happen. They had underestimated our determination to ensure our survival and they would not live to regret it.

*　　*　　*

Chris and Captain O'Donnel looked over their part of the directive.

The Captain passed the decrypted message over to Chris. "Those coordinates will take us to a place just north of Antarctica."

Chris continued to read.

The Captain continued on. "That second set is in the middle of nowhere. Does it make any sense to you?"

Chris flipped through the last couple of pages, and then set it aside. He thoughtfully watched the Captain for a moment. "I'm gonna tell you a story that began twenty-five years ago."

*　　*　　*

Sometimes all you really need is a little luck. The rest of the Blue Ridge Mountain command had made it out to sea. Their first order of business was to recover and deliver the containers to New Atlantis.

The Attack Submarine Commanders were reading their orders. Each had launch codes, times and coordinates. A few thought the orders were crazy, or at least nothing more than a drill.

A failsafe system was built in, and the key to making it work relied on the two broadcast stations remaining online. Each command had a unique verification code it would transmit. If they received a unique verification code back, it was a go.

After that, the psychological profiling used to pick and assign these Commanders would be relied on to ensure their final orders would be carried out.

*　　*　　*

It had been three days and these architects of world domination rested easy in their underground bunker. The only thing that concerned them was the lack of any word about our submarine fleet. Their surface fleet and their submarines had detected nothing. Surely not all of the submarine Commanders had scuttled their boats.

Every hour that went by without any kind of retaliation reinforced the idea that they had won. Even they had no idea that American Military Commanders could be so easily demoralized.

On September the fourteenth, Twenty seventy-three, at ten o'clock in the morning the ambient air temperature outside the bunker was a cool forty-eight degrees. In less than a second it went to ten thousand degrees Celsius as three twenty mega-ton warheads vaporized the mountaintop.

To the planet, we were nothing more than parasites existing inside a wafer-thin environment on its skin. The more than forty-three hundred warheads that blanketed the eastern hemisphere, Australia and South America did nothing more than scratch the itch.

*   *   *

The USS Georgana was on station twenty miles north of Antarctica. This location was the only rendezvous point given to the Submarine Commanders. If Chris's boat had not been available, then another of the Blue Ridge Mountain subs would have gotten the pied piper assignment.

Twenty-four of the twenty-eight submarines on station had delivered their payloads. The other four were still not accounted for and never would be.

The orders were simple and clear. Launch, and then plot the most direct course to the rendezvous point. The orders stated that they had four days to reach the rendezvous, after that there would be no safe haven to go to.

Chris and Captain O'Donnel were on the external conning tower bridge. The air temperature was just above freezing. The Captain, and the two lookouts above, were using glasses to scan the sea around them.

They transmitted a weak beacon signal that the subs could pick up when they were just a few miles out. Radio silence was being strictly maintained. Our missile attack had eliminated land-based forces but the enemy still had submarines and surface craft that might pose a threat. It was hoped that without direct orders they would hesitate long enough for us to complete the next step.

Chris had his gloved hands in front of his face using his breath to warm his nose. "Anything?"

The Captain looked away from the glasses. "No, not yet." He looked at Chris. "How deep is this place?"

"Thirteen thousand feet, about two and a half miles."

"And you've been in it?"

"Yes, twenty-five years ago. I designed it," Chris answered.

The Captain scanned another arc with the glasses, and then looked back. "How do we know it's still there, I mean that's a long time and a lotta water."

Chris pulled a small hand held receiver out of his pocket. A green light was flashing in the corner of a small screen. Next to the light were map coordinates. "I'm receiving the beacon. Our communications satellites are still functioning. It's being relayed to me over a secure channel from the broadcast station in Maine."

"Ahoy, a conning tower," came from above them.

The Captain went back to his glasses. "I see them. Flash the signal." He picked up a sound powered communication system to the inside. "Standby tube number one."

He and Chris watched as the lookout used a hand held strobe to flash a coded signal, and then went back to his glasses.

A moment later the lookout looked down. "Signal confirmed."

"Stand down number one," relayed the Captain. He replaced the mike.

Chris had, had enough of the cold. "Well, this southwest boy is freezing his ass off. I need a cup of coffee. You want anything?"

"No, thank you."

With that, Chris retreated into the warmth of the sub.

Through the rest of the day, and the night that followed, fourteen submarines took up station keeping at the rendezvous point. The next morning four more joined them. That still left ten unaccounted for. Late that morning a meeting was held in the wardroom of the Georgana.

A Submarine Captain does not like being kept in the dark, especially when it concerns the safety of his crew.

The moment Chris walked into the room he was verbally accosted.

Captain O'Donnel stepped up. "Wait, wait a minute. Mr. Wincrest will fill all of you in on what's happened and what's about to happen next."

One of the Captains said, what everyone else was thinking. "Mr. Wincrest is it. It's pretty obvious what just happened. We just killed nine billion people and turned most of this planet into a nuclear wasteland. What we don't know is what's happened to *our* homes and families?"

Chris began. "I know that question had to be asked, but stop and think about it. If our country, our way of life still existed none of *this* would have happened."

Everyone at that table, in their own way, had to come to terms with the reality of it all.

Another Captain asked, "Why are we here? If the entire world has become a graveyard what's left for us?"

Chris looked from face to face and then began. "Twenty-five years ago, looking forward to this eventuality, we created a place that would be untouched by what's happened today."

He spoke uninterrupted for the better part of an hour. When he was done he fielded the questions the best he could. He said nothing about the underground sites. That was irrelevant. In the end, a glimmer of hope existed where none had been before.

Through out the day and into the night four more subs showed up. The Captains were briefed.

At eight o'clock the next morning the Georgana set out for New Atlantis.

Chris and Captain O'Donnel were on the external conning tower bridge.

Chris looked up at a cloudless, blue sky above them. "Take a good look. It'll be the last time you'll see it with your own eyes. Once we submerge this world ceases to exist for us."

Captain O'Donnel looked toward the east. "Look!"

On the entire eastern horizon a dark cloud had formed.

Chris knew what it was. "We better get below."

"Right." Looking up, "Clear the bridge."

The lookouts clambered below.

The Captain picked up the mike, "Dive, Dive."

The alarm sounded. Chris slipped through the hatch. Captain O'Donnel followed pausing to take one final look at a world he would never see again. He pulled the hatch closed above him just as the ocean spilled onto the bridge.

*   *   *

Half way to their destination sonar made a contact. The Captain was piped to the bridge.

Captain O'Donnel and Chris stepped onto the bridge. "Captain on the bridge," was announced.

The Captain responded, "As you were. What've we got?"

The Executive Officer, Lieutenant Commander McReynolds had the con. "Ronan class sub-killer bearing one six zero range ten thousand yards," he said. "Depth six hundred. They're paralleling us."

"Have they seen us?" Asked Chris.

"No," answered the Captain. "They can't penetrate the shield. Is he alone?"

"Yes," replied the Sonar Watch. "They're not getting a sonar return but there's a lot of us bunched together. Their Hydrophones might be picking up the water displacements or the cavitations from this many props churning things up."

The Captain looked at Chris. "They're having the same problem we are, no one left to talk to."

The Executive Officer weighted in. "We may look like a school of whales, but with what just went down they may shoot first and ask questions later. If they fire a full spread they might get lucky."

"Sir," said the Sonar Watch. "They're changing course. They're turning into us."

"Shall I break radio silence?" Asked the Executive Officer.

Before the Captain could answer the Sonar Watch came back. "The Oklahoma just broke ranks. It looks like he's going after him."

"Damn it," said the Captain. "Flash a signal to the others. Tell them to disperse."

The Executive Officer went to the periscope and began using a high intensity strobe light to pass the signal back through the water.

"This close together," said the Captain, "if he gets one of us it could take out someone else."

The submarine flotilla began to break up, each sub changing direction and depth.

"They're arming weapons," said the Sonar Watch. "They're opening outer doors." He looked back. "They're gonna fire."

The Captain said, more to himself. "Come on Pete kill this mother-fucker."

The Sonar Watch spoke up. "They fired. Weapons armed themselves as soon as the left the tubes. I have four high-speed props. They have not acquired. The Oklahoma just fired tubes one, two and three. They're running hot and true and have acquired the target impact in thirty seconds. The Ronan is taking evasive action and releasing counter measures."

The Executive Officer looked at the Captain and Chris. "They sure as hell know we're here now."

The Captain asked. "The other torpedoes?"

"Circling, looking for a target," replied the Sonar Watch.

"Shit," came the Captain's reply.

"Impact in ten," came the Executive Officer's voice. "Nine, eight, seven, six, five, four, three, two, one."

The seawater carried the death throws of the Ronan back to them.

"Nice shooting Pete. Can we get firing solutions on those torpedoes?" Asked the Captain.

"I don't know," answered the Executive Officer. "I've never tried to shoot a torpedo with a torpedo before. Give me a minute."

The Executive Officer walked over the fire control. A few minutes later he looked back at the Captain. "Whenever you're ready."

"Fire," said the Captain.

The Executive Officer looked back at fire control. "Fire tubes one through four."

You could hear the launch.

"They've acquired," said the Sonar Watch.

A few seconds later you could sense the impacts as one after another the torpedoes found their targets.

The Executive Officer glanced at the Captain. "That's something I'm happy to say I should never have to do again."

"Let's get 'em back and continue on course," said the Captain. "You have the con."

The Executive Officer threw him a quick salute. Chris and the Captain left the bridge. The subs regrouped and continued on toward their rendezvous with the future.

The Pied Piper arrived on site above New Atlantis with the mice in tow. The sister ship to the Georgana was there along with three other Blue Ridge Mountain subs. They gathered together one thousand feet down. The radiation levels on the surface were still in the safe zone but they weren't taking any chances.

The only things capable of reaching New Atlantis were the Blue Ridge Mountain subs and their drones. Once the crews, and anything of use, were removed from the other subs they would be scuttled.

Fourteen of the containers were in place. It would still take days for all of them to be located and delivered. None of the dome airlocks had been opened. All of the Research submarines carried four drones. Each drone could seat ten people. With about two thousand people to transfer they were looking at three days to get it done.

The first one was the most critical. Chris insisted on being the first to crack the airlock. There was no way to know what he would find. There was no radio communication with the inside. That was one of the fail-safes put in place to insure the complex would go undetected.

The process was simple. The drone docked with the container. There were four airlocks. One faced the dome, and one faced away. It was that one they docked with. The other two would be used to connect each container to the one next to it, thus forming a continuous ring around the complex.

Once inside the container Chris extended the docking mechanism until it sealed to the airlock leading into the dome. The dome airlock had two locking systems for safety. One was mechanical and one was magnetic. The fact that the beacon was transmitting indicated the dome had power so he decided to release the mechanical lock first.

Once the seal was made he opened the hatch on the container, walked to the hatch on the dome, turned the wheel and released the mechanical seal. All he had to do now was release the magnetic seal from the control panel back in the container. He turned and walked back. Just in case he resealed the airlock door on the container.

He stood looking at the control panel. Until now he had kept thoughts of Andy out of his head. Now the thoughts and images he'd blocked out for so many years came rushing back. He swiped a card that brought up the touch panel he would use to input a code. He took a deep breath and entered the code. The system began to cycle through numbers locking each one in until the access code was completed. The magnetic seal was broken and a twenty-five year old time capsule was opened. He heard and felt a rush of air hit the other side of the airlock door.

He looked at the readouts. Everything was in the green. He spoke into his headset. "I've got a green panel. I'm going in."

The answer came back. "Roger that. I'll pass it back."

He opened the container door. Light came through the airlock from the dome. Clinton's power source had survived the test of time. He reported in. "They left the lights on for us."

"Roger that."

He wasn't sure what he expected, maybe the smell of death from corpses lying unattended, in a sealed environment for a quarter of a century. No, the air filtration system would have long since taken care of that. That first breath was musty but otherwise seemed okay.

He stepped through the airlock, back into his past. What he saw stopped him in his tracks. A wide eyed five year old was staring back at him. The little boy turned and ran for the open door in one of the three two-story buildings apparently constructed from material left behind twenty-five years ago. He disappeared inside. A few moments later he reappeared dragging his mother with him.

"What," she asked without looking up.

He pointed at Chris.

She looked up. "Oh my God. You've returned!" She shouted. "Mom, you better come out here."

Her mother stepped into the doorway. She watched Chris. "You better go find your father," she said to her daughter.

She gave her son to her mother and headed off around the building.

There was something else behind the buildings. He moved to his left for a better look. What he saw was a fully functioning hydroponic garden. It stretched for several hundred feet.

He looked back at the woman standing in the doorway. "Hello, I come in peace." How stupid, but it was the first thing that came to mind.

"Well, you took your own sweet time," came a voice from inside the building entrance. It was older, but it was familiar.

A much older and bearded Andy stepped around the woman and her grandson and into the open. Chris took two steps forward and then ran to his old friend he honestly thought to be long dead.

They both embraced. Chris was in tears. Andy, being a bit less emotional asked "You didn't happen to bring a soft drink with you, did you?"

*   *   *

The only disappointment for Andy, and the other surviving members, was they weren't getting out, just a lot more company. Andy made the comment; he now knew how the Indians felt when Columbus bumped into America.

The Commander had suffered a heart attack five years earlier and one other had died in an accident a year after that. In anticipation of that event, a way to jettison the bodies had been provided.

The surface readings above New Atlantis had risen slightly but were still well within acceptable levels. Andy asked to be taken to the surface.

Chris piloted one of the drones with Andy beside him. Nothing much was said on the way up. Andy asked about his family. Chris told him that he had made sure that their names appeared on the list for one of the underground sites, but he had no way of knowing if they made it in. Andy thanked him for the effort. The trip only took a half hour. The drones were heated and the air inside was a simple oxygen-nitrogen mix at one atmosphere.

The drone broke the surface. Chris released the magnetic seal and opened a hatch to the outside.

Andy glanced around. "Anything in this bucket that'll float."

"I don't know, why?"

Andy watched his friend for a moment. "For the last quarter of a century I've been a genie in a bottle. You just pull the cork and let me out. I'm not going back."

Chris could have argued the point, but deep inside he understood. "You know, if you do this you're not gonna make it."

"I don't know, if I dog paddle long enough in the same direction I'll bump into something."

"Not that. The radiation level is up and it's gonna keep going up. You can't survive."

Andy watched his friend's face. "Yes, but I'll be up here, free. Not just another sardine in that can."

Chris didn't say anything.

"Look, I don't see the last twenty-five years as something I lost. It was a great adventure. And I proved that what you *have* to do now, has a chance. All I want for my time is the right to end it on my own terms. Is that too much to ask?"

Chris stepped up and put his arms around him. Andy hugged him back. Chris pushed back. "There's enough juice left in this thing to get you closer and get me back. Now let's see, something that'll float."

*   *   *

The water temperature was in the seventies. On the horizon, the mountains of the Yucatan were visible. Chris watched from the open hatch as Andy paddled away clinging to a seat cushion. Andy never looked back and Chris never called after him.

A few minutes later the drone was headed back and this chapter in human history, closed.

Five Hundred Years Later
A New Beginning

Chapter eight: From out of the depths

The Gulf was calm today with gentle swells running two to three feet. The sky was clear. Just below the water's surface the light was faceted into a rainbow of colors.

A hundred feet down the light began to fade. A thousand feet down the light was gone. Deeper down something began to change. A distant glow began to form in the blackened depths.

The bottom of the sea began to transform. As far as the eye could see, a huge translucent blister covered the sea floor. Quanterra was a city with a population of over two million all of whom were descended from the original inhabitants of New Atlantis.

This undersea masterpiece supported an almost sterile environment. Nuclear powered generators had long been abandoned. The force of the sea around it was re-channeled and provided hydroelectric power. Sitting on top of one of the largest oil reserves in the Gulf provided the raw material to construct the city itself. Everything taken from the ground was used to produce the polymers that went into the surface construction and almost everything else. Some of the buildings were hundreds of feet tall. Vehicles used to move around the city were electrically powered by hydrogen fuel cells.

*　　*　　*

Aaron Colure ran down the steps of "The Hall of The Ancients." In his hand, the proof he'd been looking for. Well, maybe not absolute proof, but close enough.

Aaron conducted historical research. The company he worked for used his findings in different ways, mostly marketing. He could trace back almost anything to its origin. Today he was looking for his own beginnings.

The people of Quanterra had a general knowledge of how they got there. Their forefathers had the presence of mind to bring with them a library of reference material, literary classics and an accumulative history of the world up until the moment they left it. What wasn't included was a lot of images of that world. "The Hall of The Ancients" contained all of it. But not all of it was available to the public.

Aaron spent a good part of his free time sifting through the archives, over and over, in hopes of finding something. Somehow, over the years, he had missed what he carried with him today.

Today was a National Holiday, Founders Day. The streets were not as busy as usual. The date was September fourteenth, twenty-five seventy-three. Events would be taking place all over the city for most of the day and into the night, celebrating the five hundredth anniversary of the founding of the original site, New Atlantis.

His way home took him past the dome, a preserved historical site. From the dome, the world he knew was born. It stood as a reminder of the courage and determination of his ancient ancestors to preserve their way of life and ensure the continuation of mankind. From that, this vast undersea city had grown to rival anything that had ever existed on the surface.

The glow of day was cycling into night and lights were coming on around the city. The translucent blister that held back the blackness of the sea would soon be masked by the images of constellations normally seen from the surface. Tonight they would reflect exactly what was above this site on September fourteenth twenty seventy-three.

The blister was everything. It allowed all of this to exist. It exerted no pressure on the sea around it. It was created through a molecular manipulation of the water itself. Once the reaction started all it needed was the introduction of an atmosphere under it. As the film expanded, the sea was repelled away from it. It bonded with the sea floor, or anything it touched, forming a watertight seal. There were actually two blisters one just out side the other. When a section of the external blister expanded time was given for it to seal to the ocean floor and insure watertight integrity. After that the internal one would expand reclaiming the sea bottom.

The two things that made it safe were first, it required no form of energy to maintain it, and second if struck, it would give and then return to its original shape. Nothing could actually penetrate it from either side.

Aaron's wife Emma waited at home. Of all the national holidays, from the ancient ones of Christmas, Easter, and the Fourth of July to those that celebrated the events and the lives of people from their own time, she enjoyed this one the most. It breached the class barrier. For this one day and night, people from every level came together as one.

She was an Assistant Editor, their version of an investigative reporter for the city newspaper and would submit an article covering this yearly event.

The celebration would reach its peak with a huge crowd gathered around the dome waiting for the exact moment to arrive when an ancient ancestor named Christopher Wincrest first set foot in the dome.

Aaron's apartment was on the thirty-fifth floor of a residential tower. This was considered the Public Class. About a third of the city fell into this class. The class below it was the Worker Class and the one above, a much smaller one, was the Ranking Class.

Unlike ancient times, today there was no stigma attached to any of the classes. They simply indicated what you did to support the whole. Just because you were born into one didn't mean you couldn't excel into another. What generally segregated the population was the human desire to congregate with others like themselves.

In the beginning, when resources and space were limited, the population was controlled by a strict adherence to a stipulated birth rate and the removal of those who had reached a certain age or were unable to contribute to the whole. The general population understood the necessity and as a whole looked the other way.

In those darker times your class did determine your level of ration, but all of that changed four hundred and fifty years ago with the advent of the bubble. As more and more of the ocean floor was claimed; more and more resources became available until now the needs of the population could be met at every level.

The city beneath the sea had everything. Hydroponic gardens, huge fish farms and cloned livestock brought from the surface fed the population. Desalting plants produced millions of gallons of fresh water. Cracking plants extracted the elements required to support the environment and their industry. Unlike their ancient counterparts the heat required to support the process was geothermal or electrical. The hydroelectric generating plants provided the power to support the needs of the city.

Aaron stepped in front of his front door. The sensor read his body's electrical signature and the door to his apartment slid open. He stepped through and it resealed.

"Hey I'm sorry I'm late. I needed to look for something at the Hall."

He walked into their family area, no Emma. He checked the bedroom, the kitchen, and then the patio outside, nothing. Then he noticed the message center. It was flashing.

He touched the area to retrieve the message. Her voice came across. "Honey, Terri and Walt came by. We've gone to the Central Terrace. Change and get there as soon as you can. Love you."

Aaron sat at the dining room table and pulled a small viewing device out of his pocket. He held it and watched the play back.

It was about fifteen seconds of intermittent digital audio and video. You couldn't make out the face and there was nothing to identify the surroundings. The words were that of a very old, dying man. "It's been twenty years. Still nothing from the under... sites on the... land. I've decided... tell them."

He listened to it several times. There were a few other surviving videos in the ancient archives. All of it was taken in the dome. He had watched most of it over and over. This was the only reference to sites and land.

He sat the device on the bookcase and went to the bedroom to change. He would take this to his next meeting with "The Dry Earth Society".

*   *   *

Through the centuries sensors had been floated to the surface. About three hundred years ago all the readings had come back in the green. At least the area above the city would now support life. The governing body had no real interest in investigating the landmasses. After all, they represented a small percentage of the planet. According to the ancient text all human life had been wiped out there centuries ago.

The sea, and the rich oil deposits that lay beneath it, provided all the raw materials they needed. Their technology could extract and use it. Quite simply there was no reason to go.

"The Dry Earth Society" had formed about a hundred years ago. To casually cast aside the birthplace of humanity was, in a way a sacrilege to them.

The government paid little attention. A craft required to take an expedition of any size to the surface wasn't available, or so they thought. Relics from the past had not even been considered.

Quanterra didn't function under a monetary system. You received credits good for certain things, services and basic goods as payment for the work you performed. Consequently there was no way for anyone in the private sector to purchase or construct a vessel. The city itself maintained a half a dozen small submersibles, which were seldom used.

"The Dry Earth Society" had become at best a nuisance. As of late their voice had gotten louder. There was some talk in the general population about revisiting the home of their ancestors.

When Colin Becker, a respected member of the Ranking Class, six feet tall, in his middle fifties with pale blue eyes that literally jumped from the olive complexion that surrounded them, came to the council with a plan to revisit the surface they decided to listen. What he laid out before them was workable, if he could put together a team that could pull it off. In their minds, where else would he go but "The Dry Earth Society?"

Chairman Kyler carefully considered the proposal. It was a win, win situation for them. This would quiet the rumblings about their interference with efforts to revisit the surface, and all but disarm "The Dry Earth Society."

The one stipulation they put on him for their cooperation, was that once the expedition left the confines of Quanterra they could never return. The reason being there could be no chance of viral or bacterial contamination from the surface getting back.

They had a legitimate concern. After half a millennium of isolation, exposure to the surface could prove fatal. For that reason Quanterra did very little exploring outside the blister. Why should they? If they needed more room they would just expand the blister. Two and a half miles underwater, there were no disputes over territory.

Colin suspected Chairman Kyler and the others had their own agenda, but who cares when they just gave him what he wanted. If that one stipulation became an issue before they left he would deny any knowledge of it. Once they were on the surface he would handle it when, or if, it became a problem.

*   *   *

"The Dry Earth Society" held meetings once a month. Once a year they accepted new members. New members to the inter-circle were few and far between.

Tonight was different. Colin Becker had requested permission to address them. Colin was the Curator of Antiquities at "The Hall of the Ancients." Like most groups supporting a cause, there were several core members and a host of subscribers. The society thought Colin would bring an air of legitimacy with him. With that, their ranks might grow. What he brought with him was the answer to their prayers.

94

Word spread quickly about Colin. Instead of the twenty to twenty-five that normally attended, the hall had well over a hundred biding for seats. Aaron was the host for this event. He planned to show the clip he'd recovered, and then introduce Colin.

"Quiet, quiet everyone," Aaron began. "We have a lot to talk about tonight."

That went generally unnoticed.

"Hey," he shouted. That got their attention. "I know the seating is a little tight. Find an open spot and sit. We have several things to discuss tonight."

"Where's Colin Becker?" Came a male voice from the audience.

"Yeah," came a female voice. "You know we love you Aaron, but someone like Becker doesn't move among the little people unless something's about to happen."

Aaron looked off to his left to another member standing by a door. He lipped "Have you seen him?"

The answer came back. "No."

Aaron put his hands up. "Listen, listen everyone, Mr. Becker will be here, but first I want you to see something I discovered in the archives a few days ago. I think it supports what myself and others, have been saying."

He picked up a controller and aimed it at a section of white wall behind him. The audio and video clip he had brought with him played on the wall.

When it finished Aaron said, "We've all been taught that life ended on the surface five hundred years ago, that the nuclear winter, and the lethal fallout that followed a massive attack by our submarine fleet, killed everything." Pointing to the still image on the wall behind him, "What was said there, the reference to what I believe to be underground sites, tells me that maybe some did survive and may still be there today."

Betheny Lender in the front row, stood up. She was in her late twenties with a slender build and dark shoulder length hair. Something about her caught Aaron's eye. "That may be, but what chance do we have of really proving any of it. And even if we could, why do we want too?"

A voice came from Aaron's left. "What's your name?"

Aaron and the rest of the room looked toward the voice. Colin Becker stood just inside the entrance

"Mr. Becker, my name's Betheny Lender."

Colin moved toward Aaron. "Ah yes, I know who you are. You lead an evolutionary, investigative research group at the university. Of all people, I would have never expected that question from you."

Both embarrassed by what he said, and honored that he knew who she was, she defended her position. "Bad choice of words. What I meant was, why do we *need* to. We've cataloged the remains of those that founded the dome. They looked very much like we do today. Their DNA is..."

Colin interrupted her. "You're missing the obvious." His gaze moved to the entire audience. "Five hundred years have passed. We have no idea what survives on the surface today. But believe me when I say, something does. Life almost always finds a way"

Steward Macon, mid forties, stood up next to Betheny. "I'm Steward Macon and I'm not an anthropologist. I run a clothing store in the Middleton Sector. Unlike this young lady, who only showed up here tonight because of you, I've been part of this gathering for a very long time." He glanced around the room. "I think I'm speaking for those of us who understand what "The Dry Earth Society" really stands for. Our history started, for all intents and purposes, five centuries ago. All of us know the history of humanity goes back a great deal farther than that. I personally would embrace any opportunity to find out where I came from."

Colin watched the crowd's response. "I see."

Betheny spoke up. "That's all well and good, but first we'd have to get there."

Colin reached out to Aaron. "May I have the controller?"

Aaron passed it over.

Colin took it and re-addressed the crowd. "The reason I was late tonight was because I was putting something together to show you."

He pointed the device at the wall. The image changed to that of a nebula. "Does anyone know what this is?"

A murmur passed through the crowd but no one came forth with an answer.

After a moment Colin continued. "This is a picture of the Crab nebula. It's a natural occurrence in the universe around us. It was one of the many things that could be viewed from the surface."

He had their attention.

He brought up another image. It was a picture of Mount Rushmore. "When it became obvious that we weren't going to return to the surface for many generations our founding fathers, I guess we could call them that, decided that it would serve no purpose to remind future generations of things they might never see."

He flipped through pictures of mountains and lakes and a couple of skylines of large cities. The entire audience was by now pointing and talking amongst themselves.

Betheny broke in. "Why are you showing us these things that don't exist anymore?"

Colin looking at her said, "We don't know for certain if they exist or not. We don't know what kind of contact our ancestors may still have had with the surface. They chose to hide most of this from us. Until two months ago I knew nothing about any of this myself. We were repairing a section of the floor in the dome and came across all of this, and a lot more. Did all of it come with them, or could they still receive transmissions from the surface for a while."

Eric Bickel stepped forward. "My name is Eric Bickel. I'm a doctor. This is all very interesting, but let's look at the practical side of what we're talking about. I've spent a good part of my life studying medicine and the human body. The basis of my profession stems from the knowledge of human anatomy our ancestors left behind. Where *they* came from they suffered from disease and starvation. Compared to their world we live in a near sterile environment. If we became exposed to what lived in the air they breathed, we'd all die."

Betheny shook her head. "This is all just an exercise. We have no way to return to the surface."

Colin pointed the controller at the wall. The image of the Georgana popped up. It sat afloat with nothing distinguishable around it.

Now it was Aaron's turn. "The Georgana. That was the submersible that Christopher Wincrest came to New Atlantis on. I've seen pictures of it many times."

Colin looked at Aaron. "Not this picture." He looked back to the crowd. "I took it this morning."

The crowd surged forward for a better look. Aaron pulled Colin aside. "It still exists?"

"Yes, and I've been given permission to refit it for an expedition to the surface."

Chapter nine: It could happen

To use an ancient phrase, news of the Georgana and its new mission spread like wildfire through the population. Requests to join the expedition were coming in from everywhere. The ruling body just sat back and watched. No matter how this went, even after it failed, they would be looked on as heroes.

The word "hero" did not describe Aaron when he told Emma he wanted them to join the expedition.

"Are you crazy," were the first words out of her mouth? Everything went down hill from there.

"It's a chance to find out where we came from," he argued.

"I'm from the Kolanees sector and that's as far back as I need to know."

He followed her around. "This chance may never come again. It's been my dream for as long as I can remember."

She faced him. "And what about my dream. A family and a chance to grow old with you."

"It's not going to be forever. When we get back we'll have all that."

There were tears in her eyes. "I guess it's time for choices. If you go, it's without me."

He'd never even considered doing this without her. He loved her so much and in the end he had to back off. "Nothing in this life means more to me, than you. There are no choices there's just us."

Her face brightened. She kissed him, hugged his neck and took him to bed.

*   *   *

For the next couple of weeks Aaron went to work, came home and went through the motions. The Georgana carried a crew of eighty-five. He was sure it was filling up fast.

One night he received a call from Colin. Emma was in the kitchen and heard the call come in.

"Colin, how are things going?"

"Aaron what happened to you? I thought you would've been first in line to sign up. You're part of the reason all of this is happening."

What had been a light hearted greeting faded into something more somber. "I'd love to be there when the Georgana breaks the surface for the first time in five hundred years, but I have other commitments here at home, maybe the next trip. Now, tell me everything."

Emma listened at the doorway as Colin and Aaron talked and joked about the adventure of a lifetime. She had never seen him so happy.

That night at the dinner table Aaron ate while Emma picked at hers. She finally laid down her fork. "Will they let you call?"

He looked at her. "What?"

"Can you send messages," glancing up, "from way up there?"

When it finally registered what she said, he stood up and walked around the table. She stood up.

He hugged her. "Why?"

She held him tight. "When I told you to make a choice and you did, a light went out inside of you. Tonight, on that call, I saw it come back on for just a little while. I realized without that light I only have part of you and I fell in love with all of you."

"You're not coming, are you?"

100

"This is your adventure," she said. "Go and find whatever it is you're looking for, and then spend the rest of your life with me. That's mine."

He took her in his arms and kissed her holding her as close as he could.

Pushing him back she said, "Now, answer my question, will we be able to talk?"

"Every day." He knew what she was giving up and in his heart, he would never love her more."

*   *   *

Aaron met with Colin the next day in Colin's office. The office was filled with items from the past some dating all the way back to the dome. Quanterra had a cumulative history of its own. Most of it dealt with the construction and expansion of the city itself.

Aaron looked across the desk at Colin. "I wasn't sure there'd be any room left."

Colin passed a contract across the desk. "I needed you to be with me on this. I needed "The Dry Earth Society" to become the focal point, something for people to identify with. But most of all I needed your passion to know and understand our past beyond the dome. If you hadn't decided to join us, the Georgana would've sailed with an empty seat."

Aaron picked up the paperwork Colin had placed in front of him. "What's this?"

"It's a release of sorts. What we're about to attempt is very dangerous. It guarantees certain things from you and releases the council of any liability. They're requiring it from everyone."

Aaron read through it. He got to the last page, signed it and handed it back. In all of the contracts, Colin had left out the part about not coming back. In his mind it was still negotiable and that allowed him to sleep at night.

Forty-seven people were accepted based on the expertise they could bring to the endeavor. The one thing none of them brought was the ability to pilot the sub. When the question came up Colin assured everyone that had been taken care of.

*   *   *

The day came for everyone to be relocated to a secure area of the city. A place where medical teams, already in place, would attempt to adjust their immune systems to give them a better chance of survival on the surface. DNA samples were available from the original inhabitants of New Atlantis. Antibodies extracted from these samples would be used to boost their immune systems. Even with this, there were no guarantees. It was an eventuality everyone chose to ignore.

Emma and Aaron looked at each other, each not really wanting to say goodbye to the other.

Finally Emma broke the silence. "What are they gonna do to you?"

"From what I'm told it's an adjustment to our immune system to protect us from bacteria or viruses that may still exist on the surface."

She placed her head on his shoulder. "I'm sorry I asked." She looked up at him. "I want you back. You understand me? I want you back."

"There will be stories for our grandchildren," he said. "I'll be back. I promise."

With that he kissed her goodbye, and he and the others boarded the bus.

Midway down the isle Betheny Lender had a seat next to the window. The seat next to her was empty. Aaron asked, "Betheny, isn't it? Do you mind?"

She smiled at him. "It's Beth and no, I don't mind."

Aaron took the seat. Beth went back to looking out the window.

Most of the city structures were away from the blister itself. The hydroelectric facilities were partially exposed to the sea around them allowing access to the water pressure required to drive the turbines. The desalting plants, and some other industrial facilities, needed the ocean to produce the fresh water and other elements required by the population.

The bus pulled up to a restricted area. It was clearly marked "off limits to the general population." Colin left the driver's seat and approached the entrance. Next to the entrance was a keypad and card reader. Colin made several entries on the keypad, and then swiped a card. The door slid open, followed by the sound of air being released. He returned to the bus and drove through the gate. As soon as the bus cleared the entrance the door resealed followed by the sound of the magnetic security lock resetting itself.

A huge facility spread out before them. Beth asked, "Did you know anything about this place?"

His eyes had never left the window. "No, I don't think many do."

The bus continued toward the back of the complex. Everyone they passed seemed to be wearing a uniform of some kind. The city had no standing army. The police, charged with protecting the population, had nothing much to do other than provide a sense of security. Crime was almost non-existent. The hopelessness and helplessness that fed criminal activity in most societies just didn't exist here. It had been more than two years since the last homicide and that stemming from a jealous confrontation.

Criminal prosecutions were conducted before the Council. Their decision was final. Those convicted of capital crimes were executed, sealed in containers and dropped into vertical shafts going down thousands of feet. I wasn't practical to support the space required for a conventional cemetery. Huge mausoleums were maintained where families could place plaques and pictures to remember their loved ones.

Beth looked at Aaron. "I've seen pictures of the ancient armies. These people look a lot like..."

He finished her comment. "Them."

The complex covered about three hundred acres. The lack of military presence in the city was not exactly true. None of them ever showed up in uniform.

The bus pulled up in front of the housing selected for the new guests. Everyone filed out and lined up. Colin was met by what appeared to be a military officer. They talked for a moment and then the officer left.

Colin turned to everyone. "Okay folks, this is going to be your home for the next six months."

Aaron spoke up. "Six months? What's gonna take six months?"

Colin directed his answer to everyone. "A fair question. First, the vessel we'll be traveling in hasn't functioned for five hundred years. It requires some major refitting. The nuclear power plant onboard won't work and it's going to take a while to convert it over to electrical. On top of that it's gonna take time to train the crew."

The crowd murmured among themselves.

Colin continued. "They have to begin adjusting our immune systems. That can't be rushed. Now, I need all of you to pick up your personal belongings and follow me inside. In about an hour we all go over for physicals."

They were met in the lobby by another military type. They were being housed two to a room. He called off the names and assigned the room numbers. Gender didn't come into it. The people of Quanterra had long since given up gender segregation. That didn't mean that everyone wanted to share their space, especially married couples, with everyone else. It just meant casual contact didn't really matter. Public restrooms for instance were unisex.

As chance would have it Aaron and Beth having been designated as team leaders were assigned to the same quarters. Beth being single didn't care. Aaron was married and should have spoken up, but something in the back of his mind said this would be okay.

Beth stepped up to the door to room 416 and it slid open. The room wasn't too bad. The walls were off white and the carpet was light gray. Against one wall were two beds. A desk with computer access was provided. There was one bathroom and storage space for clothes and personal belongings. A window looked out over a courtyard landscaped with trees and shrubs. Parks with trees and shrubs were common throughout the city.

Aaron stepped around her. "Not too bad."

Beth entered after him and the door slid shut. "Which bed do you want?"

"I don't care, you pick."

Aaron stepped into the bathroom. Beth sat on the bed up against the wall in the corner.

Aaron stepped back into the room. "I hope you're a shower person there's no tub."

"What do you think about all this?"

Aaron sat on his bed "What do you mean?"

"Colin seems to gravitate toward you more than anyone else. I thought maybe you might have a little incite into what he's planning."

"Not really. I literally caught the bus at the last minute. I've spent a lot of time in the Hall. I'm sure he's checked the logs."

A knock on the door, "Hey we need you downstairs. It's time to get poked and prodded."

They both stood up and left the room.

*   *   *

The clinic was state-of-the-art. The roommates were paired up together. Aaron and Beth waited their turn, second in line. The two ahead of them were taken in. Twenty-five minutes later they left through another door wearing just a piece of tissue paper. They were escorted down the hall. Beth blushed a little at the prospect. It was their turn.

The room was filled with devices to probe and scan every part of the human body. They were both handed a white bag, told to disrobe and place everything in the bag.

Beth blushed. "Here?"

"Ma'am, this is a military base. We don't have private dressing rooms."

They both made every effort to avoid looking, but in the end when you're standing naked next to someone it's going to happen.

They sat Aaron on a table while they placed Beth in front of a number of devices that literally told them everything there was

105

to know. While he waited, they took blood and tissue samples. While the scanners were used on him they took blood and tissue samples from her.

The last thing she had to endure was a vaginal exam with very little privacy.

This was embarrassing for Aaron. He could only imagine what it was for her. He looked away.

When they were done she could hardly look anyone in the eye.

Then it was over. They were given their tissue paper gowns and sent back into the hall.

As they were led away Beth smiled and glanced his way. "I guess sharing the bathroom isn't gonna be a major issue after all."

"Just don't leave your underwear hanging all over the place."

That brought a laugh. "You're assuming they're gonna give us any."

That brought a smile from him.

At the next stop they were in fact given a lot of things including clothes, and allowed to change.

Aaron wanted to talk to Emma but was told that as long as they were inside the facility there could be no communication with the outside.

He wasn't happy. He'd made a promise and wanted to know why he couldn't keep it. Colin needed to supply that answer. He cornered him in his quarters.

"I was told I can't talk to my wife or anyone else. You never said anything about this."

Colin had been waiting for this to come up. He was surprised it took so long. "There's a lot of very sensitive research going on here. Things that no one needs to know about until they're sure it's safe."

"Research huh, I think it has more to do with an *army* no one knows we have and *why* do we need one anyway? It's not like we're subject to attack."

"Not today, but old habits die hard. The paranoia that created all of this still lingers. As for the communications black out, I was assured that family members were informed and if there were any kind of emergency, exceptions could be made."

Aaron still wasn't happy about breaking his promise, but there was nothing he could do about it now. The conversation turned to the mission. He and Colin went over the time line for the next several months.

Chapter ten: Adjustments

The next couple of months were spent pulling their teams together. Beth headed up a team of bio-researchers that would have the job of identifying, classifying and naming whatever they find. Aaron, and his group would be responsible for creating a time line of past and present events and filling in the blanks. Beth began keeping a hand written journal. The journal was her personal, private feelings about what was happening and she didn't want it to be part of the electronic record.

They, and the others, had been getting weekly injections. Preserved DNA samples from the original inhabitants of the dome were used. It was thought that someday future generations might want to trace back their linage. Some members of the Ranking Class had done that just to establish bragging rights.

Their bodies were changing. Because of these changes they were kept in general quarantine away from the base population. The building they lived in was hermetically sealed. At first some of them developed symptoms. They had to be placed in close quarantine until it could be determined if, or when, it was safe for them to rejoin the rest of the group. Colin was careful to leave out the "if" part. Beth and Aaron had not reacted to the injections and continued to work on their projects.

*   *   *

It had never been the Council's intent to inform the families about the blackout assuming Colin had already covered that with them and Colin had simply needed to appease Aaron for the moment.

Emma became concerned when she hadn't heard from Aaron for such a long time. Attempts to contact him were being blocked. She went to "The Hall of the Ancients" in an attempt to contact Colin. She was told that a blackout was in force by order of the Council and that no form of communication was being allowed.

She managed, through her sources at the paper, to come up with a list of names of those chosen for the expedition.

She ran down some of the family members and found out there had been no contact with anyone from the day they left. Everyone was in the dark as to why.

Her nose for news told her something was up and with the paper to back her, she managed to contact a member of the Council who was willing to meet with her.

Edward Langston was newly selected to the Council. He had been directed by Chairman Kyler to meet with this reporter, and first to find out what she knows, and then to double talk his way around any probing questions that might come up.

Emma was escorted into Mr. Langston's office. He Stood and walked around his desk to greet her. "Mrs. Colure, please have a seat. It's always a pleasure to meet with the press."

She took the seat. "Please, it's Emma."

He moved back to his chair behind the desk. "Okay, Emma, I understand you have some questions about our attempt to make contact with the surface." He took his seat.

She settled back in the chair. "I'm more concerned about making contact with those chosen for this little quest to top of our world."

"That's an interesting way to put it. Why do you need to talk with them? I mean we're releasing information as we get it from the facility where they're being trained and conditioned to make this trip."

Smiling at him she said, "Well I guess you haven't gotten any information because as far as I can tell you haven't released any. I'm here on behave of the paper, but I also have a personal stake in all of this. My husband is one of those being conditioned, as you put it, and I haven't heard from him since he left."

"Well if you'll leave him a message I'll see that he gets it."

She leaned forward to make her point. "What's going on? Why can't I get a call through to him? What's this *facility* you spoke of?"

"It's a research facility. What's developed there isn't released to the public until we're sure it's safe."

"What has that got to do with my husband or the others?

"Nothing, but for the reasons I just spoke of protocols are in place that prevent outside communications. If we breach those protocols for the benefit of your husband, or anyone with him, it could compromise the entire facility."

What he said sounded good, maybe a little too good. A little voice in the back of her head was speaking to her and it told her something else was going on.

Edward stood. "If that's all, I have someplace I need to be."

She stood. "That's all for now. Oh yes, tell my husband I love him and miss him and to contact me as soon as he can."

"I'll see that he gets the message."

With that she left. Edward sat and pondered his next move.

Emma left the building. She had her sources. Somewhere someone knew exactly what was going on.

* * *

A few days later Colin knocked on the door to Aaron and Beth's living quarters. After a few moments he knocked again.

Aaron popped the door. "Hey, it's Saturday. What's up?"

Beth appeared from the bathroom. She closed her robe.

Colin smiled at her and then asked, "May I come in?"

Aaron stepped back. "Sure, the place is sort of a mess."

Colin came in and stopped just inside the doorway. "I need to talk to you, in private."

Beth spoke up. "I was just about to take a shower."

She stepped back into the bathroom and closed the door. Colin stood for a moment. All he could think to say was what he had come to say. "There's been an accident. It's your wife."

Aaron stepped back. For a moment his mind went blank. He stammered. "I, I have to go to her." He began turning this way and that. He picked up a pair of pants off the floor, and then turned to Colin. "How bad, how bad is she?"

"From what we know there was an electrical short somewhere in your apartment. There was a lot of smoke and gas released. I'm afraid, your wife died in her sleep. I'm so very sorry."

Aaron's eyes glazed over he started to say something, but nothing came out.

"They're taking care of everything," Colin said in a consoling tone. "There's nothing you have to do."

Aaron's mind began to function again. He went to the closet and began to pull out his clothes. "I have to see her. I need to be there."

"You can't."

An armload of clothes fell to the floor. Aaron looked back. "What do you mean, I can't?"

"You've been exposed. You can't reenter the city at least not for a while."

Aaron's mental state went from mournful to rage in an instant. He grabbed Colin, and being much stronger, carried him across the room and slammed him into the wall.

Beth had been listening at the door and if not for her intervention Colin might have been hurt. She pulled Aaron back and they both sat on the bed. Aaron was hyperventilating.

She looked at Colin still trying to catch his breath. "We haven't been exposed yet."

Colin regained his voice. "The injections, all of you including me, are carriers. Three of those in quarantine have died." Colin addressed Aaron. "What we're doing here will change this planet and the future for all of us." He went to the door. It slid open. He paused in the doorway. "I can't make you get on that sub, but if you don't, you may never leave this place. Don't waste the chance

I'm giving you. I'm very, very sorry for your loss." With that he left.

Aaron just sat on the bed staring straight ahead.

Beth sat with her hands in her lap. "What can I do?"

Aaron began to cry. He looked at her and placed his head on her shoulder. She put her arms around him and let him cry.

Colin felt he had to do something so he arranged for Aaron and the others to view the funeral proceedings. A one-way communication was allowed so the service and the eulogy, delivered by Emma's father, could be heard. It was all Aaron could do to keep from breaking down. Beth noticed and took his hand in hers. He squeezed it and managed to control his emotions at least until the screen went blank. Lowering his head he began to cry. Beth waved those with them, off.

When they were gone he looked at her. His eyes were almost swollen shut. "She really didn't want me to go. Maybe if I'd stayed..."

She looked him in the eye. "None of this is your fault. It was an accident. You would've probably died with her. Unfortunately sometimes things happen we can't control."

He looked down.

"Look at me." He looked back at her. She continued, "I've known you long enough to know that if she really hadn't wanted you to do this you wouldn't be here. What we're about to do will make a difference to every generation that follows. She'll be right there with you, in your heart. The two of you will share in this adventure together."

Aaron looked at her for a moment, put his arms around her and hugged her. She hugged him back and for a few moments they supported each other.

*　　*　　*

For the next two weeks Aaron buried himself in his work. Beth stayed by him, but at the same time kept her distance. The day came to meet the rest of the crew.

From the day they started the inoculations they had not mixed with the rest of the complex. Today the remaining forty-five sat in a hall waiting for whatever was going to happen.

In front of them was a raised stage. Aaron and Beth sat in the front row, each at the head of their respective teams.

Colin walked to the center of the stage. "Ladies and Gentlemen, I would like to introduce the crew members that will pilot the Georgana and the security team that will come with us." He stepped to one side. "Captain Zackery Ulysses Kemp."

The Captain walked out on stage and kept going to the other side. He was five foot ten inches, mid forties, slightly overweight, with chin whiskers.

Quanterra didn't have a navy. Captain Kemp was a ship's captain in name only. What he was, was a military officer capable of leading the men who would pilot the ship. He and those under him had to be educated from the ground up.

Captain Kemp stopped next to Colin and extended his left arm toward the other side of the stage. The crewmembers marched across the stage, twenty of them in all. The group included two females. They were all dressed in blue jumpsuits with their name stitched over their left breast pocket and a patch on their left shoulder depicting a landmass with a rising sun behind it. They stopped and faced the audience.

Beth leaned toward Aaron. "You think we'll get a patch for our sleeve?"

He smiled at her. It was the first time she had seen him smile since he'd gotten the news about his wife. She smiled back.

Colin continued. "Lieutenant Colonel Fredrick Hathaway."

The Colonel entered the stage and walked with a heel-toe military step over to Colin and the Captain. The Colonel was mid fifties, six feet, short cropped hair, and a build that reflected a lifetime of workouts. What instantly set him apart was his uniform. A deep green, with his pants legs bloused around the top of a pair of laced, high top black boots. He stopped next to the Captain and extended his left arm.

Twenty-two men and six women entered and marched to center stage. They stopped in front of the ship's crew and did a left face in unison clicking their heels together. Worn over a uniform similar to the Colonel's, was a black vest. Slung over their shoulders was a weapon similar to those seen in the ancient photos.

Colin addressed them. "These are the people who will get us there and protect us if need be." He paused for a moment to let that sink in. "From this point on, until we launch, everyone will relocate aboard the Georgana."

The Colonel faced those on stage. "At ease."

In unison they relaxed their stance, moved their feet apart and placed their hands behind their backs.

The Colonel gave his next command. "Dismissed."

Everyone, including Captain Kemp's crew, broke ranks and walked off the way they came talking amongst themselves.

The audience began to file out. Aaron and Beth approached the stage. Colin stepped down to meet them.

Aaron addressed Colin. His tone was without emotion, just business. "When do we launch?"

"In five days. I take it everything is a go on your end."

Beth answered. "It's as ready as it can be without knowing for sure what we'll be walking into."

Colin looked at Aaron. "I've had your personal items moved on board. We're short of space so you'll both be sharing a cabin."

Beth looked at Aaron who had never moved his eyes from Colin. "That's okay."

Aaron looked at Beth and grinned slightly. "We're used to each others bad habits."

"Very good, we'll transport in two hours, if you want to take the time to relax there's food and drink in the next room."

Colin stepped up on stage and left the way the military had. Aaron watched him until he was out of sight.

Beth took his hand. "Come on I wanna make sure they didn't miss anything."

He looked at her hand in his, squeezed it, and then let it go. They walked out together.

* * *

114

The Georgana was two hundred and fifty feet long. For centuries it had sat off by itself too big to move to "The Hall of the Ancients." The Tiridium hull had held off the destructive forces of the seawater. Time had passed it by and everybody had forgotten about it.

For a couple of months, before Aaron and the others had arrived, the technicians and repair crews had been checking every seam and updating its control systems. It had never been intended for war. There were no missile tubes. It was armed with four torpedo tubes in the bow and two in the stern. These were defensive only. It had been a construction tool. Now it would be an ark for a different kind of cargo.

A new electrical power plant was installed. The storage batteries had to be recharged from modified hydrogen fuel cells. The problem was the power requirements of a vessel this big would drain the batteries faster than the power cells could be recharged. The batteries could supply propulsion and life support for only twelve hours.

Once on the surface, propulsion would be shut down so the distillation system, that separated hydrogen from seawater, could catch up. Without having to recycle the atmosphere the system could supply the power needed to maintain forward motion.

The bus arrived carrying Aaron and Beth and their teams. It passed into the dock area and the doors were magnetically sealed. A connecting tunnel was supplied to affect the transfer. They still weren't allowed any outside contact.

Beth and Aaron were taken down the narrow passageway to their cabin.

Beth reached out with both hands and rubbed the bulkheads on each side of the passageway. "I had no idea it was going to be this close."

The crewmember escorting them commented. "You should see what we have. A piece of webbing stretched inside a frame stacked three high."

They came to a stop and were each handed an access card. The crewmember walked away mumbling to himself, "Enjoy the suite."

Aaron swiped his card and the door slid open. He waited for her to enter and followed. The door slid shut.

The cabin was about ten by ten feet. The door to the left led to a private bathroom. Built into one bulkhead was a small workstation on the other were two bunk beds.

They glanced around. Aaron said, "You want on top?"

Before she thought, she grinned and said, "Is that an invitation?"

Aaron just stared at her.

She stammered trying to find a way to take it back. All that came out was, "I'm so sorry."

Aaron stepped up to her. His eyes searched her face. He lightly brushed her hair back with his hands and then he gently kissed her.

All the emotional walls she had so carefully erected between them evaporated. She returned the kiss with every ounce of passion she could muster.

The months of pain and sense of loss lifted off him and were replaced, at least for the moment, by the simple human need to hold another human being.

He picked her up and placed her on the bottom bunk. She lay there moving only enough to allow him to undress her. Afterward she watched him do the same. She moved over against the bulkhead to make room. He stretched out beside her. She closed her eyes and let him explore. When the time was right they melted into each other's arms and made love.

*   *   *

With nothing much to do, Aaron and Beth spent most of the time in their cabin. The times they did leave were for meals and the occasional briefing.

116

On the third morning, right after breakfast, there came a knock on the door. Aaron answered it. A member of the military stood at ease.

Aaron asked, "What do you need?"

"I need you and the young lady to come with me."

Beth joined them at the door. "Where?"

The soldier stepped back. "Target practice."

Aaron and Beth looked at each other and both said, "Target practice?"

* * *

The sealed bus took the three of them to a building on the other side of the complex. Before they left the bus all three slipped into environmental suits. The suits fit well and allowed for normal movement. The helmet filtered the air in both directions.

A practice range for firearms was something Aaron and Beth had never even thought about let alone stood in the middle of. There were several lanes each with a bench to place the weapons on. Each lane had a transparent shield separating it from the one next to it. Seventy-five feet away each lane had the shaded outline of a human being.

The Range Marshal walked up and introduced himself. To his left and right stood a man. Each carried a Mark-18 assault weapon.

The Mark-18 had been fashioned after weapons carried by their military ancestors. It fired a 10-millimeter case-less, light armor-piercing cartridge. Its effective range was two hundred yards. Each magazine carried seventy-five rounds. It supplied four modes of fire; fully automatic, eight round burst, three round burst and semi-automatic each selectable by a switch on the right side of the gun.

Beth and Aaron were both handed one. Beth reacted to the weight. Aaron asked, "Why do we need one of these?"

The Range Master explained, "You're both considered squad leaders. The Colonel insists that if it becomes necessary, you both be able to defend those under you."

That being said, the Range Master introduced them to their next best friend, the Mark 18.

After adjusting to the noise, Aaron had no problem using it. Beth, on the other hand, was terrified of it and almost dropped the damned thing the first time she fired it. But as the morning wore on they both got better and better and in the end Beth emptied her magazine into the plastic person at the end of the lane, and with ease of motion dropped the empty magazine, snapped in another, chambered a round and emptied that one. The Range Master certified them both and they returned to the sub in time for lunch.

* * *

The mess hall could handle about a third of the crew at a time. Aaron and Beth sat at the table poking fun at the food in front of them and their marksmanship. Aaron was laughing again. Beth was falling more in love with every passing day.

Colin's voice came across the PA system. "Everyone, to your launch stations."

Beth looked at the speaker, "What?"

All the military personal sitting around them, scattered.

Aaron grabbed Beth's hand and pulled her to her feet. "Something's wrong." They pushed their way out of the room.

Aaron and Beth hurried down a passageway to a ladder that led to the bridge. That was their station. They both looked at each other when they felt the ship's main power system come on line.

They climbed through the hatch onto the bridge. Colin and the two military leaders stood in the center. The rest of the bridge crew was busy bringing the ship to life.

Aaron asked first. "What's happened? What's goin' on?"

Without taking his eyes off the activity around him Colin answered, "The Council has scrubbed the mission."

"But why," asked Beth?

"Who knows," said Colin. "Maybe they're afraid of what we might find."

Aaron jumped in. "I don't think they ever thought we could do it; that we could take it this far."

"Someone's trying to shut down the main power grid," said Captain Kemp.

"Override them," said Colin. "This ship's leaving if I have to pull it outta here myself."

The dock was rapidly filling with water. Law enforcement invaded the control room. The man leading the invasion shouted at the controllers "Shut it down, now."

One of the controllers looked back. "We can't. They've overridden our consoles."

"Get down to the dock. Breach it if you have to."

Everyone started out. The controller jumped up. "No, look." He pointed at his console. "They've opened the outer lock."

The leader walked over to the console and looked. The outer lock indicator showed green.

The Controller looked at him. "You do that and you'll flood the city. You'll kill us all."

The Georgana backed out of the flooded dock and into the Gulf. When it was clear it made a slow turn to port and moved away. As long as the override remained, those wanting to stop them couldn't follow. By the time they could run a bypass it would be too late.

The ship's Captain walked over to the Colonel, Colin, Beth and Aaron. "We're clear. Navigation is working. Where to?"

Colin looked from face to face and then said, "Take her up."

A New World
Awaits...

Chapter eleven: Next, a breath of fresh air

For the first time in five hundred years a US Submarine broke the surface of the Gulf of Mexico. It was May 23rd, 2574 at 8:30 p.m. Quanterra time and the sky was clear and filled with stars.

The Captain stood at his position next to the periscope. "What've you got?"

The crewman manning the console that received the reading from the sensors outside the sub looked back. "Everything looks fine. No radiation readings at any level. The air temperature is eighty-two degrees Fahrenheit. A slight breeze at ten knots." The nautical training was showing.

*   *   *

Beth and Aaron were in their cabin trying to figure out how to get everything they needed into the little backpack each had been given.

As Beth fiddled with her stuff, "You scared," she asked?

Aaron paused. "To death."

There was a knock on the door. Aaron opened it. It was Colin. "Come on you two. The rest of the crew's takin' turns on the forward deck. Join me on the external bridge."

Aaron looked at Beth, and then back to Colin. "We're there?"

Beth asked. "We're on the surface?"

Colin stepped aside. Beth and Aaron left with him to have a look at something last seen by their ancestors half a millennium ago.

*   *   *

The Georgana made fifteen knots on what was determined to be a northerly heading. With the electric motors having to just supply forward motion, and not a breathable environment, the run time could be extended. For safeties sake they wanted to put a little distance between them and Quanterra. The use of a sextant had been re-mastered in order to use the stars, the horizon and the sun to navigate. The original aids to navigation required GPS satellite triangulations. That wasn't going to happen.

Beth, Aaron and Colin climbed through the hatch onto the external conning tower bridge. Colonel Hathaway, and Captain Kemp were already there. The lookouts were not being used; after all there should be nothing to look out for.

Beth and Aaron were like two little children seeing their Christmas presents for the first time. The sky was filled with an ocean of stars. The bow of the ship sent a micro mist up to them as it plowed through the gentle swells. The smell of the sea was much stronger now with it all around them.

Aaron moved over next to Colin. "Where're we headed?"

Colin had a folded map showing the Texas/Louisiana gulf coast. He pointed to a small island off the coast of Texas. "There, off the coast. It was called Galveston."

Beth stepped over, put her arm around Aaron and snuggled up to him. She was actually a little chilled. "How long till we get there?"

The Captain stepped over. "We're making about fifteen knots. I'd say three days."

Aaron leaned over and watched the last of the crew reenter the sub through the forward hatch. "Then what?"

Colin answered. "We knock, and see if anyone answers."

*   *   *

For the next two and a half days Aaron and Beth organized and reorganized, checked and rechecked everything. They held briefings with their teams.

Beth's group had prepared several lists of all the species of animal, plant, and insect life known to exist in this part of the world as per the ancient archives.

Aaron's group had prepared a chronological time line of events taken from the private journals of the original inhabitants of New Atlantis and the volumes of historical text brought with them all preserved in digital form in "The Hall of the Ancients." They had downloaded most of it into the data banks at the facility and then moved it into storage on the Georgana when they relocated. Colin had used his access codes to release facts and information not available to the public.

With the destination known, Aaron divided the crew into two groups and held a history lesson that covered major events and people from the Galveston/Houston area dating from the year 2000 up until the world ended in September of 2073.

At that point they were as prepared as they could be when the Texas/Galveston coastline appeared on the horizon.

What they saw, they weren't prepared for. Much of the evidence of human existence didn't exist any longer. The images and pictures they had were from another place in time, a place that had been erased, first by the destructiveness of man, and then by the reclamation processes of the planet itself.

*   *   *

Galveston Island was a jungle. Whatever human construction might have been there had long since vanished into a sea of vegetation. The Georgana stood offshore about a quarter mile. The water depth wouldn't allow them to get any closer.

Below decks a meeting was held in the ship's wardroom. The time for making decisions was here.

Colin had a chart hung on the bulkhead at the end of the table. It showed the bay to the northeast of the island. The Captain, the Colonel, Beth, Aaron and the crewmen that would handle the inflatables all sat around the table.

Colin put his palm over Galveston Bay. "We need to go here. It'll shelter us from the open water and make transferring men and supplies safer and go faster."

The Colonel asked, "Can we get in that close?"

Colin pointed to the spot where the bay joined the Gulf. "This shows what looks like a manmade channel leading into the bay." He traced it with his finger. "This boat draws about thirty feet of water. The depth indicators show the channel to be forty-five feet deep. However time and tides and weather may have brought the bottom back up to a point where we can't use it."

The Captain asked, "How do we find out? The inflatables aren't fitted with sounding equipment."

Aaron answered. "We do it the old fashioned way. We measure it."

Everyone watched and waited for him to explain how.

He continued. "We take a coil of rope. We tie a knot in it every foot. We then tie a flag to every sixth knot and label them. We weight it down and let it sink to the bottom. That establishes a point of reference. As we move along we add or subtract knots that are covered by the water compensating for wave action."

They all just looked at him. He said, "I read a lot. And in case you're wondering about the six knots, they used to measure water depth in fathoms and a fathom is six feet."

Colin looked at the Captain. "Well?"

"We'll set it up."

Colin addressed the room. "I guess we stay here until we know."

Everyone got up. The Captain left in need of rope. The Colonel and the two crewmen left to prepare the inflatables.

Beth and Aaron walked up to Colin and blurted out together, "We wanna go."

"NO, not until I know it 's safe." He wouldn't listen to the pleading that followed and left Beth and Aaron standing alone in the empty wardroom.

*   *   *

Aaron, Beth, Colin, Captain Kemp and Colonel Hathaway watched the forward deck from the external conning tower bridge as two inflatable boats each twenty feet long were slipped into the water and tethered off to fittings on the forward deck. The sea was running at one to two feet and made the transfer of men and equipment fairly simple.

The two boats, each with a crew of three, moved away from the sub. They were powered by small but powerful electric motors. One crewman would take the soundings and the other would keep watch around them. All of them were armed with Mark 18's. Communications would be maintained through handhelds.

The two boats sped along, the only sound coming from the impact of the boats with the light sea running before them. The slight hum of the electric motors was lost to the wind.

The boats slowed their approach to the point where the channel should have joined the Gulf. It took more than an hour of probing with their rope depth finder to finally get a reading that looked right.

The Colonel used the glasses to scan the coastline. Beth and Aaron had climbed up to the lookout positions. You could hear her laugh from time to time. Colin had retreated below to work on his strategies for taking a landing party ashore.

The crew taking the readings reported in. They had a starting point.

The Captain acknowledged. "Roger that, report in every half hour."

The response came from the handheld. "Yes sir, will do."

The rope depth finder was tedious, but it worked and after six hours of soundings and dropping markers a channel was posted allowing the sub to venture about ten miles into the bay around the northeastern point of the island. That was as far away from deep water as the Captain was willing to go.

The crews on the inflatables requested permission to approach the shore and see if they could spot anything of interest.

The Captain gave his permission for a two-hour sortie followed by an order not to go ashore under any circumstances.

The inflatables moved slowly along the coastline about a hundred yards off shore directly to the west of the channel they had marked. While one drove the boat another used field glasses to scan the jungle line.

On the shore inside the tree line an animal, unknown in its present form to the ancestors of those on the sub, watched and waited for its dinner to appear on the beach. For more than an hour it had stalked its prey waiting for the moment to strike.

This creature was the product of hundreds of years of nature trying to adjust for the damage caused to its ancient ancestor's DNA.

Standing upright on powerful hind legs it was eight feet to the top of its head. Its upper body leaned slightly forward and was covered with fur. A thick stubby tail counter balanced its weight. The upper back was heavily muscled and its forearms were short with powerful, taloned fingers. The eyes were intense and set deep into the skull above its wide, slightly protruding jaw showing one inch overlapping canines.

During the season this beach area would be teeming with other forms of life, mating and giving birth to their next generation. It, and others of its kind, would raid the nesting areas and feed. The season had passed and the feeding grounds had moved inland.

This was a young rogue driven away by the alpha male. He bore the scars of that encounter. He was a pack hunter and on his own, had not fared very well. He was hungry and would kill and eat anything he could catch.

Two small creatures ran onto the beach. They were four legged mammals and were playing, running and jumping at one another.

Those on the boats were looking in another direction when the attack came. A high-pitched squeal drew their attention. The attack only lasted a second. When asked later no one could be sure of what they saw. They did see a small animal run down the beach and turn into the jungle. One thing was certain. Life did indeed still exist on the surface.

*   *   *

The submarine slowly maneuvered its way into more sheltered waters running between the channel markers. The Captain backed down and stopped just short of the final set of markers. The last thing he wanted to do was run her aground. Anchors were fired into the bottom and the sub was tethered off forward and aft. Each of the lines had an explosive disconnect to allow for a speedy retreat if necessary.

Beth and six of her team members, three of them female and three of them male and Aaron and five of his, all of them male, were preparing to complete the cycle their ancestors had begun half a millennium ago. Colin, the Colonel and fifteen of his troops would accompany them to provide security and assist with the setting up of a base camp. Three inflatables would be required to transfer the personnel and three more to deliver supplies to the beach.

Beth and Aaron were in the forward hold making a final check. Aaron finished his checklist and then watched as Beth kept checking and rechecking hers.

He finally commented. "In a way it's like setting foot on an alien planet for the first time."

"Yes, and I just know I'm forgetting something."

"Hey, the mother ship isn't going far. And once we have a chance to look around, and establish there's no threat, the Captain will bring it back and park it right here."

She put her arms around him and pulled him close. He could feel her heart beating against his chest and was sure she could feel his.

She looked up at him. "From the first day I've been so excited about this moment, and now I'm scared to death of what we might find, or what might find us."

He grinned. "Well, I've seen you shoot and I think the safest place for me, is behind you."

She laughed and pushed away. "Idiot..." She glanced around, took a deep breath and let it out. "Let's tell' em to load it up." She tucked away her list, took his hand and led him back through the opened hatch.

It still took a few hours to prepare the inflatables for travel. Colin directed everything from the external conning tower bridge. Hydrogen power cells would be used to supply power to the camp.

The time had finally come. After five hundred years the descendants of the brave men and women who founded New Atlantis would once again set foot on dry land.

The three inflatables, carrying the explorers, pushed off and started for the beach. A few minutes later three more inflatables followed. One of the largest they had carried the supplies, and the materials to construct the shelters.

When everything was clear the tethers were blown and the sub began to back out the way it came. The Captain would lay off shore and wait for the all clear to return. A communications time schedule was established for the shore party to check in. If for any reason they failed to do so the Captain was under orders to wait for seventy-two hours and then proceed down the coast and try again to land.

Beth and Aaron had both prepared a member of their respective groups to take over if anything happened to them. The Colonel also had a second in command in the wings if necessary.

Chapter twelve: On solid ground, again

The beach lay ahead. The bow of the inflatable slapped the small swells sending back a spray. The small breakers rolling up on the beach would not pose a threat to the landing. At the last second the power was cut and the incoming waves carried the small boats up onto the beach. Each boat carried part of the military contingent. Four of the soldiers jumped out, two on each side. They waited for the next breaker and then shoved and pulled the boat farther up onto the land. Two lines, each with a stake attached, were tossed onto the sand. These stakes were driven into the beach to secure the boats.

Sandy beaches were virtually non-existent on Quanterra. The bottom of the Gulf around the city was made up of salt domes and hard sediment. As the blister recovered more and more of the gulf floor it was resurfaced to support the architectural requirements of its builders. Where plants were needed as decoration or as food crops they were sustained by a vast network of hydroponic reservoirs.

Everyone piled out. A number of them had a momentary problem keeping their balance. And everyone having never seen or touched beach sand before, picked up handfuls of it and let it fall through their fingers. They began to laugh and toss it into the air.

Colonel Hathaway put a stop to the horseplay. "Alright enough. Unload and set up the encampment."

The spot they chose left an open area of ground between them and the jungle. The Colonel wanted to be sure they could see anything coming.

Colin, Beth and Aaron stood with the Colonel while everyone else pitched in to erect the shelters that would be their home for a while.

Colin watched the sky. "It'll be close to dark before everything's ready."

The Colonel stepped in. "Let's fix an evening meal, then I'll let you three do whatever you need to do. We'll start out first thing in the morning."

Aaron ask, "Which way?"

The Colonel answered. "You choose. You know more about the area than anyone else."

Aaron looked at Colin, technically the leader of this little expedition.

Colin motioned. "Which way?"

Aaron stepped away. "About sixty miles from here was one of the largest cities in the country. I think that should be our ultimate destination."

Beth spoke up. "Yes well, we don't know what lies between here and there. I took a reading when we left the boats and there's still some residual radiation in the soil. It's not enough to harm us now, but a few hundred years ago it altered or killed every living thing here. I think we need to look at what's a hundred yards ahead of us before we think about what's sixty miles away."

The Colonel looked from Aaron to Colin to Beth. "I think she's right. After we eat let's the *four* of us sit down and think this through, beginning tomorrow morning and ending sixty miles north, okay?

"Okay," came their collective answer.

The rogue sat on its haunches well inside the tree line and watched the events on the beach. The hair around its mouth was stained with the blood of his last victim. These creatures were similar to some he had encountered before. These didn't smell the same, but their sounds were the same and they moved in the same way. By themselves, or taken by surprise, they were easy to kill.

However they also had a way to kill at a distance. The meal he'd made earlier had satisfied his immediate need for food. He would wait in hiding and watch for a chance to carry off one of these.

Lighting had been set up around the perimeter, guards were posted and the camp settled in for the night. Beth, Aaron, Colin and the Colonel tossed around ideas. Aaron ran down what he knew about this immediate part of the country.

Beth speculated about what may have happened to the human population. "We know that the population died quickly. I base that on the journal entries made by the original inhabitants of New Atlantis, but nothing I've read really ties it down."

"It was biological not nuclear," said Colin.

"I don't think so," said Beth. The readings clearly indicate that at one time this area was contaminated."

"That came later. After their submarine fleet delivered nuclear payloads to three quarters of the planet." Not giving them a chance to respond, "There were communiqués between the surface and New Atlantis for a time after most of the population on the land masses were already dead."

Aaron spoke up. "I knew it! I just knew it! There *were* underground sites that survived."

Colin answered. "Yes, and one of them was near that city sixty miles from here.

The other three exchanged glances.

Colin continued. "Now don't get too excited. There's no way to know if anyone has managed to survive until now. Eventually the radioactive fall out blanketed this part of the world as well."

Beth had a revelation. "That's why the Council tried to stop us. They were afraid we might actually find something. But if that's so, why did they agree to this in the first place?"

Aaron was confused. "Or why would they care?"

Colin looked at the Colonel. "Colonel?"

"Control and power, or the fear of losing it."

Colin continued on. "I would've never started this if Colonel Hathaway hadn't been my "Ace in to hole.""

"What, in a hole?" Beth asked.

"It's an old card game expression," Colin said. "Anyway, the Council saw "The Dry Earth Society" as a threat."

Aaron was confused, "A threat? A threat to what?"

The Colonel answered, "You had an idea, an idea that something existed outside of Quanterra. When people begin to pose questions sooner or later they want answers. It was fortunate that the engineers affecting the dome repairs recognized the ancient military markings on the containers and passed them over to us. I glanced through some of it and happened onto a reference to the underground sites. I turned it over to Colin expecting him to pass it along to the Council."

Colin picked it up. "After reading through most of it, it was obvious that maybe someone had survived on the surface. I also knew that if the Council found out, these records would disappear forever and maybe anyone who knew anything about them. I had nowhere to go with it, so I went back to the Colonel." He glanced at the Colonel. "I was surprised when he showed the same interest and brought up the Georgana. I went to the Council with a plan to revisit the surface if we could make the Georgana operational again. I hadn't expected them to go along, but I now suspect they knew I would involve the leadership in "The Dry Earth Society. With you out of the way the movement would die and the world of Quanterra would remain theirs to control for another five hundred years."

Beth said, "Out of the way? How, out of the way?"

Colin answered, "Through the Colonel I found out they were assured that as soon as the bugs from the past were introduced into our bodies we would all die."

Aaron looked at the Colonel, "You were trying to kill us?"

Colin shook his head. "No, actually it was necessary or we couldn't have continued. They were just assured everyone would die."

The Colonel added, "but most of you didn't. So I was ordered to make sure it ended in a tragic accident somehow evolving the Georgana outside of the city. Once outside the city the hull would be breached and the problem would be solved. They would simply say that all efforts had been made to revisit the surface, but it had ended in a tragic loss of life and the only vessel capable of making the trip."

Beth looked at the Colonel, "And they really thought you would kill yourself along with the rest of us?"

"No, they thought I'd be standing safe on the dock with a detonator. And I'm sure an accident of some kind, would've tied up the loose end I posed."

Aaron was confused, "So why did they send in the troops?"

Colin answered. "Once they found out the injections weren't going to do the job they needed someone on the inside. The Colonel volunteered to be that someone. They accepted and he joined us in quarantine. That played right into our hands and then somehow they found out about our first meetings. We barely got the word in time, but if you'll forgive the expression *that's all history*. We're *here* and it's *now*, so let's look to tomorrow."

With that, all of them went back to tackling the problem at hand, the best way to get from here to there.

*   *   *

Overnight the sea breeze had put a slight chill in the air. Aaron and Beth were cuddled together inside of a large version of a sleeping bag in the back room of their enclosure. The closeness had kept them warm.

Colin shook Aaron. "Hey, wakeup. We had a visitor last night."

Aaron, still half asleep, "What? What visitor?"

"Get your pants on and join me outside". He stood up and left.

Beth, her eyes still closed, "Was that Colin?"

Aaron pushed back the covers. "Yeah." He leaned down and pecked her on the lips. She grinned. "They need us outside." With that he climbed out of the bag.

Everyone was gathered inside the tree line looking at a two-inch deep track with four clawed toes.

133

The Colonel was kneeling beside one. He stood up. "Whatever this is, it's big and moved without making a sound. The tracks cover the entire length of the camp and no one heard a thing."

Beth looked back toward the encampment. "Why do you suppose it stayed out of the camp?"

Colin answered. "Maybe the lights, or maybe it didn't know what we are or didn't want to tackle this many of us."

"Or," said Aaron, "it *did* know what we are and didn't want to tackle this many of us."

Colin, the Colonel and Beth glanced back down at the track.

The Colonel checked in with the Georgana, reported the visitor and filled them in on the decisions that were finalized the night before.

The first sortie into the unknown would involve the Colonel, Colin, Beth, Aaron, three members of each of their teams and five armed escorts. The Colonel carried a Mark 18. The weapons were offered to Colin, Beth and Aaron. Colin took one but Beth and Aaron declined saying they would just get in the way. The Colonel reminded them of their leadership role and they each slung one from its strap across their backs.

Quanterra had trees and even a small forest. What it didn't have was heat, humidity and bugs. Thirty yards into the wilderness they lost the sea breeze and ran into all three.

Aaron's team recorded what they observed. Beth's team set about collecting specimens. Part of the encampment included a small mobile laboratory to analyze and catalog what was recovered. It was decided, at least in the beginning, every two miles they would break down and reestablish their base camp.

The civilians were able to resist the heat and humidity only because their clothing was loose and light weight. The military uniforms were of a heavier material and the vest just added to the problem. Finally the Colonel ordered them to discard the vest and allowed them to cut the sleeves off above their elbows.

The jungle was close at times, and a machete like knife was used to widen a path. Each member carried a device that would home in on a signal being transmitted by the base camp just in case someone got separated from the group.

Colin carried a rangefinder that used the beacon signal to determine the distance and direction covered and after about two hundred yards he decided to call for a rest period. "Let's stop for a few minutes. Everyone take some water."

Two of the military took up positions on either side of the group to keep a watchful eye. Everyone else found a place to sit and each took a little water.

Back at the encampment a small reclamation plant was set up and could produce about twenty-five gallons of fresh water in a twenty-four hour period. One of the things they were looking for was another source of water, salt or fresh. Without it they would remain tied to the beach or at worse would have to reclaim their own urine. They felt sure they would find water. All this vegetation needed a constant source of fresh water from somewhere.

One of Beth's team saw something move in the brush to her right, and without thinking got up and wandered away in that direction.

The rogue had shadowed this small group from the time they had left the beach. He was getting hungry again and sooner or later he would separate one of them from the rest. He watched the female move away and knew this was his chance.

The young woman watched the ground and foliage around her for any movement. She didn't see the danger moving in on her left until the last second. Every nerve in her body reacted at the same time. The rogue's teeth missed her neck, which would have been snapped, and sank deep into her left shoulder. She screamed.

Beth's heart jumped. The two on guard reacted instantly.

The Colonel was with them. "This way."

Everyone followed with Beth, Aaron and Colin bringing up the rear. The way was suddenly blocked when everyone ahead of them pulled up short.

Beth tried to push her way through. After all she had the only females; it was one of hers that was in trouble.

The Colonel blocked her way. "You don't want to see this."

"What?" She pushed past him and froze. She grabbed her stomach and turned away. The head and part of a shoulder was on the ground. There was blood everywhere.

Aaron took her by the shoulders. "What is it?"

She pulled away, ran a few steps and threw up all over the ground and herself. Aaron looked at the remains for a moment, and then went to Beth.

Colin walked up to the Colonel. "What are you gonna do?"

The Colonel's eyes were following the blood trail that disappeared into the undergrowth. "About what?" He glanced back at the ground behind them. "That? Nothing. What we *can* do is try and keep it from happening again."

The Colonel moved back. Most of his men were shaken. He shook the first one he came to. "The remains go back with us." Then he said to everyone, "From now on we stay together. No one wanders off alone."

The soldier looked down at the woman's head. "How do we..? What do we put it in?"

"Use your shirt," was the Colonel's answer.

Aaron helped Beth away from the scene. Colin followed. Two of the soldiers began to remove their shirts.

Colin caught up with the Colonel. "How do we protect the camp?"

"Fire. Most wild animals have an inborn fear of fire, or so I've read."

*   *   *

Some distance away a tower stood with vines growing up its legs. The jungle had been pushed back to afford a clear field of view.

Its lone occupant watched for movement. He was humanoid, seven feet tall and heavily muscled. He wore leather pants. A twelve-inch wide leather panel extended from the back of his pants up his back, to a hole for his head and then extended down in front and attached to the front of his pants.

In spite of his animalistic appearance he used a very sophisticated viewing device to observe his surroundings.

His mouth opened for a breath. His teeth were very white, pointed with slightly extended canines. His eyes were dark and his jaw was wide and square. His fingernails were claw like. He was barefoot, and the soles of his feet were very thick. His toenails were also claw like. Portions of his exposed body were covered with short velvet like hair light tan in color.

This watchtower sat along an invisible border that formed the boundary around the territory claimed by a species genetically engineered, almost three hundred years ago, to survive in a highly contaminated world. As time passed and the levels of contamination fell their bodies adapted. It was what they were designed to do. They now formed a large percentage of the intelligent life that occupied the surrounding area.

A voice came from below. "We patrol." The sound of the voice was very guttural and course, but it was definitely English.

The Humanoid in the tower waved to the two on the ground. They returned the gesture and moved off. They were dressed similar to the one above. They carried very sophisticated crossbows, machined out of metal with what appeared to be a magazine mounted underneath allowing the bow to be reloaded quickly. The hair color of these two varied from the one in the tower.

*   *   *

The activity in the camp was at a heightened level. Firewood was gathered and stacked around the perimeter. Fire was still used in Quanterra but only for its decorative effect and only on special occasions. The smoke and gases it gave off had to be filtered out.

Beth sat on the floor of the enclosure, her legs crossed in front of her, her face in her hands sobbing. Aaron paused just inside the doorway.

He watched her for a moment and then said, "We took care of her. I mean... you know what I mean."

She looked up at him; her face wet, her eyes red and recessed. "I've never seen anyone... like that before."

He walked over, sat down and placed his arm around her. She immediately laid her head in his lap. He stroked her head and face while she continued to quietly cry.

*   *   *

The two Humanoid scouts moved effortlessly through the jungle. They were at home in the tangled undergrowth. They listened and watched for anything out of place. The one in front stopped, moved his head right and then left and sniffed the air. He looked back. The one behind him had already moved off to the left.

The rogue had dragged his kill for more than two miles before pausing to feast. Normally several would feed while others watched and listened to the jungle around them. This young male was too busy ripping the body into smaller pieces to notice the approach of the two Humanoids.

They knew what lay just ahead. The air was thick with the scent of the beast but there was something else, the scent of human blood.

The rogue only realized his mistake in the moment before the bolts from the crossbows struck. He dropped the body fragments he was holding and turned in the direction of the attack. Another bolt struck him in the throat and another in the chest. He faltered back and fell on his side. He tried to lift himself and then fell back to the ground. After two labored breaths he lay dead.

The Humanoids slowly approached. One went to make sure the beast was indeed dead; the other one examined what it was eating.

The one kneeling with the remains looked up. "Subhuman." He stood with a piece of the body. He placed it close to his nose and took in the scent. He looked at his partner with a somewhat confused expression on his face.

The other one walked off, back tracking the blood trail. The second one dropped the body part and followed him.

*   *   *

Movement in the camp had slowed. No one was aware of the two sets of eyes that watched them. After a moment one of the Humanoids backed away and left. The other one remained hidden and watched.

That night fires burned and formed a perimeter of light around the camp. Everyone went about his or her duties. Aaron had finally settled Beth down. Colin sat in his enclosure and prepared his nightly report to the Georgana. Guards patrolled the edges of the encampment.

Aaron and Beth sat in the small research enclosure. She listened to the verbal notes recorded by her team during their brief excursion. She had elected to use earphones so as not to disturb Aaron as he recorded his thoughts on an input pad. So when all hell broke loose outside she didn't know until Aaron spun her around and pulled out the earpieces.

Gunshots rang out. Shouts and screams poured in as Colin pulled open the enclosure.

Aaron pushed Beth back. "What the hell's going on out there?"

Colin glanced back out. "We're under attack."

Beth was shaken. "Attack. Attacked by who?"

Colin grabbed Aaron by the arm and pulled. "Come on. We have to get to the boats."

Colin, Aaron and Beth emerged from the lab just as Colonel Hathaway and six of his men backed into them. They fired their weapons into the darkness just beyond the perimeter fires. Several of the military lay dead with crossbow bolts protruding from their bodies.

Another barrage of bolts drove most of the camp to cover.

Colin was armed but wasn't firing back. "Who the hell are they?"

The Colonel returned fire at nothing. "I don't know but if we stay here they'll pick us off one by one."

Colin peered into the darkness. "We have to get to one of the boats"

The Colonel pointed with his weapon. "That way. I'll cover you."

The Colonel stood his ground while his six men, Colin, Aaron and Beth moved toward the tethered boats. The assault from the jungle had subsided, as had the weapons fire from the camp.

Everyone, including the remaining military, had crouched behind whatever was convenient. The Colonel backed in the direction taken by the only members of the team still moving.

The tide was in and the water was close. One of the boats was being moved slightly by the incoming surge. That was the one everyone made for.

A voice came from the darkness. It was deep and very coarse. "Drop weapons or all die."

The Colonel looked back at everyone. "Keep moving."

Colin and the others had reached the boat. Two of the soldiers pulled the stakes from the beach. Everyone grabbed the inflatable and pushed.

The Colonel still covered the retreat. "Would you look at that?"

Everyone looked. More than a hundred Humanoids moved out of the darkness into the firelight. Most were armed. There was no escape other than the gulf.

One of the soldiers rose up from cover with his weapon and was instantly cut down. The others tossed out their weapons and slowly stood up with their hands in the air. The rest of the encampment did the same.

Until the wave action began to toss the inflatable up and down the Colonel, and the others with him, had gone unnoticed. The boat was free of the beach and everyone clamored in.

Colin shouted to the Colonel. "Come on, hurry."

More than a dozen Humanoids broke ranks and charged the boat. The Colonel opened fire spraying the beach in front of them causing them to pull back. The Colonel ran for the boat. A bolt from a crossbow pierced his left leg just below his hip. He screamed and went down.

Beth grabbed Aaron. "The Colonel," she shouted above the surf noise.

The boat was too far into the surf for anyone to help him. "There's nothing we can do," answered Aaron.

Colin shouted. "Get us outta here."

All anyone could do was watch. The batteries were fully charged and the motor sprang to life. The soldier on the helm swung the boat around and opened the throttle.

The Humanoids moved quickly to the water's edge and opened fire. One shot found its mark and pierced a primary chamber on the inflatable. Each boat was self-sealing and carried a reserve bottle of compressed air. This hole was too big for the fail-safe system to fully function. Their escape would be short lived if they didn't find a safe place to re-beach the boat.

The shaft protruded from both sides of the Colonel's leg. He grimaced with pain, rolled over and stared up into the animal like faces surrounding him. One of the humanoids was dressed to indicate some kind of rank.

The one next to him asked, "Why would Subhumans break treaty?"

The one in charge knelt in front of the Colonel. He placed his face very close and drew a long breath through his nose. After a moment he stood. "Not Subhuman. Bring him." He turned and walked off.

Two others pulled the Colonel to his feet.

The Colonel's face registered the pain. "Take it easy."

Another picked up the Colonel's weapon, while the two holding the Colonel all but carried him off. The rest of the survivors two women and eight men were herded into the center of the encampment.

Chapter thirteen: Run for your life

As the lights of the encampment faded in the distance, two members in the boat tried forcing cloth into the puncture in an attempt to extend the life of the inflatable. It was a losing battle. After a half an hour it was beach the boat or go swimming.

Colin pointed toward land. "I think that looks okay."

The helmsman swung the bow into the beach.

* * *

When the two carrying the Colonel reached the staging area they sat him down. He was in a lot of pain. The shaft still protruded from both sides of his leg. The Leader approached with another. This one had a satchel slung from his shoulder.

The Colonel couldn't hear what was said and at this point didn't care. After a few moments the one with the satchel knelt next to him, took hold of the bolt and moved it around. The Colonel almost passed out.

The Humanoid opened his satchel and removed a container, placed it next to the injured leg, and then took out snipers and cut away the pant leg. He opened the container and removed two fingers of the contents.

The Colonel had reached the point of losing consciousness. The Humanoid rubbed what was on his fingers into the wound on both sides of the leg. The amazed look on the Colonel's face said the pain was instantly gone. At that point the bolt was pulled out.

Blood from the damaged vessels sprayed into the air. More oint-
ment was rubbed into the wound on both sides and the bleeding
stopped. The Colonel's breathing returned to normal.

Another Humanoid approached the one leading the raiding
party. "Some got away. Go get them?"

"No. Not last long in feeding grounds." The Leader looked
at the Colonel and then around at the other captives. "Bring them.
Need to know where from." He walked off.

The Colonel was lifted to his feet. He placed weight on the
injured leg and flinched, but it held him. Favoring the limb he was
led to the others and everyone was escorted into the jungle. One
Humanoid or another carried away everything of interest. All of
the weapons were taken.

*   *   *

There was little integrity left in the inflatable when it was
pulled onto dry land about two miles down the coast from the encampment. Beth had the presence of mind to grab the small survival kit from the boat while the others moved from the beach to
the tree line. The members of the military had their weapons so,
for the moment, security wasn't an issue.

Colin stopped, turned and faced the others. "Who's the
ranking military?"

A soldier stepped forward. "I guess that would be me. Corporal Hickman, sir." He was very young and definitely had no idea
what to do next.

Colin sized him up. "Well first of all I'm not in the military
so you can drop the *sir*. It's Colin." Pointing, "That's Aaron and
this is Beth."

The Corporal touched his headgear. "Ma'am," and then to
Colin, "What do you need us to do?"

Colin answered. "We'll have to wait for daybreak. It's too
dangerous to chance the jungle at night. We can't light a fire either
so I need you set a perimeter. Take turns every four hours in
threes. You decide who and when. In the morning we'll get our
bearings and take it from there."

143

The Corporal glanced around. "Sounds like a plan. Get some sleep. We won't let anything get past us." With that he went back to his men and they set about securing the site.

Colin addressed Aaron. "What's the name of that city?"

"Houston."

"You really think anyone could've survived in all this time?" Asked Beth.

Aaron answered. "Who knows, either the radiation mutated survivors on the surface into what just attacked us, or those creatures represent a new branch in our evolution. I'm really hoping for the latter."

Beth yawned and sat on the sand. "I really need to shut my eyes for a while." She glanced around at the three manning the perimeter. "I just hope the guys with the guns can keep us from becoming something's midnight snack."

Aaron joined her. Colin stretched out a few feet away. In a matter of minutes all three were sound asleep.

*　　*　　*

Even though the Leader of the Humanoid contingency was sure he had captured a completely different species from that of his old adversary he wasn't taking any chances. He had sent a runner back to report to the ruling body rather than risking the airways.

The runner left the jungle and crossed into a huge open expanse. Rising before him was an enormous city. The city of Anorphia.

It was almost primal in appearance, but one thing was for sure. The mind that conceived it and the technology that constructed it was highly advanced.

The entire Humanoid population lived within its boundaries. There were no outlying villages. Generations before, a war had been waged and nothing had been left exposed to their enemy. Today each side tolerated the existence of the other and a three-mile buffer zone had been established to insure the sovereignty of each.

The runner delivered his message and a response was returned with the messenger. Just in case, the Ruling Body ordered the city sealed and placed on alert.

* * *

Voices awakened Aaron. He immediately thought of Beth. She was still tucked in next to him. He glanced over to see the Corporal reaming out one of the perimeter guards. He later found out the man had dosed off.

He looked back at Beth and in a very quiet voice said, "Hey, you awake?"

He got no response. He nudged her and repeated his question. She stirred in her sleep. He moved and her eyes came open and her head came up.

She glanced around. "What... what is it?"

"Time to wake up sleepy head."

She smiled, and then suddenly remembered where she was and sat up. "Are we alright?"

He rose up. "As alright as we can be, considering..."

Colin's voice came from behind them. "We need to decide our next move."

Aaron and Beth both looked back in his direction. Aaron pushed himself to his feet, steadied himself and stretched. He put his hand down for her. She took it and he pulled her to her feet.

Aaron pointed. "That way, I'd say."

She began to move her feet around and glanced toward the jungle. "Guys, I need to pee." The term had carried over from the past.

Aaron waved one of the military over. "Me too."

The soldier stepped up. Aaron reached out his hand. "Me and the young lady need to relieve ourselves. Let me have the weapon."

The young soldier hesitated. "I don't know. I shouldn't give this up. What if I come with you?"

Beth took the gun out of his hands. "I don't think so."

The soldier reached for her and Aaron's hand stopped him. The Corporal stepped in. "What's going on?"

Beth handled the Mark 18 like she knew what she was doing. The Corporal noticed.

"Tell him, when we get back I'll give it back," she said.

Colin added, "They need to use the head." He was apparently up on naval terminology.

So was the Corporal. He looked at his man. "It'll be okay."

The soldier still wasn't happy but backed off. "Yes sir."

*   *   *

Beth and Aaron both stepped through the undergrowth and around the trees until they were out of sight of the beach.

He glanced around. "This looks okay."

He watched as she laid down the weapon and began to loosen her clothes.

She noticed and grinned. "I guess sharing this bathroom isn't quite the same."

He was embarrassed a little. "I don't think I've ever actually seen you, go."

She used her index finger in a circling motion to tell him to look the other way. "The wind is coming from the left. I suggest you point it to the right."

He laughed at the comment, turned away, opened his pants and relieved himself. He turned back just as she stood back up bringing her clothes with her.

He looked back toward the beach to get his bearings and then back ahead of them. She finished and picked up the gun.

"Let's have a look," he said.

"I don't know. Maybe we should go back for the others."

He took her unarmed hand. "We're not going far."

It wasn't something she wanted to do, but she shifted the Mark 18 in her grip and made sure the safety was off. "Not far."

He led her into the jungle.

Once they began to move her scientific instincts took over and she began to investigate one thing and another.

146

*　　*　　*

The inland feeding grounds had not yielded as much as in past years. Four of the beast had broken off and moved back toward the coast. Working as a team they had managed to pull down several smaller animals, but were still in need. The wind changed and another scent was carried to them on the breeze.

Normally this would have caused them to move off, but they were hungry and what they detected told them it was a small number.

*　　*　　*

Aaron and Beth had moved ahead for several minutes when Aaron stopped. She noticed and moved back to him.

He seemed a little nervous. She asked, "You think we should start back?"

The sound of the wind moving the treetops around covered a lot of the sounds coming from the forest. Humans, even five hundred years removed from the surface, were still predators and certain instincts had begun to reawaken.

Something moved in the forest in front of them and then to either side. They both sensed it and reacted.

Beth brought the gun up. "There's something out there."

Aaron looked quickly around. A group of trees were clustered together to their right. It was defendable. "This way."

They both ran for cover. The beasts moved in from several directions. The small natural fort was the only thing that would stand between them and a meal. With fangs and claws they converged on their fleeing prey.

Beth and Aaron squeezed between the trunks just as the four beasts slammed into the living barrier. They slashed and ripped at the wood. Beth stepped up aimed and fired point blank into the belly of the creature in front of her. The burst sent that one onto its back.

The gunfire backed the other three off. The injured one thrashed around on the ground spraying blood everywhere. The smell of blood enraged the others and they began attacking the wounded one. It fought back until its belly was ripped open, its entrails pulled from its body, shredded and consumed.

Beth and Aaron could do nothing, but watch. The blood feast had removed all fear of the weapon and the remaining three, covered in blood, charged the enclosure. Beth fired again. Two rounds discharged and then the Mark 18 jammed. The two rounds hit a tree trunk splintering it. The beasts sensed the weakness and attacked. They were going to get through. Aaron wrapped his arms around Beth and buried her face into his chest.

Gunfire erupted from two directions. Colin and the rest of the military moved in with their weapons on full automatic. All three of the animals sustained multiple hits. Two went down. The third rushed the man closest to it severing the man's head before joining the other two on the ground.

Beth and Aaron left the cover. She had trouble catching her breath as she stepped through the blood and gore all around her. Aaron moved to her.

She waved him off. "I'll be okay. Just give me a minute."

Colin and the others joined them. Aaron asked, "How did you find us?"

Colin glanced at Beth. "When you didn't come back we came looking. Of course, all hell breaking loose over here did help."

Beth walked up. She'd cleared her weapon. She checked the readout on the magazine. "This one is half gone. How much do we have left?"

The Corporal checked and then said, "Not much, between us maybe six magazines."

Beth adjusted her selector switch. "Set the weapons to fire three round burst."

The Corporal responded. "Yes Ma'am."

She tossed it back to the man she'd taken it from.

Aaron added, "We can't stay here. The smell could attract others." He turned away and pointed, "Houston was north of here. That way."

"And we know this, how?" Beth asked.

He turned back. In his hand was an ancient compass. He held it out. Everyone gathered around.

Colin looked at the compass. "That was part of the collection at the Hall. You stole it?"

"Liberated," Aaron pushed it back into his pocket, "Not that I thought I'd need to use it. It was symbolic more than anything else. It was used by our ancient ancestors to find their way in the wilderness."

"How does it work?" Asked Beth.

Colin answered. "It uses the planet's magnetic poles." Then he grinned. "Just make sure you return it when you're done."

Aaron and Beth both grinned at the comment. Aaron led the way. The Corporal paused long enough to remove the ID from the dead soldier.

*   *   *

The evening before when the Colonel and the other survivors were led into the open area leading to the city the hole in his leg wasn't bothering him at all. Whatever they rubbed into the wound had accelerated the healing process.

A lock down had been put in place and the human and humanoid procession was stopped at the gate. The energy force that blocked the way distorted the air. It took on an almost reflective aura that prevented the depiction of any detail of what lay beyond it.

After clearance was granted the gate was turned off and the raiding party and its captives were permitted to enter.

Just inside the gate the Colonel was separated from the other members of his group and led away.

"Where are you taking me? I want to stay with my men."

The four armed escorts, two on each side, weren't interested in what he wanted and when he tried to hold back he was pulled along. They had two or three times his physical strength. It was useless to resist. He looked over his shoulder as the rest of the party continued on into the city.

He concentrated on the details around him. If given the opportunity he wanted to be able to find his way back to the city gate. The surface he walked on was smooth and hard with subtle changes in color imbedded in it. The architecture was utilitarian, but with an unexplainable appeal to the human eye. The one thing that stood out was the total lack of windows. Not a single building appeared to have an external window and everything he could see was clean to the point of being almost antiseptic.

He attracted the attention of those they passed. Like the buildings, the clothing worn by individuals was similar, but with different blends of color. Everything had a pastel, earth tone look to it.

Even though they all had animalistic features the females were less dramatic. A few even shied away when approached. A few with young blocked the view of their offspring as though protecting them from something known only to them.

He was taken through a building entrance with a pale pink cross imbedded in the wall above it. Once inside it was obvious this was a clinic of some kind. The walls were off-white and Humanoids, dressed in their version of scrubs, assisted the ill and injured.

He looked at the Humanoid walking on his right. "If I'm here because of my leg, it feels fine."

There was no response. They turned into a wider hallway with rooms leading off on both sides. All of the doors were closed. At the end, an area opened up. Several males stood waiting. From their dress they looked to be in charge. The Colonel, and his escort, stopped a few feet away.

One of the Humanoids stepped forward and waved the escort aside. He walked slowly around the creature in front of him and then unceremoniously sniffed the Colonel's neck.

The Colonel pulled back. "What are you doing?"

The one that had circled the Colonel stepped back with the others. "Not sure. Need test."

The others nodded.

The first Humanoid looked the Colonel in the eye. "Remove clothes."

The Colonel moved back a step. "This has gone far enough. I want to see whoever's in..."

The Colonel never knew exactly what happened just that his world went black.

* * *

Colin, Aaron, Beth and the five soldiers moved through the jungle that surrounded them. The infinite shades of green had begun to look pretty much the same and the heat and humidity had begun to take its toll. What they needed was water.

Aaron raised his arm and everyone stopped. He checked his bearings. He looked back toward Colin. "How far have we come?"

Colin reached into his pocket and produced the device used to measure distance. Colin replied, "Three point seven miles."

Beth put her hands on her knees to catch her breath. "Three point seven. That's all?" She looked at the both of them. "You sure that thing's workin' right?"

Colin looked at it again. "As long as the beacon on the beach keeps transmitting this will work."

Beth pulled at the front of her shirt. It was stuck to her skin. "It's so damned hot."

Aaron asked, "Who has a knife?"

Each of the military held up a hand.

"Good, we need to cut the sleeves off at the elbow and pants off at the knees."

Knifes were passed around as each helped the other shed some of the sweltering cloth.

The Corporal began to sniff the air. "You smell that?"

Everyone took a moment to take in a long breath through his or her nose.

Beth spoke up first. "Water?"

Colin started off. "I think I hear something. This way."

The sounds of the jungle came from the wind in the tops of the trees and the unseen movement of insect life on the forest floor. The air was wet against their skin and the radiant heat coming off of everything made it difficult to catch your breath.

Colin made his way through the dense undergrowth. Everyone followed behind him. The sound of running water was plain now. The heavy smell of wet and decaying foliage had been replaced by the fragrance of fresh water.

Colin stepped from the entanglement of the jungle onto an open precipice over looking a running stream. Everyone piled in behind him.

This pause in forward motion only lasted for an instant. The instinct for survival overrode the need for caution. Those with weapons dropped them and all eight slid down the embankment into the flowing water.

Some used their hands to pull handfuls into their mouths while others buried their face in the cool flowing water and drank.

Aaron finished first and pulled himself back onto the bank. He watched Beth roll over on her back and float with her face just above the surface. She submerged and resurfaced a second later sending a stream of water from her mouth in his direction. He laughed as he rolled out of the way.

The others were splashing around and throwing the water at each other. Aaron glanced up. Colin had climbed out on the other side and intently studied the ground around him.

Aaron called out. "What do you see?"

Colin looked into the jungle ahead of him. Another sound was carried to them on the breeze.

Aaron could hear it too and stood up. "What is that?"

Colin turned and ran back into the stream. "Out of the water, now. Back into the jungle."

Beth and the others could hear it now.

Before they could ask the question, Colin answered it. "We're about to have company."

Everyone scrambled up the rise. The soldiers grabbed their weapons and everyone disappeared back into the jungle.

A few minutes later the Alfa male led several dozen beasts to the water's edge. A number of them carried the shredded carcasses of smaller animals. The air became heavy with the smell of death.

Some drank from the stream while others began to tear the kills into smaller pieces. The leader glanced around, and then let out what sounded like something between a bark and a growl. Several beasts took up positions around the pack and watched and listened to the jungle while the rest began to feast. In a surprising act of intelligence several carried meat to those keeping watch.

Colin and the others lay on their stomachs above the stream out of sight. The slight breeze was into their face so their scent was undetected by the feeding animals. They watched and listened to the sounds of tearing flesh and cracking bones. No one spoke a word.

* * *

It was late afternoon before the herd of beasts followed the leader back into the jungle on the far side of the stream. The remains of their meal littered the ground at the water's edge.

While they ate the male moved among his harem stopping from time to time to nuzzle one or another. One of them, a smaller one, pushed him off and was struck hard enough to put her down. He then forced her to her feet and mounted her.

Colin and the others were totally exhausted and several had dozed off.

After half an hour Aaron rose up. "I think it's safe."

Beth, standing, qualified that statement. "It's not *safe* anywhere."

Colin stood up and looked around, "Wake 'em up."

Aaron nudged the sleeping members.

Colin started down toward the stream. "Come on, we need to hurry."

"To do what?" Asked the Corporal.

Colin kept going. "To pick up some of what's left, while it's still fresh enough to eat."

The Corporal shook his head. "You're crazy it you think we're gonna eat any of that."

Colin paused and looked back. "You'll eat it... or this jungle's gonna drain the life out of you and what's left will feed something else." Colin continued toward the stream.

"He's right," said Aaron and started down after him.

Beth followed, "And we need to find a way to carry water."

The other four soldiers followed Beth. The Corporal watched, and then brought up the rear.

*   *   *

The Captain paced around the bridge of his ship. The look on his face said it all. The shore party had missed their check in time and no one was answering the com-link.

Second Lieutenant Charles Avery had been left in charge of the military contingent. He stood to one side and watched. "What are you gonna do? The orders are..."

"I know what the orders are," interrupted the Captain. "We'll wait."

Chapter fourteen: Friends are made

It is said that your hearing is the first of your five senses to return. The chatter down the hall brought Colonel Hathaway back to consciousness. He slowly opened his eyes and took in the room around him. He was lying on a padded table. The walls were the same off white color he'd seen in the hall. The place was spotless. There were various pieces of equipment; he assumed were used for some medical purpose. The encouraging thing was none of it was attached to him. His uniform had been replaced with a light green, one-piece seamless jumpsuit. He was barefoot.

The next thing he noticed was the lack of restraints. He rose up and moved his legs. Everything seemed to work so he moved into a sitting position with his legs hanging off the side of the table. It wasn't until then that he noticed he was missing the little toe on his left foot.

"What?" He brought his left foot up onto his right thigh. There was no open wound. The skin covered the vacated area as though the toe had never been there.

He slid off onto his feet. His knees buckled slightly and he caught himself on the table. After a moment to gain his balance he headed for the open door. Just as he got there his way was blocked by a female Humanoid.

From the way she was dressed it was obvious she worked there. Her eyes were dark. Auburn, velvet like hair covered her head and ran down the back of her neck. The backs of her hands and the tops of her feet were also covered with hair.

155

The Colonel pulled up short. He was furious. "You animals cut off my toe! Get outta my way!"

He put his hand on her to push her away. She didn't move. He bumped into the front of her and bounced back. He went to go around her. She took him by his right upper arm. He tried to pull away and she tightened her grip. He flinched, tried again and this time she put him down on one knee.

She spoke in a soft voice. "Not animal, and still have *nine* toes." She pulled him to his feet and released him. He rubbed his arm. "Must stay here. Someone come soon."

He watched her for a moment, turned back into the room and then looked back. She still stood in the doorway. "All of you speak my language. How is that possible?"

"Language of creator."

He turned back toward her. "What do you mean? Your God speaks English?"

"Don't know God. Don't know English. Subhuman like you. Well, not like you."

He turned and walked back to the table. He hesitated, placed his hands on the table, jumped, turned in the air and sat on the table. It was his way of rebounding, so to speak, from being put on the floor by a female.

She still stood in the doorway, with something that resembled a smile on her face. "See, don't need toe"

He wasn't smiling.

Hers faded away. "Don't leave room." With that she left the doorway.

He rubbed his sore arm. Subhuman, he thought. If anyone deserved that title it was the inhabitants of this place.

The Colonel slipped off the table and moved around the room taking the time to examine each piece of equipment. Curiosity was part of it, but what he really wanted was something to use as a weapon. Nothing presented itself.

Two armed Humanoids appeared in the doorway and motioned him out. He joined them and was escorted away.

"Where's the rest of my people?" He asked.

Neither Humanoid gave any indication they heard him or understood him.

They took several turns and stopped in front of another door. This one was closed. One of the escorts touched a panel and the door slid open. The Colonel stepped into the room. This room was a little more hospitable. There was what appeared to be a bed and a table with an attached bench. More important, was the meal and something to drink that sat on the table.

The door slid shut behind him. He turned to the door and tried to move it with his hands. It wouldn't budge. He walked to the table and sat down. Apparently the food in front of him was intended to be eaten with the fingers due to the lack of any kind of utensil. He picked up a piece and sniffed it. Hunger replaced his need to know what it was and he pulled it apart with his teeth. Whatever it was, it wasn't bad.

*   *   *

Again someone had the presence of mind to grab the survival kit when they left the beach. Because of that they were able to build a small fire under what appeared to be a stone arch sealed on both sides by thick undergrowth. Colin, Beth, Aaron and the others huddled around the fire. Strips of meat cooked in the heat. An armed soldier sat at each side of the shelter and kept watch.

Whatever each was thinking was surely intermixed with the images that danced in the flames.

Beth broke the silence. "Anyone need water?"

One of the soldiers held out his hands. She reached behind her and brought out a stomach she had rescued from the pile of uneaten entrails. She had washed it out in the stream, tied off one end and filled it with water.

At the time no one liked her choice of containers, but as the heat and humidity wore on, what was in it became much more important than what it was in. She poured a little into his hands and he drank it.

Aaron turned the strips of meat. "Best I can tell we're near where we need to change direction to the Northwest."

The Corporal stretched out his legs. "What happens if the submarine doesn't hear from us?"

Aaron answered, "After three days they move on to another location."

"We can't think about the sub," said Colin. There's nothing we can do about it. Right now it's tomorrow we have to worry about."

Aaron pulled a piece of meat from the fire and tasted it. He nodded and each of them took a piece. Beth carried a piece to the two watching the front and back doors, and then returned to her place by the fire. If the truth were known, nobody wanted to think about tomorrow.

*   *   *

Beth dreamed about a trip she had taken to a city park with her father and little brother right before her father had died in an accident. She missed him very much and often thought about those happier times, when she came under a lot of pressure. The last few days certainly qualified. The Corporal kneeling over her suddenly replaced her father's smiling face.

"Ma'am... Ma'am, the sun is coming up. You asked me to wake you first."

She rose up and rubbed the sleep from her eyes. "Thank you. Have your men check around outside. I'll get the others up."

"Yes Ma'am."

"It's Beth not Ma'am. Every time someone calls me that I look around for my mother."

He smiled and got to his feet. "Yes Ma'am... Beth."

She looked to her left. Aaron was on his side facing her. She watched him sleep for a moment and then leaned over and gently kissed him on the lips. He jerked and swiped his hand across his face as though to swat away a bug.

In her case it had been love at first sight, but he was married. Even after the death of his wife she had suppressed those feelings. Now she treasured every moment they had together. Even if their lives ended here, in this awful place, the way she felt inside when he was near by made everything somehow seem okay.

She shook him. "Hey, wake up."

He rolled on his back and opened his eyes. "Wow, I don't even remember closing my eyes."

She noticed him staring straight above him. She glanced up. "What?

He pushed himself up on his elbows. "The rocks above us aren't rocks."

The stone beams above them had square corners and nearly flat sides.

She stood up and followed the overhead with her eyes. "You're right. Nature didn't form this."

He stood up and moved away following the beams. In the darkness at night you couldn't make out much detail. Now with the pale light of morning invading their sanctuary the columns that supported the roof they had slept under were visible.

He ran his hand up and down their surface. He looked at her. "You're right. A man made this.

*　　*　　*

Everyone stood together. Two kept watch in all directions. They stood on the ground above where they had spent the night. It rose above their surroundings. Colin rubbed the earth away with his boot. A few inches down he hit something solid. He knelt down and began digging with his hands. Aaron and Beth did the same while the Corporal kept watch.

In a few minutes they had cleared an area a couple of feet, square. Over the centuries wind and rain had kept the earth fairly shallow, but that thin covering had kept the concrete, forming the overpass, from wearing away.

They all stood back up. Aaron offered an explanation. "Hundreds of years ago people traveled across the land on what was called a road or highway much the way we get around Quanterra. Look there."

Everyone followed his gaze. Leading off through the jungle was an erratic but discernible path through the dense foliage. Where the road had been, the earth was too thin to support most of the larger plants.

Colin walked a few feet, turned and looked back. "I read a story once. It was part of the library in the Hall. It was about a young girl and her dog. They were carried away to a mystical land by a phenomenon called a cyclone. In this land there was a road. This road led to a great city." He looked off into the distance. "I think we've discovered the road that will take us to our destination." He looked back at the group. "I suggest we follow it." He started off.

Aaron checked his compass. The direction taken by Colin was Northwest. The way they needed to go. They all followed him.

The Corporal asked Aaron, "What's a dog?"

"A small mammal kept as a pet by those who lived here hundreds of years ago."

The Corporal thought for a moment. "A pet. Like a Takus?"

"But without the tentacles," Aaron added.

Beth and the Corporal both nodded their understanding and everyone hurried to catch up with Colin.

*   *   *

The light in the room holding the Colonel had dimmed a short time after he finished his meal. He had moved over to the bed and stretched out.

The next thing he remembered was being pushed. He opened his eyes to the face of the female Humanoid he'd spoken with the day before. She again had her version of a smile on her face.

He glanced over to the table and another meal waited for him. He glanced back to her. "I need to pee."

Her face went blank and she tilted her head slightly to her left.

"You know..." He swung his legs over the edge of the bed and stood up. He grabbed himself between his legs. "Pee."

A light went on behind her eyes and the smile came back to her face. She motioned for him to follow her.

They left his quarters and moved down the hall to another door. There was a symbol above the door he didn't recognize. They approached the door and it slid open. She followed him in.

This room was like the rest he'd seen, purely utilitarian. Along one side was a shallow trough that ran the length of the wall. A stream of water entered at one end and left at the other. Along the other side was their version of toilet seats. A bench ran the length of the wall with four holes each surrounded by what looked like a raised ring. She motioned to them with her hand.

He walked over to one of the openings. He began to feel around the front of the garment he was wearing. There didn't seem to be a way in. She walked up behind him, took the seam around the neck on both sides, stretched it out to his shoulders and pulled it straight down. The entire suit fell to his ankles. He stood there naked.

She stepped back. "Now can... *pee*."

He heard what sounded like a giggle behind him. He looked back at her. "Very funny."

She smiled. He peed.

*　　*　　*

The audience chamber for the ruling council, like everything else was done in a blend of earth tones. A long elevated desk, resembling the bench used by the old U.S. Supreme Court, spanned one end of the room. It was done in highly polished hard wood. The walls of the room were decorated with patterns composed of inlaid wood and other natural elements.

Behind the desk sat five older looking Humanoids, older, but no less imposing. They all wore what would have resembled the ancient robes worn by human judges eons ago. The color again was a blend of dark earth tones and graduated into a deep cream.

They all talked amongst themselves until the large double doors slid open at the far end of the room.

The Colonel entered followed by an escort. He was taken to the center of the open space in front of the bench. The Chief Council member, seated in the middle, waved off the escort. Nothing was said for a moment. The Colonel and the Chief Council went eye to eye.

The Colonel broke the silence. "I'd like to know where, and in what condition, are the rest of my men?"

"Not all male. Two female," came the answer.

"You know what I mean."

The Chief Council member watched the man in front of him for a moment. "Need to know where from and how got here."

"From what I'm hearing there are others like me."

"Look like you, not like you. Need answers."

The Colonel seized the moment. "I'll tell you what you want to know, but not until I know the rest of my men... and women are safe."

The Chief Council member appreciated a commander that thought of his men first and pointed to a section of the wall to the Colonel's left. The Colonel looked; the wall section became a view screen. It showed his people milling around in a large room. They were all dressed the same as him and all appeared to be okay. The screen went blank and then transformed back into the wall.

The Chief Council member continued. "Answer questions. Who are you and where from?"

The Colonel took a deep breath. He glanced around. "I'm gonna need a chair? This is gonna take awhile."

Chapter fifteen: At last we meet

The submarine had moved back into its original mooring position in the channel. Captain Kemp and the Military Commander stood on the external conning tower bridge. The Captain scanned the beach with his glasses. The remains of the beach encampment were visible, but there were no signs of life or bodies.

The Military Commander asked, "Well, what do you see?"

Glancing at the Lieutenant, and then back to the glasses the Captain said, "It's what I don't see that bothers me. The camp's been overrun, but there are no bodies. Whoever or whatever attacked them cleaned up after themselves."

The Lieutenant looked toward the beach. "I'd vote for *whoever*. That means we're probably dealing with intelligent life. What do you want to do? Send another party ashore?"

The Captain thought for a moment. "No. Let's cruise down the coast a ways and see if we can spot anything. If not we'll come back here and wait. My gut feeling says at least some of them are still alive."

"Alright. We'll give it a little more time. But at some point we'll have to write this one off and move on."

The Captain picked up the mike. "Bridge to the engine room. All back one third."

The answer came back. "All back one third."

The water churned behind the stern and the sub began to back down the channel.

*   *   *

Colin, Aaron, Beth and the others had been moving steadily northwest all day. Other than some strange looking birds and a few smaller animals they had not encountered anything threatening. Not even the inevitable Cockroach long believed by their ancestors to be the only thing that would survive a nuclear holocaust.

Aaron had them overcook some of the meat from the night before which basically turned it into jerky. In the middle of the day they had stopped for a meal. The stomach Beth carried was two thirds empty. They would need water soon.

Moving along in silence, Colin checked his distance device. He pointed it toward Aaron. It read 15.6. "Without having to cut our way through, we're making better time."

Aaron looked at the sky. The light was beginning to fade. "The next time we reach one of those man made elevations we need to stop and make camp."

Beth moved over. She shook the stomach. "We're gonna need to find water soon. Tomorrow maybe."

Aaron answered. "There were small streams of water called bayous and somewhere ahead of us was a place called Clearlake. There was a large body of water there. Of course that was five hundred years ago now, who knows."

Beth pointed. "Home at last."

Just ahead the ground began to rise again.

*   *   *

Everyone gathered around the fire burning beneath the overpass. No one said much. The last of the jerky was passed around. Afterwards the guard was set and Colin moved away and stretched out. Corporal Hickman sat just inside the perimeter of light and checked and cleaned the weapons. The other two soldiers were already asleep. Beth and Aaron were left at the fire.

She moved over next to him. "I guess tomorrow we'll have to shoot something."

Aaron put his arm across her shoulders. "Yeah, I hope the noise doesn't attract the bigger ones." The odor from under his arm suddenly hit him. "Sorry," and he started to pull it back.

She smiled, grabbed his hand and put it back. "We're all a little ripe."

He squeezed her shoulder. She placed her arm around him.

She didn't intend to say it, it just came out. "I love you."

"I know. I've known from the first day we met."

She just watched for a moment. "How could you? You were married."

"Don't get me wrong. I loved my wife as much as any man ever loved anyone. But now..." He watched her face. "I think she would have liked you. And, I think she'd be glad I've found someone else to give my heart to."

There were tears in her eyes. She leaned over and gently kissed him on the lips. He placed his hand behind her head and returned the kiss.

He took her hand and stood up bringing her with him. He led her away from the fire and into the darkened reaches of their shelter. There he held her and quietly made love to her. At that moment two souls became one.

It was the sound of thunder and pouring rain that woke everyone. A small stream of water coursed through the camp killing the embers that were left from the fire.

Beth didn't hesitate. She grabbed the stomach and shoved it into the stream. It began to fill. Everyone else moved to the sides of the camp and watched the storm. This was real rain not the kind supplied to parts of Quanterra to simulate this wonder of nature.

*   *   *

It began as a cooling rain, but by noon the sun had reversed the effect in the form of steam rising from the drenched jungle around them. Colin and the others moved along with their heads down forcing their feet to take the next step.

The attack came without warning. A human scream ripped through the humid air. Everyone jerked around to see one of the beasts holding the soldier bringing up the rear in the air while two others grabbed his body with their teeth, and between them, ripped him in two.

The soldier standing next to Beth was frozen. She grabbed his Mark 18, and opened fire. One of the beasts lunged and went down. Another took several hits. With that, a dozen moved in from all sides. The other four with weapons opened up, but with so many they didn't stand a chance.

Beth fired her last round into a beast only a few yards away. As the animal closed she grabbed the weapon by the barrel and prepared to use it as a club when the monster's head exploded in a blinding flash. It dove into the ground in front of her, its headless body thrashing around. The searing heat generated by whatever decapitated it had cauterized the blood vessels in the neck producing minimum blood spray.

Everyone stood huddled together and watched as the creatures were blown apart. In just moments the few that were left broke and retreated to the cover of the jungle. Whatever was killing them allowed them to escape.

The carnage covered the ground all around them. It took several moments for any of them to get their voices back.

Beth was first. "What just happened?"

A voice from somewhere behind them answered. "I believe the battle was won. Welcome home."

Everyone turned as four electrically powered vehicles fueled by solar energy approached them from out of the brush. Two pulled in on the left and the other two crossed their path and stopped on the other side. The front passenger's side door, on the vehicle closest on the right, opened. A very tall, very human man got out and made his way to the front.

Several others stepped out of the other vehicles some of them carried weapons. The two soldiers, with ammunition left, brought their weapons to bear.

The tall man spoke. "Steady now. My name is Terrance Lieberman." He glanced around at his men and motioned for them to relax. "We're from New Houston and I think you could use a lift."

Aaron stepped forward. "You said New Houston?"

"Yes. And I believe you're from," he paused to get it right, "Quanterra. Did I pronounce that correctly?"

Colin answered. "How do you know that name?"

Terrance motioned toward his vehicle. "It's not a long story, but an interesting one. Let's get back to the safety of the city. We have a lot to talk about."

Aaron glanced at Colin who nodded. Aaron looked around at the beleaguered group and motioned for them to do as they were asked.

Terrance opened the back door of his vehicle for Aaron and Beth. Colin and the others split up and climbed into the back of the other three vehicles. As soon as all were aboard the caravan swung around and headed back the way it came.

Terrance offered both of them a drink of water, first to Beth and then to Aaron. The fresh water was something they both needed and drank deeply.

Beth was the first to break the silence. "How *do* you know where we come from?"

Facing her Terrance replied. "You have our neighbors to the south to thank for that. Apparently some of your friends are guest of theirs."

"Guests," Aaron injected! "They invaded our camp. They killed some of us."

"Well," Terrance continued, "That was a slight misunderstanding. They thought you were us."

"Misunderstanding," Beth lost her temper! "Tell that to the ones they killed."

Terrance took a breath. "Look Beth, you are Beth right?" Glancing at Aaron. "And you're Aaron, right?"

"Your friends to the south?" Aaron asked.

Terrance ignored that. "Okay, you guys just stepped back, I think the word *onto* applies here, a world you left hundreds of years ago. As you've noticed. That world can be rather lethal."

"It's been five hundred years," Aaron said. "You'd think by now you could've fixed some of it."

"There weren't many of us left. There still aren't. We spent the first two hundred years underground. That's not to say there aren't versions of human life wandering around."

"Like the ones that attacked us," asked Beth?

Terrance thought a moment about his answer. "Well, not exactly. We created those."

Beth and Aaron were amazed. "You created them!"

"That's something we can get into later. Right now let's get you back so our medical staff can check you over. Make sure you haven't contracted something nasty from your little walk through the jungle. After that I'll introduce you to something my Ancestral Grandfather helped create a long, long time ago."

Beth yawned. "Ancestral Grandfather?"

"Well, it's been twenty generations and that's a lot of *greats* to put in front of anything. You both look like you could use a nap. It's gonna take us a while to get back."

Beth looked at Aaron. His head was resting against the seat. He was fast asleep.

Her eyelids were drooping. "I guess you're... right. We've all been... a little... stressed out."

Her voice trailed off and her head went down next to Aaron's.

The driver looked at Terrance. "I was beginning to think that stuff was never gonna kick in."

Terrance watched his two sleeping guests. "It'll be a lot easier to find out what they are with them out."

Terrance picked up a small communicator. "Well?"

"Out like a light," came the response.

"Same here," came two other responses.

The vehicles bounced their way across the rough terrain until they came to an opening in the jungle. In front of them was an open expanse of ground. The Jungle had been cleared back from both sides of a paved road. A set of towers formed an entrance to the road. The air distorted for a moment. The vehicles passed between the towers. The shield was reestablished. In both directions, for as far as the eye could see, a fence made of energy separated this world from the one next door.

*   *   *

Colonel Hathaway sat at the table in his room. He'd been given some history books. Their language was very similar to his own with some slight variations. Their language seemed to drop a lot of connective words and phrases when both, spoken or written. There were some words he didn't know and some symbols he wasn't familiar with, but for the most part he was able to decipher it.

The one thing he had observed, and their history suggested it, was that despite their animal like appearance they were passive unless provoked. And provoked they were three hundred years ago. A war had raged for almost a year between the Subterranean Humans, they had shortened the term to Subhuman, and the Humanoids a name given to them by their creators.

Those who voiced the reason for the war said it was over territory, but underneath it all it boiled down to the right to exist. In the end someone remembered why humanity had all but reached the brink of extinction. Put simply, the failure of one people to except the right of another people to exist within their own beliefs had all but eradicated mankind from the face of the Earth.

The leaders on both sides decided history did not need to repeat itself. Treaties were signed, boundaries were established and the two worlds had lived apart, but in peace, for hundreds of years.

One of the provisions of the treaty was that neither would encroach upon the other. When, what appeared to be Subhumans were found so far inside Humanoid territory it was assumed that the agreement had been broken. Fortunately the Humanoid ability to detect even the slightest difference in scent prompted them to look closer and in the end that saved the lives of most of the landing party.

From what he had read, even though they peacefully coexisted they almost never interacted. Consequently much of the culture of one people was all but unknown to the other.

This recent chain of events was about to change all that. Unfortunately, in most cases there will always be a few that mistrust the motives of the other.

The door to the Colonel's room opened. He looked back and the female Humanoid who kept showing up was there again. She had his uniform across one arm and his boots in her other hand.

"If you keep showing up," he said, "I'll have to send you a Christmas card." Again he got a blank stare. "It's a human holiday."

"Don't know Christmas card. Don't know holiday. Thought might like." She held out the uniform he had arrived in. "Needed repair."

He rubbed his leg where he was shot, got up and walked over to her. Everything was there, pants, shirt, underwear, socks and the belt. The severed pant leg had been replaced.

He reached over and took them off her arm. She held out the boots and he took them. "Thank you," he said.

"Change. Take you somewhere out of here."

"You sure it's safe letting me loose?"

She smiled. "I not afraid. Where you go anyway?"

He smiled at her, reached up and took the jumpsuit on each side of the neck, stretched it out to his shoulders and let it drop to the floor.

She watched him dress without comment. Afterwards she walked to the door, opened it and invited him into the hall.

They walked through the hallways to their version of an elevator. The few Humanoids they passed only took passing notice of him. The elevator was circular in design. When she touched the wall next to it, it rotated open. They entered and it rotated shut.

Inside she keyed something into a pad on the wall next to the door. There was a slight surge and the elevator quickly rose. The pattern she had punched in on the panel kept changing until the panel was blank. It stopped and rotated open. She stepped out and he followed.

They were on the roof of the building. They were alone. It was nighttime and the sky was filled with stars.

She took a few steps, stopped and looked back. "Come."

He followed her to the rail at the edge of the roof. It was one of the tallest and the view of the city was spectacular. Even the nighttime lighting on the streets below was subdued as though it was designed to blend rather than highlight. The nighttime breeze, this high up, was cooler.

He broke the silence. "Why do you keep coming around?"

"Never met Subhuman before."

"First of all my name is Fred and I'm not a subhuman."

"Fred good name. Subhuman live underground. You live under water. What difference?"

It's hard to argue with the logic, he thought. "Let's just go with Fred. What's your name?"

"Kera."

"Just Kera?"

She smiled at him. "How many names need?"

He laughed slightly. "Just one, I guess. What do you do when you're not looking after me?"

"Look after others."

"Like me?"

"Not like you."

He was curious now. "Do you ever bring the others up here?"

She looked away from him. "No. Not others up here."

He reached over and turned her face toward him. "Thank you for bringing me up here. I think it's special."

He watched her large dark eyes. Something resided there different from anything he'd ever known. For just a moment he forgot about her appearance. Instead she was just someone who was trying to be nice to him.

She turned away. "Need go back. Got others look after."

He reached out, took her hand and turned her back. "I meant what I said. This was very special."

She seemed a little embarrassed and didn't make eye contact with him. He released her hand and started past her. She reached out, took his hand back and they both left the roof.

Once they entered the hall she took her hand back. Nothing was said all the way back to his room. She opened the door and he stepped through. She stood in the doorway.

"If need pee. Door not locked." With that she stepped away and the door slid shut.

He walked to the door and it slid open. He stepped into the hall and looked both ways. It was empty.

He stepped back in and went to his bed, pulled off his boots, stretched out and closed his eyes. Something had just happened. He just wasn't sure what.

Chapter sixteen: Distant cousins, meet

The first thing Beth became aware of, after she passed out in the back seat, was muffled voices and soft light.

In a few seconds her hearing and vision returned to normal. A man and a woman, she didn't know, stood at the foot of the bed she was in. They were discussing something they were holding between them. She put her hands on her head and discovered she had no hair.

That brought her straight up in the bed. "Where's my hair? What did you do to me?"

Startled, the man left the room in a hurry and the woman came to her bedside.

"Please," the woman said, "You need to lie back."

"I'll lie back when someone tells me why I'm bald."

"A very nasty form of mites." Terrance stood in the doorway. "That will be all," he said to the woman. Who seemed very happy to leave the room.

"Mites? What's a mite?"

"A parasite. You shouldn't go swimming in strange bodies of water. They take up residence anywhere there's hair. We were lucky. They hadn't had time to burrow into your skin and lay their eggs. That would have been a great deal messier."

Beth still had both hands on her head. "Hair? Everywhere?" She lifted the sheet with one hand and her gown with the other.

"There too, I'm afraid."

She dropped the sheet. "We drank some of that."

He continued. "They can't survive in your digestive system. If it makes you feel any better the others suffered the same fate.

She lay back on the pillow. "Not really. What did you give us?"

"Just something to relax you."

"Relax... I don't remember a thing until I woke up here." She touched her head. "Without any hair."

He started for the door. "Get some rest. Tomorrow will be a busy day."

"What happens tomorrow?"

He paused at the door. "We both get caught up on five hundred years of history. Oh yes, it's late but if you're hungry I can have them bring you something."

"That's alright. I don't seem to have an appetite."

"Good night then." With that he left.

She rubbed her head again then raised the sheet for another look. The lights in the room dimmed. She relaxed, laid back and watched the ceiling for a moment. If the truth be known the bed felt great. She closed her eyes.

*   *   *

The next morning Beth's breakfast arrived with a woman named Rose. With breakfast came a change of clothes. The bacon and eggs were a new experience. They weren't bad. The chickens and pigs that arrived at New Atlantis with her ancestors had not survived the test of time where the cattle had. The concoction called coffee she didn't like at all and asked for water. Afterwards she took a shower and dressed. The sizes were right. The pants, the pullover and the shoes even the underwear fit perfectly. With the clothes came a scarf for her head. With Rose's help they tied it in place.

She was concerned about the others especially Aaron. She asked Rose about them. She didn't know. They left the room and passed down a corridor to the end, took a right and entered a large atrium.

Aaron and Colin sat at a large round table. The moment Aaron saw her he left his seat and met her half way across the room. They entered each other's arms. It felt so good to feel his heart beating against her chest.

They leaned back and looked at each other. He smiled and looked at the scarf on her head. "It's very becoming," he said.

She grinned and rubbed his baldhead. "I kinda like this... on you."

She took his face in her hands and kissed him. He kissed her back and then took her hand and led her back toward the table. "What have they told you?" He asked.

"Nothing really. Something about catching up on history," she answered. "Where are the others?"

"I don't know."

They took their seats and began to talk amongst themselves until Terrance and three others entered the room.

Terrance smiled. "Good morning. I hope everyone's feeling well this morning. I'd like to introduce you to some folks."

At the table Terrance began his introductions. Pointing to the man beside him, "This is Michael Chanell. He's the head of security for this complex." He continued with the woman next to Michael. "This is Kora Parkins. She's the head of the medical facility you're currently in and our Chief of Genetic Research. And last, but not least, Benjamin Peck he's the head of the department of anthropology at our University."

"Before we go any farther where's the rest of our people?" Colin asked.

Terrance answered. "They were part of your military, am I right?"

"Yes," Colin answered.

"They're being debriefed by members of our military. I assure you they are fine and will rejoin you soon. Now, would you do the introductions?"

Colin looked at his two colleagues. Indicating Beth, "This is Betheny Lender. She led a group at our university that researched and chronicled the evolution of our people from the time of New Atlantis."

Benjamin broke in, "Betheny, we definitely have to talk."

"It's Beth and yes we do."

Colin continued. "This is Aaron Colure he's our historian and that brings us to me. I'm Colin Becker. I am, was, the head of "The Hall of the Ancients." It contains all the artifacts and records chronicling our past."

"Well ladies and gentlemen," Terrance began, "Shall we begin? Everything that we'll discuss this morning will be recorded and added to our historical database. Afterwards I have some video records dating back to our beginnings that I'm sure all of you will want to see. I'll start. I'm going to give you a brief accounting of what we believe happened right before life ended, as we know it. If you know anything different please speak up."

Terrance began. He spoke of the time before New Atlantis. He talked about the Blue Ridge Mountain Group and about the specialized submarine fleet.

It was then that Colin told them about the Georgana. "The Georgana was the vessel we used to return to the surface."

Terrance stopped him there. "The Georgana still exists?"

"It's sitting off shore," Colin answered. "It's imperative that we contact them. Their orders are to continue up the coast if they loose communications with us for more than seventy-two hours. We updated the communications equipment onboard for our use. Unfortunately we don't have any of our com-link communicators, but there may still be a way. Some of the receivers are stilled tuned to the frequencies used back then. The thing is, we need to try now."

Terrance touched an area on the table in front of him. An area of the tabletop lit up. "I need the old submarine broadcast frequencies linked to this console."

"Give us a minute," came the response. Everyone watched and waited. "Try it now."

Terrance motioned Colin over. Colin moved around next to him.

Colin took a breath and let it out. "Georgana this is Colin Becker. Come back."

*   *   *

The Captain was stretched out on his bunk in his cabin. The speaker on the wall came to life. "Captain to the bridge. We've contacted the shore party."

The Captain entered the bridge and went directly to the Com-link communications console. "When? Who?"

The Communications Office answered. "Colin, about ten minutes ago. It came in on one of the old broadcast channels."

"Really," said the Captain. He flipped on the mike. "Colin where are you? What's happened? The beach camp was destroyed. Why and how are you transmitting on this frequency?"

"Long story," came the reply. "You disobeyed orders. Where are you?"

"Sitting at the mouth of the channel. I'm the Captain. This ship goes where and when I say. Shall we send over another landing party?"

Terrance took over. "Captain, my name is Terrance Lieberman Governor of New Houston."

"You found people, alive?" Interrupted the Captain.

The entire bridge crew reacted to the news.

"I assure you, we are alive and well," came Terrance's voice. "Captain, do not send anyone else ashore. We do not control those beaches. There are *diplomatic* channels that have to be traversed before that can happen."

"Colin, what do you want us to do?"

Colin took over. "He's right. Through a *misunderstanding* we've lost some of our team. But I'm assured that's been cleared up and no one else is in danger. Just stay where you are until you hear from me. Understood?"

"Yes, I understand. We'll wait here." With that he closed the communications channel.

Several of the crew spoke at once. "They found people. After all this time."

"It would seem so." replied the Captain. He switched to the shipboard com-system. "I need team leaders and officers in the wardroom now."

He started out and looked back. "Route that frequency to the ward room speakers and keep it open."

"Yes sir," came the reply.

The Captain left. The bridge crew began to speculate on everything.

*   *   *

"I can't believe a Blue Ridge Mountain submarine still exists," Terrance said. He could hardly contain his enthusiasm. He would now be able to touch a direct link to his distant past.

Terrance spoke of the events around the creation of New Atlantis and the underground sites. He described the effects of the pulse and the unprovoked missile attack that followed. He spoke of the message transmitted to the submarine fleet that gave them the order to launch their payloads. Some of this information had been preserved and passed along to the descendants of New Atlantis and some had not. Only those ancient ancestors would truly know why they did that. He did not go into much of what happened right after the underground site was sealed. He said the videos would better tell that story.

Beth asked. "And the creatures that attacked us?"

Terrance allowed Kora to field that one.

She began. "First of all they're not creatures just another intelligent life form that exists alongside us... It took a while for the radioactive cloud that formed from the missile attack to filter in above the site. But once it did every living thing left on the surface suffered in one way or another. We had no way of knowing how many people may have survived the biological attack. We're pretty sure there weren't many."

Beth stopped her. "But these beings are not part of that." She indicated Terrance. "He said you people created them."

Kora continued. "Our ancestors did. That was almost four hundred years ago."

178

"Why," asked Colin?

Kora glanced at Terrance. He nodded. "First of all they are genetically engineered human clones."

Aaron jumped in. "Wait, what I saw was defiantly not human."

"Our ancestors didn't know what would be required to survive above ground in a contaminated eco system. It took years to develop an immune system that would ignore the destructive, and mutating effects, of a highly eradiated environment. Early attempts failed miserably. What some of those people went through defies description. Then one day the adjustments worked. But in order to *make* those adjustments work certain modifications had to be made to the DNA helix. The end result is what you ran into out there. They are stronger, faster; their senses are five times more sensitive to their environment and don't let their appearance fool you. They are highly intelligent. In some ways their technology is superior to our own."

"Again, why," Aaron asked? "I'm sure the intent wasn't to simply create a new branch in human evolution."

"In a way it was," Terrance said. "We needed to know what was going on above ground, and the best way to find out was to go look. Of course until we actually sent them up, there was no way to know if anything could survive."

Kora stepped back in. "Well, survive they did and at first everything went as planned. They recorded what they saw. They collected and returned samples. Unfortunately like every intelligent life form their ideas and believes evolved. The mistake we made was producing both genders thus giving them the ability to reproduce. They finally broke away and made the world above their own."

"You have to remember," said Terrance, "At their core, they *are* human, with certain lower animal characteristics spliced into their DNA that allowed them to survive in a very savage world."

"And like I said they are very, very intelligent," continued Kora. "As for their reproductive cycle, the fetal gestation period is about two months and they mature to adulthood in less than two years."

"Less than two years," broke in Beth. "Over several hundred years their numbers could be in the... hundreds of millions."

"If not for the failsafe system we built in," said Kora. "Their lifespan is only from twenty to twenty-five years. Their birth rate is controlled by the fact that the females, after the first time, only ovulate once every eighteen months and only release one egg."

"And you don't think they've gotten around that?" Asked Colin.

"Like she said," answered Michael, "if that were the case there'd be an awful lot of them."

"And these... *people* have the surviving members of our team?" Asked Aaron.

"Yes," answered Terrance. "Once they determined *you* weren't *us*, they contacted us. That's what brought us to you. It's out of *our* hands and into the hands of the negotiators. We'll make sure you know what we know. Now, if it's okay with everyone, let's get back to why we're here."

He then turned the floor over to Colin, Aaron and Beth to fill in what they knew of their beginnings.

For the next two hours Colin, Aaron and Beth took turns providing a history lesson to Terrance and the others. They were particularly interested in the blister that allowed for the expansion of New Atlantis into what it is now.

Colin and the others related to everyone, the wonders that made up their world. And then they described the events that led up to the launch of the Georgana and the steps that had been taken to stop them.

"Then getting back in could be a problem?" Terrance asked.

"It's an almost sterile environment," Colin answered. "It's not likely they'll allow it after having been exposed to the surface. We could kill them all."

Terrance thought for a moment. "I see. Well, we've been at this a while. Why don't we get something to eat? Then I'll line up the videos you need to see."

They all stood. Beth asked. "When do we get to see more of this place?"

Terrance glanced at Michael. "That's up to Michael."

Michael answered. "We should be done with all the interviews today. Let me arrange for the necessary clearances. Maybe tomorrow."

Everyone left the room. Michael held back with Terrance. "You sure you wanna release them into the city?" Michael asked.

"The tests prove they *are* our distant cousins. The weapons they carried were designed after those in our archives... Let 'em visit the public areas for now."

"What about the Humanoids?"

Terrance and Michael moved toward the door. "They're as curious as we are. This could be the event we've needed to open some serious talks between us."

They left the room.

*　　*　　*

Kera and Colonel Hathaway approached a doorway. She wasn't wearing her uniform. Her clothing actually suggested a human female figure underneath. She touched the wall section to the left and the door slid open. The Colonel stepped inside. The rest of the Colonel's people were there. They all reacted at once to his presence and rushed toward him.

"Colonel, we thought you were dead. Where are we? What are they gonna do with us?" Came their collective response.

"Settle down," he began. "Nothing is going to happen to us." He looked back out the door. "Kera..."

She stepped into the doorway. The others moved back a step.

"This is Kera."

She looked at their faces. "Good morning... to you all. I hope... all of you... slept well." She had spent most of the night listening to recordings of the way these people spoke their version of her language. She wanted to get it right.

The Colonel watched her. She glanced at him and said quietly under her breath "I practiced."

The Colonel quietly responded, "Perfect."

She smiled, turned back to the door and motioned. Several Humanoid females moved into the room. They carried the clothing and boots worn by the Colonel's group when they arrived. Each walked up to its owner and offered it to them.

At first no one moved. The Colonel nodded. "Go on."

Each member took his or her belongings. With that Kera and the other Humanoids left the room and the door slid shut.

The Colonel began. "Get dressed. There's a lot to talk about."

Everyone went to separate places in the room and began to change.

Chapter seventeen: A history lesson

The video archives dating back to the day the underground shelter was sealed were extensive. Terrance selected those that would depict a thumbnail view of what happened on the day that changed the world. Colin, Aaron and Beth were left alone to witness a part of their past that until this moment would have been hard to imagine.

The image was projected from a pedestal and came to life in the air in front of them. There was no audio at first. Janet and Daniel and members of the military pushed back toward a building and went inside. Police stormed the entrance. A few moments later a blinding flash of light cleared the projection in front of them.

Aaron spoke up. "What just happened?"

"I'd say," answered Beth, "the camera just melted."

The image returned. It panned across the inside of the shelter. It showed hundreds of people, men, women and children, milling around in small groups. This image came with sound and the tone of their collective voices indicated confusion and uncertainty.

A voice on a PA system quieted them down. "Everyone... Everyone listen to me. This is Janet Crowley. There are some things I need to say... I know what's running through the minds of each and every one of you... I'm afraid what we've been rehearsing for all these years has come to pass."

"Wait," came a male voice from the crowd, "What are you saying? Everything up there is gone?"

The voices in the crowd faded waiting for the answer. After a few moments that seemed like forever, she answered. "At five am this morning this facility was sealed and will not reopen for at least the next one hundred years."

The silence was deafening and then a lone female voice summed it up. "May God have mercy on us all?"

Janet answered. "God has shown us his mercy by giving us this place and this chance to survive. But, as of this moment, whether we *do* survive is strictly up to us. We have what we need and the knowledge to make it work. Everyone here knows exactly what needs to happen next. Our only purpose *now* is to make sure our children, and grandchildren, have the chance to reclaim a world that *our* shortsightedness just destroyed."

Beth said, what they were all thinking. "If they had only known."

Time lapse allowed the site to morph from one form to another, and then another. People changed and life moved forward. Through the images, which moved on and off the display, they got to know Janet's family, her son-in-law and granddaughter and eventually found out about Liz and what happened to her.

The four walls that formed the boundary of the underground site were pushed back as the population grew. Colin and the others got a first hand look at human ingenuity at its best. The almost limitless power provided by the underground reactor had allowed them to recycle almost everything and in some cases use the raw material obtained from the site's expansion.

The last video was an image of Janet thirty years later. She sat at a desk speaking into the recording to whoever might be watching. Her desk, and the wall behind her, was covered with what must have been personal mementos. At eighty-six her hair was almost white and her skin reflected the years of stress brought on by having to be responsible for so many lives for so long.

"My personal diary," she began, April twenty-third, twenty-one, Oh-three... The only site I've had any contact with was Blue Ridge Mountain. They were experimenting with a process that allowed the electrical impulses that form the memories of who we are, and what we know, to be recorded and stored. In effect they want to put the genie back into a bottle. Years later a clone can be created using stored DNA from an individual. In less than a week the clone will mature into adulthood. At that point reversing the process will imprint the clone with the memories and hopefully the essence of the donor. The last transmission I received stated that the fifty or so people that make up the site were going to undergo the process... That was more than twenty-five years ago. There have been no farther transmissions. I kept trying for as long as our communications satellites remained up. I fear something went terribly wrong... Unfortunately we may never know". Janet's image faded from view.

Terrance's voice came from behind them. "The cloning process we've perfected, obviously."

Everyone turned to face him. He walked up and continued. "The rest of the process we haven't been able to recreate. That last clip was only discovered a few weeks ago. It had been buried for eons in the tens of thousands of hours of recorded history. That brings us to the Georgana".

"The Georgana?" Asked Colin."

"Yes, we need the Georgana to reach that site."

"Wait a minute." Aaron was confused. "The Blue Ridge Mountains are in what was Tennessee. The Georgana is a submarine."

Terrance sat with them. "Well the relay site was in Tennessee. But according to other diary entries, the complex is, or was, a couple of hundred feet underwater off the west coast of an island called Culebra. It would seem *your* home wasn't the only underwater facility they created. It was going to take us years to develop anything that could reach it and then you showed up."

Colin thought for a moment and then said, "That's all well and good, but we're not going anywhere without the rest of our team."

Michael entered the room. He carried a small device in his left hand. He approached them.

Terrance stood. "I understand that. Michael has arranged for the clearance you need to gain access to most of the city."

"Most," Aaron asked?

Michael held out the device. "Well, we all have our little secrets. This will plant a small-encapsulated chip under the skin on the back of your hand. It will open doors and allow you to move about. If you try to enter an area that's off limits it will notify security. Those areas are clearly marked. Understood?"

They all nodded and Michael went about tagging them. Beth asked for writing material. She said she kept a personal journal and what she had with her was lost in the attack. Terrance said he would see she got what she needed.

*   *   *

The Colonel and those with him were being allowed to mix with the general population. They were still being viewed with a certain amount of uncertainty, but as the day wore on they were approached and spoken to.

All of them had been assigned private quarters. Each of them, including the Colonel had been offered a change of clothing. The Humanoids had reproduced items more in keeping with the style they had arrived in. It was a welcomed change.

While all of this was going on out front, a lot of things were going on behind the scenes. A long overdue dialogue had opened up between the ruling body of the Humanoids and Terrance's people.

For three centuries the two predominant species that existed in this part of the world, had ignored each other.

Fortunately their ancient ancestors had recognized the bloody and destructive path being taken for what it was, and did something all those who came before them, had not. They learned from the mistakes of the past.

Unfortunately live and let live had been taken to an extreme and because of that, both societies had missed out on the technological and social growth that had occurred on both sides. The introduction of the Quanterrians was about to change all of that.

The Humanoids had never recognized the Subhumans ancestral beginnings as their own even though they were directly descended from them. As far as they were concerned their existence on Earth began when they were sent to the surface to fend for themselves.

Certain factions, on both sides, thought that fissure should never be bridged. Even though these clandestine groups had no reason to trust each other, they now had a common cause; destroy this link in a way that each side would blame the other.

*   *   *

Aaron and Beth had left together. Colin and Terrance walked off in another direction, talking.

The city above the ground flourished. It went on for miles. The jungle all around it had been pushed back. The energy fence they had passed through earlier completely encircled this marvel of human engineering. The architecture was clean and functional with some of the buildings extending over a hundred stories into the sky.

In the distance a new building was under construction. Prefabricated pieces were being lifted into place by a huge device extending from the top of the site. The construction material, to produce all this, had to come from someplace that neither Aaron nor Beth had seen yet. So far they had not run across any type of industrial complex that might have been used to produce the building components.

There was traffic. Some of the vehicles were obviously designed as private transportation while others moved things from place to place. In a lot of ways it reminded them of home and in others ways it was completely alien.

The inhabitants of New Houston knew and understood the theory of flight. The technology existed to create it. However from the moment they regained the surface laws were passed outlawing its creation and use. The events that brought about the near extinction of mankind had rained down from the sky. The ban was looked at as a religious edict. It would take another hundred years for the need to circumvent the fear.

Again there were no settlements outside the city. Even though both groups had the technology to extend their influence well beyond their borders they had remained encapsulated consuming only what was necessary to support their own population.

As Aaron and Beth wandered along they attracted little attention at first. In fact everyone seemed to move with a purpose. There was almost no casual interaction. It was Aaron and Beth taking the time to stop and observe that attracted attention. People began to glance their way and slow down as they passed. Some even began to comment amongst themselves.

Aaron noticed and asked, "What are they staring at?"

"Us, I think," she answered.

"I think we need to keep moving."

"I want to find something."

"What," he asked?

She pointed. "Maybe that."

He looked. There was an entrance across the street that apparently led underground.

*   *   *

Colin sat with Terrance in an office. One entire wall was glass and looked out over the city below them. A young lady entered and handed Colin, and then Terrance something to drink. They thanked her. She smiled and left.

Colin's attention was drawn to the items decorating the office. "I've seen some of this before."

"Yes, in the files you and the others viewed this morning."

"You're right. Some of this was sitting around Janet's office." Colin's attention returned to the man across from him. "I need to know the disposition of the rest of my people. You said something about negotiations."

"You have no idea what the real significance of your being here is," Terrance said. "You may have literally changed the course of history."

"My people."

"In a moment; first another small history lesson. We spoke briefly about how and why the Humanoid population came to be. They broke away and formed their own nation and for more than a century there had been no real communication with them. It took that long for the surface to clear enough," pointing to the window, "for all of that to happen. When contact was finally made the Humanoid population approached with a hand out to greet us and I'm embarrassed to say my ancestors tried to reclaim what they thought was still theirs. When that happened the Humanoids defended their right to exist as a people and many died on both sides. Fortunately someone remembered what caused all this in the first place and cooler heads prevailed."

"But I don't see what any of that has to do with us," Colin said.

"It's simple. In all this time there hasn't been one single contact with anyone else from anywhere. We had truly begun to believe that we, the Humanoids and ourselves, were the only remaining pocket of intelligent life left on the planet and then you showed up."

Colin just looked at him.

"Don't you see; if your people made it there may be others, or at least now there's hope there might be. Our ancestors had ways to communicate around the world, but today that can't happen. Without going to look we will never know. I've received word that in a few days a contingent of Humanoids will arrive at the gate with your friends. Here's what I want to discuss. I want to put together a crew for your submarine made up of members from all three groups."

Colin spoke up. "You want to try and find the Blue Ridge Mountain complex."

"For a start. We may be able to revive some of them. Their knowledge of what the world was like before would be invaluable."

"I'll speak with the others. If we decide to do this I want to try and contact Quanterra first. They need to know about all of this."

189

"Deal..." An area lit up on his desktop. He removed a device attached to the top of his desk and placed it to his ear. "I see... No I'll be there in a little while. Just hold them there... Okay." He replaced the communicator into its holder. "It would seem that Beth and Aaron have wandered into someplace they weren't supposed to be. Let's go and, I think the ancient term was, *spring 'em.*"

He got a blank stare from Colin.

Terrance smiled and stood up. "Come on. We'll talk some more on the way."

Colin stood and accompanied Terrance out of the office.

* * *

Earlier Beth and Aaron had walked into a street entrance that led underground. The angled walkway led to a door a hundred feet below street level. It was marked "Restricted, Authorized Personnel Only."

Beth tried holding her hand out, but nothing happened. "I guess this is one of those places."

Aaron glanced around. "This entire society evolved from a few hundred people trying to survive in an underground shelter. That's where the real story is."

The sound of footsteps echoed off the walkway that led down to them. To each side of the door was a corridor. He took her hand and stepped into the passageway to their left. They stood close to the wall and watched the sealed entrance.

Two men, dressed in street clothes, approached the door. One held out his hand, the seal was broken and the door slid open.

Aaron pulled Beth with him and fell in with the two men. They looked at them.

Aaron spoke to the one nearest them. "Hello," and then to Beth. "The next time Terrance Lieberman tells you to do something I suggest you do it." They walked past the other two and entered the restricted area. The moment that happened, security was dispatched.

The area just to the other side of the door was very busy. The immediate area was elevated above something much, much larger. People, by themselves and in groups, moved around them. No one took any particular notice of them. Beth and Aaron moved over to the railing. What spread out before them was nothing short of spectacular.

Stretching as far as the eye could see, a subterranean city that rivaled anything they had seen above ground. The buildings weren't as tall reaching up maybe sixty or seventy feet above street level.

This wasn't a relic of the past. This city was very much alive and bustled with street activity.

Beth commented. "Look at that. You were right. Everything we've seen so far started right here."

A very large, very pale hand took each of them by a shoulder. They both jumped and looked back and up behind them stood a giant of a man well over seven feet tall. His skin was almost white and he was bald. His uniform indicated he was security of some sort.

He spoke in a very deep, but very soft voice. "You both need to come with me."

*   *   *

Beth and Aaron had been taken to a detention center in the subterranean city. They had passed a number of these giants mixed with normal human beings going about their business.

Beth and Aaron sat at a table across from several empty chairs in a sealed room. They waited for whatever was going to happen. They had commented to each other that all of these large beings looked pretty much the same.

The door opened and Terrance and Colin entered. The room resealed itself.

Terrance smiled and shook his head. "Children, Children, just couldn't resist taking a peek."

Aaron started to say something to defend their actions, but Terrance cut him off. "That's okay. I was going to bring you both down here tomorrow anyway." He and Colin took a chair. "There's something we need to discuss."

*   *   *

At about that same time Colonel Hathaway stood outside a door in one of the Anorphian high-rise apartment buildings. He started to knock and the door opened.

Kera stood in front of him. She was dressed in a floor length robe. The top of the robe formed a vee coming down from her shoulders exposing some of her breast. The sleeves draped from her shoulders to just above her hands. "Please, come in Fred. Thank you for accepting my invitation."

He stepped past her and took note of her chest. The velvet like hair that covered her shoulders thinned out down the front. Her skin was milky white "How did you know it was me?"

"I knew it was you... when you got off... the lift," still trying to form complete sentences.

The door slid shut. It was obvious he was confused. She touched her nose and continued. "I recorded your scent."

She walked past him into the room. The back of her robe, well, there wasn't much to it. The back was open to just above her hips. Again the hair on her shoulders thinned out a short ways down her back leaving her skin exposed. Despite her animal like characteristics she was beautiful in a way he couldn't explain and he felt a strange attraction to her. He followed her into the room.

The room was furnished in what appeared to be leather. There were several places to sit. A strange form of artwork, representing the natural world around them, decorated the walls and stood around the room. The walls themselves were covered in pastel colors that blended together much the same as everywhere else. The room was well lit, but he couldn't tell exactly by what. The aroma of something cooking filled the air.

She faced him. "I've pre... pre..." she couldn't find the word for a moment. Then she smiled, "prepared a meal."

"It smells very good."

"Please sit. I... I'll get us something to drink."

192

With that she left the room. He walked over and sat down. Whatever they called this it conformed to his body and was very comfortable.

After a few moments Kera reentered the room. She carried two ornate, metal cups. She handed him one. For a moment he was caught up in her presence and didn't take it.

"Here," she said.

"Oh, sorry." He took the cup from her.

She walked over and sat across from him. "The meal will be ready soon."

There were a few moments of awkward silence. He didn't really know what to say.

She broke the silence. "It is called qulara."

He blinked. "I'm sorry, what is?"

"The meal." She took a sip from her cup.

He suddenly remembered his and did the same. The color of the contents was creamy yellow. The taste caused him to squint. It was very tart but sweet at the same time. "What do you call this," indicating the cup?

"Taquree. Difficult to get."

"I feel honored."

"Special time," reverting to her old speech pattern. She smiled. "It is," taking a moment to think, "a special occasion."

He raised his cup to her. She did the same. They both took a sip.

Chapter eighteen: Death comes in many forms

Terrance and Colin sat with Beth and Aaron. Terrance said,. "Please wait until I'm finished before asking any questions."

He then went back over everything he had discussed with Colin.

Aaron surprised him and asked, "The security guard, and the others like him, where did they come from?"

Colin said. "I was wondering that myself."

Terrance answered. "They have individual names just like you and me. For the lack of a better term I guess you could call them Super Humanoids."

"You genetically engineered them like the others?" Beth asked.

"Not exactly like the others. They can't reproduce, but their lifespan has proven to be well over a hundred years."

"Then they just die?" asked Colin.

"They simply decompose. It's not very pretty I'm afraid. Fortunately they seem to know when it's about to happen and seek out someplace private. "

"Why create them at all?" asked Aaron.

"Paranoia," was Terrance's answer. "Once it became apparent we weren't going to be able to control the first ones it was feared they would eventually retaliate against us. Let's face it, we'd created the perfect fighting machine designed to survive against all odds."

"But the attack never came," said Beth. "Not until you attacked them a hundred years later".

"That's true," continued Terrance. "As it turned out, our *new* creation refused to take part. To put it in their words, *we can't see the logic in it*. In the end working in the background, they helped negotiate the peace between us... Now, about the mission I've proposed."

Beth answered for all of them. "The whole reason we're here is to rediscover the world on dry land. I don't see where that's changed". She glanced around the table. "You can count me in. I can't speak for the others."

"I'm with her," said Aaron.

Colin nodded his agreement.

Terrance placed his hands on the table and stood up. "Let's go ask the rest of your friends."

Everyone else stood up and they all left the room.

*   *   *

The Colonel and Kera had talked about many things throughout the course of the meal. He spoke about the wonders of Quanterra and the history of his people. She did the same.

She finally asked, "You have a mate?"

The question took him by surprise. He in fact had been married. His wife and son had been killed when the elevator they were in dropped twenty-five floors. They had been the biggest part of his life away from the military. Even after all this time he had never considered getting involved with anyone else. "My wife... mate... died years ago."

"Sorry to hear this."

"How about yourself?"

She took a drink. "No. I've just entered that cycle." She realized what she'd said had no meaning for him. "We don't measure time the way you do." The speech pattern was becoming much easier for her. "Our lifespan in subhuman terms is much shorter than yours."

He stopped her. "How old are you, in subhuman terms."

195

"A little over four of your years," was the answer.

He didn't say anything for a moment and then asked, "How long do you usually live in our years?"

She hesitated to answer for fear of ending what had just started. Then she said, "We seldom live more than twenty-five of your years."

She half expected him to politely excuse himself and leave. To her amazement he got up, walked around the table and extended his hand to her. She watched him for a moment, took his hand and stood up.

"Explain to me how this cycle thing works, but first I'd really like some more of whatever it was you served us when I first got here."

"Taquree."

"That's it."

Her sixth sense, and the sudden change in his scent, told her he wanted something more.

When they turned to leave the room he placed his hand on her back and ushered her out ahead of him. His touch triggered a chemical chain of events inside of her she wasn't sure she could control. She didn't want to harm him but the mating ritual, when it was the female's first time, could be very violent. Males of her own kind knew this and would defend themselves but even then, on rare occasions, it proved fatal for the male.

* * *

Terrance had taken Colin and the others back to the surface and then to the military quadrant of the city. Beth had been wondering about Corporal Hickman and his men.

They all met in a courtyard surrounded by buildings of a much more utilitarian design. The Corporal and the others looked physically fine and were dressed in new uniforms that matched everyone else's. The moment they spotted each other they all moved quickly to greet the other.

Beth asked, "Have they been treating you guys okay?"

"Yes Ma'am," the Corporal responded. "Sorry, Beth. We've been poked and prodded and asked a million questions. We were assured the three of you were okay. I guess I was never *really* sure of it until now. "

There were benches placed here and there in the courtyard. Colin motioned them over. "Let's sit. You guys still up for a little adventure?"

The Corporal answered. "We've still *got your back* if that's what you're asking."

Beth smiled.

The Corporal noticed and returned it. "Yes, I read a book once."

They all sat and listened to Terrance lay out the plan again. When he was finished the Corporal got a thumbs up from his men.

Terrance stood followed by everybody else. "Fine. Tonight dinner is on me."

As they all walked off together Aaron asked Terrance. "I understand the original Houston site is south of here. Even after all this time I'd think there'd still be some evidence of it. I'd like a chance to see it."

"There was a tunnel system under part of the city. Some of the buildings were a hundred stories," Terrance replied. "Apparently the nuclear winter that followed the submarine attack changed the weather patterns. For a very long time, massive storms moved in from the Gulf. Most of the superstructure has succumbed to the elements. The jungle has long since reclaimed the rubble. What lives in the surviving parts of the underground you really don't want to meet."

Colin asked, "In all this time you haven't tried to find the other underground sites?"

"We have. Over the years we've sent out several expeditions."

"What did they find?"

"We don't know. We lost contact with all of them and *none* of them ever returned. Now you know why this is so important to us."

*   *   *

The Colonel and Kera stood in her bedroom. A nighttime glow filled the room through the window. He asked earlier about the windows. Everything was visible through them from the inside, not even the window was visible from the outside. The engineering process was very similar to that of a one-way mirror, but it had been applied to the components use to construct the guilding.

Kera's breathing was shallow and her head was down. The centerpiece of the room was the bed, carved from a single piece of wood. She stood beside the bed still not making eye contact. Her arms hung at her side.

He stepped up to her and pushed the robe off of her shoulders. It dropped to the floor. She stood before him naked. Except for her facial features, nails and the pattern of velvet like hair she was very human.

He placed his hand under her chin and slowly raised her face. Her eyes were glowing red in the dark. Her mouth was slightly open exposing her canines.

She drew in a long breath through her nose taking in his scent. Her mouth snapped shut and in a single motion a one hundred and thirty pound female lifted a two hundred and twenty pound human male and flipped him onto his back on the bed. She straddled him pinning him down.

She had warned him that the only chance he had of surviving this was to offer no resistance. He lay perfectly still and watched as her eyes moved up and down his chest.

She rose up releasing him. He dare not move a muscle. A soft growl emanated from her throat. She extended the index finger of her right hand. The nail extended to form a razor sharp claw. She pulled at the front of his shirt and the claw sliced through the material like paper. She slid back, leaned down and bit through his belt with her teeth. The claw continued down the front of his pants and the right inseam. She pealed the cloth back like a huntress skinning her prey. In a matter of minutes he lay naked beneath her.

She began to touch him and when he was ready she mounted him. It took every fiber in her body to back off enough to

198

keep from tearing him apart. Even so, it was painful for him. He closed his eyes, set his jaw and dug his fingers into the bed.

As her moment approached her body backed off for just a second and allowed him to reach his. Her head went back, her mouth opened emitting a high-pitched screech. She threw herself forward and razor sharp claws ripped into the bed on each side of him.

His eyes opened. She lay on top of him, her head on his chest. Her breathing was easy. She snuggled in and began to softly purr. He placed his hand on the back of her head and then moved it down onto her back. He could feel her heart beating against his chest. He wrapped his arms around her and held her.

* * *

The Colonel awoke covered by a cloth in the middle of Kera's bed. He opened his eyes and immediately shaded them with his hand against the piercing light that flooded through the window section of the wall.

It took a moment for reality to set in. The throbbing in his genitals was all too real. He raised the cover. His torso and upper thighs were bruised and sore.

"It would seem you survived," Kera's voice came from across the room.

He dropped the cover. She stood in the doorway wrapped in an earth tone cloth. Steam rose from the cup in her hand. The hair that ran from the back of her hands and faded away up her forearms made her look like she was wearing gloves.

He glanced at the condition of the bed on each side of him. "That's more than I can say for your bed."

She appeared a little embarrassed. "You need to bathe. I had new clothes delivered. I'm afraid your old clothes are not usable any longer. Then food, and then we need to talk."

He threw the cover off and with some effort swung his legs off the bed and stood. Her eyes moved up and down him.

She pointed to her left. "There."

A small hallway led off the bedroom. He half walked and half limped out of the room.

After the events of last night her needs had been met for the next eighteen months. She had done her research. She knew that human males required the attention much more often. It was something she was prepared to do. She smiled, turned and left.

*   *   *

Beth and Aaron woke to a much tamer scene. Except for the fact that their clothes were scattered everywhere the room was intact. They both showered and dressed in time to greet Terrance at the door to be taken to breakfast at another location.

This dining hall was different from the more public place where they had dined with the Corporal and his men the night before. This place was richly decorated in wood and leather. The table was fifteen feet long and made of solid wood and the chairs were brushed metal with leatherbacks and seats. The walls were covered with framed photos of what the area must have looked like before everything changed forever. The pictures within the frames were digital images that changed every few minutes.

As they entered the room Beth, Aaron and Colin slowed to watch the changing images of grand city skylines, parks, shopping malls and university campuses.

Terrance commented. "It's a reminder of what was lost to *our* generation due to the intolerance of our ancestors."

Servers began to enter the room. They placed food and drink along the center of the table. Others placed the plates, glasses and utensils.

Terrance motioned everyone to the table. "Let's eat. Today will be a very busy day for all of us."

Everyone took their seats and the meal was served.

*   *   *

The Colonel was dressed in something that resembled civilian clothing by Humanoid standards. The only part of his original uniform that survived was his boots, only because he'd removed them ahead of time. While he had bathed and changed Kera had changed into something more in keeping with her job.

They sat in silence across the table from each other having breakfast. Each wondered about the thoughts of the other, but neither was sure about how to begin a conversation.

She finally had to say something. "I'm sorry I hurt you last night." Her voice was soft and consoling a far cry from the shriek that preceded her bed being ripped to shreds.

He took a bite. "That's okay. I've been beat up worse teaching hand to hand combat classes back on the base." He lied. His next question took her completely by surprise. "How'd we do?"

She looked up from her plate. "How'd we..." He was smiling at her. She actually laughed. "Okay I guess. You're still in one piece, if you don't count the toe."

He almost choked on whatever it was he was eating. Now it was his turn to laugh. He continued. "What's happening next with me and my men?"

She took a drink. "In two days we all leave. You're being turned over to the Sub... other Humans."

"You said *we*."

"Since I've been in closer contact with you..."

"I'd say."

Her eyes showed a momentary pink tint and her lips pulled back for an instant exposing her canines. "...than anyone else. And because I've taken the time to master the way your people speak I've been given the position of spokesman for the head of the Council."

"Sounds important."

"You have no idea *how* important your presence really is. For a very, very long time, except for some rare occasions, which usually involved someone getting killed, we've ignored each others existence."

He watched as she spoke. Except for the body she existed in, and the fact she could literally tear him to shreds if she wanted to, she was as human as anyone he'd been with. He felt drawn to her emotionally and physically. He both looked forward to and feared their next encounter.

She noticed the detached look on his face. "Did you hear what I said?"

"Yes. I need to prepare the rest of my team"

"Finish your meal and I'll take you to them."

He continued to eat. Now it was her turn to watch and wonder what was next for the two of them.

*   *   *

As they finished their meal Terrance filled them in on the chain of events that would lead up to the meeting in two days. Then, against his better judgment, he allowed Colin, Beth and Aaron to convince him to put together a little expedition to the South. His rationalization was; it would give them a chance to meet some of what had survived outside the safety of the city.

A three-vehicle caravan left the confines of the city and for the first two and a half miles traveled quickly along a paved road surrounded by open, barren ground. As they neared the exit point in the security shield it became obvious things were going to slow down. The jungle beyond the perimeter fence was very thick. Everything came to a stop at the exit.

Terrance wasn't taking any chances. The vehicle in front and the one behind carried seasoned, trained troops. An energy field similar to the perimeter shield protected each vehicle. The shield projector was powered by its own set of batteries and could tap into the main power source for a short time. If both sets of batteries were completely drained it would take several hours for the sun to recharge them. He wouldn't use the shield until it became absolutely necessary.

Terrance turned in his seat and looked at his passengers. "Now, it's going to take several hours to reach what was considered downtown Houston. Along the way, and once we're there, you may see some pretty scary stuff. Do not, and I repeat this, do not attempt to leave the vehicle. If the shield is up you'll get a pretty nasty burn. Understood?"

Colin answered for all of them. "Understood."

Terrance turned back around and said. "We're pretty well armed. I wouldn't worry, too much."

Everyone in the back picked up on the words "too much". Terrance spoke into a headset. "Let's go. Place the shields on standby."

The energy field, inside of a framed area in front of them, dissipated. The vehicles passed through the exit and the field reestablished itself.

It didn't take long for the heat and humidity rising from the jungle floor, to make itself felt.

After about an hour of nothing but green Beth wiped her forehead with her hand. "It's so close in here all together. What if we get out and walk for a few minutes," she asked? "It'll give us a chance to catch our breath and stretch our legs."

Terrance gave an order to the other two vehicles. "Stop here for a minute."

A small biped, maybe twenty pounds, scurried from the path of the vehicle in front. It stepped onto a large plant growing close to the ground. Most of the plant life was a mutated form of its ancestor. Much like the Venus flytrap it snapped shut.

Everyone watched as the victim tried to escape. Four tentacles rose up from around the plant and slipped inside the living encasement. The animal inside stopped moving almost at once. The entire plant began to pulsate. A few minutes later the plant opened up. What was left was a bloody skeleton still partially covered by the animal's skin. One tentacle seized the carcass and threw it several yards into the jungle. It then laid waiting for its next meal.

Aaron broke the silence. "We spent a couple of days out here. I never saw one of those."

Terrance answered. "You were lucky. There's a lot of ways to die out here. That's why nobody's walking." He then gave the order to continue.

The vehicles continued to flush out various forms of life big and small. After an hour or so they no longer saw any signs of life, big or small.

Colin asked. "What about the larger animals that attacked us earlier? We haven't seen anything that comes even close to them in size."

Terrance answered. "Where we're headed the animal life avoids, and for good reason. What still survives there was once human but the radiation effects altered its DNA. It's cunning, very lethal, and absolutely fearless." He then corrected himself. "Almost fearless. The only thing they go out of their way to avoid are the Humanoids."

He had peaked their curiosity. Beth asked. "Why?"

"Well, when we sent our creations to the surface the first thing they encountered were these remnants of humanity. They were attacked almost immediately. Fortunately the modifications we'd made to their DNA allowed them to give better than they got. It didn't take them long to establish themselves as the dominate species. By the time we resurfaced the threat had been eliminated."

"If they were eliminated," asked Colin, "Why are they still around?"

"Unlike the rest of us, the Humanoids recognize the right of a species to exist as long as they don't pose a threat."

"Does this *remnant* of humanity have a name," asked Aaron?

"We've adopted the Humanoid name for them, Drakmun."

*　　*　　*

The moment the human procession entered the Drakmun range they were being tracked silently through the jungle.

These creatures were once human but apparently no longer possessed a higher level of human intelligence. They still used fire, created tools and fashioned hand weapons. They maintained a social structure of sorts, were skilled hunters and were strictly carnivores. The males stood from five to six feet tall, were heavily muscled, and except for their genitals, were completely hairless. The females were a little smaller, but no less deadly. The males in a way controlled the population growth. If given the chance they would eat the new born. Neither gender wore clothing of any kind.

Several fires burned in a clearing. Groups of Drakmun were bunched together. Skinned animal carcasses were suspended above two of the fires. Females tended these cooking pyres. They communicated in a way understood only by them.

A large rectangular opening led underground. It was apparent this was not something that occurred in nature, but was man made. The skeletal remains of past meals littered the ground around the opening. Several males moved quickly out of the jungle, through the open area and into the underground.

*   *   *

The vehicles moved across broken ground. The jungle began to change. Larger trees and plants lined an area that had given way to smaller forms of growth and ground cover.

Terrance spoke into his headset. "Stop here. Bring up the shields."

The air distorted for a moment and a faint hum set up in the background.

Aaron and the others looked in different directions, and then at Terrance. "I don't see anything," said Aaron.

"We've been shadowed for the last few miles," Terrance replied.. "Not too far from here there's a permanent encampment. The shields will protect us. I'm doing this for one reason. The world has changed. This is one example. I want all of you to see what could be waiting for us."

"The Georgana will protect us," said Beth.

"At sea," said Terrance. "But the underground sites inland from the East coast can't be reached with the sub. We'll have to move overland. Now, everyone hold on. You're about to see something you'll never forget." He spoke into the headset. "Take us in. Take it slow. We haven't been through here in a while. Things change."

For the first twenty minutes there was nothing. Beth saw them first. "There," she pointed.

Off to their right were four human like creatures moving just inside the jungle cover. Each carried a spear in one hand and a crudely fashioned ax in the other.

Aaron was next. "This side too."

Everyone looked. There were five or six more all armed. Everyone jumped when an ax glanced off the shield. Then several spears and axes were all repelled. Suddenly dozens of Drakmun rushed the vehicles throwing themselves into the shields. All fell away severely burned. They kept coming. The sound they created was deafening.

Colin shouted. "What are they doing?"

In that moment Terrance understood and shouted into his headset. "They're depleting the shields. Let's get outta here."

All the vehicles swung around. Axes and spears pummeled the shields. Each time the shield's power source had to expend energy to reinforce it. They hadn't gotten far when a large tree fell from the side of the path and landed on the vehicle in front. The shield held for a moment. The weight was just too much and it collapsed allowing the full weight of the tree to smash down onto the top pinning the transport under it. Those inside stood no chance. A barrage of spears sliced through the cab killing everyone inside.

Terrance shouted at the driver. "Go around."

The driver accelerated and swung to the left. At that moment two other trees smashed to the ground. They were narrowly missed, but the vehicle behind them was crushed. Someone inside got off a few shots, but immediately suffered the same fate as those in front.

As they sped past the vehicle in front, the occupants were being pulled out and hacked to pieces. Spears and axes continued to impact the shield. The air around them began to crackle and the shield failed. The spears continued to come. Some flew past them and some struck the back of the cab. In a matter of minutes they were out of range.

Beth was out of breath. "You said they no longer had human level intelligence. That was a planned, coordinated attack." She looked to her left and screamed.

Everybody looked. Colin sat beside her with a spear point protruding from his chest. The spear had pierced the cab and then him. He was dead.

They stopped long enough to remove the spear. All the way back no one said a word. Totally exhausted, Beth fell asleep in Aaron's arms.

Chapter nineteen: North meets south, again

The next day Colin was laid to rest in New Houston. This entire mission had been his idea and he had paid the ultimate price to see it through.

Captain Kemp was informed and it was agreed upon that Aaron would take over leadership of the civilian ground-based part of it. The death of their friend had shaken Beth, but having witnessed death several times already she managed to refocus her thoughts on what was coming. What was coming today was a reunion.

* * *

Conspiracies can create strange bedfellows. Factions from both sides were working together to keep the two worlds apart. The plan was simple. Somewhere along the way to the gate the Humanoid envoy, and everyone with them, would be attacked and slaughtered. The Humanoid members of this conspiracy would do the actual killing, and the other side would supply the weapons used and the physical evidence left behind.

The really odd thing about all of it was once the war ensued these co-conspirators would again be killing each other. What neither side had taken into account was a third group that had gone unnoticed, but who had in fact noticed everything.

* * *

Earlier that morning, as the glow of a new day began to highlight the city skyline and the jungle beyond; Colonel Hathaway had stood at the window in Kera's bedroom. He looked back into the room. Kera lay asleep in the bed.

He'd held her and made love to her and she had accepted his touch and returned it. As violent as their first encounter had been this time her body had eased into what they were doing. Her claws had extended and moved slowly down his back without leaving a mark. Kissing was something she wouldn't, or couldn't, do so he'd found other ways to arouse and excite her. When the moment was right for both of them it happened. For Kera all of this was new, but she had enjoyed it.

Afterward he lay beside her and enjoyed the nuzzling that took place. She didn't say a word. She used her face to caress every inch of his body. When she was done she settled in against him and fell asleep. It had taken him another hour to do the same.

He looked back out the window. There were decisions to be made. He needed to rejoin his own kind, but he also knew leaving her behind was something he couldn't do.

*　　*　　*

Etac, the Humanoid Council Leader, and several Senior Council Members making up his entourage, stood in front of the Chamber Building. They spoke about the historic events to follow that day.

The Colonel and Kera approached the gathering and were joined by the rest of his team. He had Kera's hand and that brought grins and a few muffled comments. A stern look and a set jaw put an end to that. He and Kera moved on and for just a moment the grins returned.

The Colonel and the others joined the Council Leader. Kera did the introductions. "Colonel Hathaway I believe you've met our supreme leader Council Leader Etac."

"Yes," answered the Colonel.

Council Leader Etac looked at Kera, but his comment was for the Colonel. "Your stay, pleasant?"

209

"Yes," answered the Colonel, "you've treated us well."

The Council Leader looked at the Colonel. "Good. Soon be with *own* kind." With that he rejoined the other members of his envoy.

The emphasis did not go unnoticed by the Colonel or Kera. There was a noise behind them. Kera took his hand and pulled him aside. Most of the population walked or rode in a very small electrically powered conveyance. What pulled up behind them had military transport written all over it. It floated a good five feet off the ground, was at least seventy-five feet long, twenty feet high and was supported by some form of energy field projected beneath it.

A compartment up front opened and a set of steps extended to the ground. The Chief Council and the rest of his advisors climbed to the open door. A rear hatch opened and another set of steps presented themselves. The Colonel and Kera waited for the rest of his team to start up, and then followed them. The Chief Council waited at the doorway. Kera was last and paused in the opening. She rubbed her stomach. The Chief Council watched her for a moment, nodded and entered. The forward hatch closed. Kera stepped inside and the rear hatch sealed.

A second similar vehicle moved into place behind the first. A twenty armed military climbed aboard, both vehicles powered up and moved off.

The Colonel and Kera occupied the first two seats next to the hatch. The propulsion system was totally silent. The ride was absolutely smooth with no actual contact with the ground.

Kera kept glancing down at her stomach. The Colonel noticed. "Something wrong?"

"Oh no, I'm fine. Just a little nervous."

"I noticed the man in charge kept looking at you."

"Maybe he's having second thoughts about me. I really don't have any experience with this sort of thing."

The Colonel smiled at her. She glanced at him. A small smile came and went on her face.

The Colonel took her hand and said, "Who does? I don't think that was it. It was something else."

She squeezed his hand a little too hard. He flinched. She noticed. "Sorry." She took her hand back.

An hour passed. They had no view of the outside, but they heard the explosion that disabled the following vehicle and they felt the surge when their vehicle came to a sudden stop.

Everyone stood. The Colonel held up his hand. "Wait." He moved toward the hatch. Kera started to go with him. He turned to her, "Wait." She held back.

As he got to the hatch it opened. He came face to face with an armed Humanoid.

A hiss came from behind him. Kera's claws extended and she made a deliberate move toward the intruder.

A Subhuman pulse weapon went to the Colonel's head. "Stop, or die."

Kera's fangs showed, but she pulled back and the claws retracted.

The Humanoid stepped away from the hatch and motioned with the weapon. "All, out." He pointed at Kera. "You stay."

The Colonel stepped back toward Kera. "I'm not going without her."

The Humanoid was angry now and his voice lowered to almost a growl. "You have same choice." He pointed the weapon at her.

Kera pressed against the Colonel. "Go. This traitor won't harm me."

The Humanoid raised his voice. "Not traitor to protect own kind, own home." With that he waved everyone out again.

The Colonel hesitated, but knew she could better protect herself without him to worry about. He indicated to the others to leave. Everyone stepped around him through the open hatch.

Once outside it was plain what had happened. Concentrated weapons fire had totally destroyed the carrier behind them killing everyone onboard. A dozen Humanoids surrounded the Chief Council's transport. The Chief Council and his Ministers stood at the bottom of the stairway leading up to their blown hatch.

The Colonel and his team started down their stairway. The Leader of the rebels was in the Chief Council's face exchanging

211

words. When the Colonel and the others reached the bottom of the stairway the exchange stopped.

Etac looked at the Colonel. "He wants destroy future."

The Leader snapped his fangs shut in frustration. He looked away and called out. "Bring."

Four Humanoids moved from the other side of the transport each carried a dead Subhuman. They had been killed by Humanoid weapons fire. The bodies were scattered around.

The Chief Council spoke up. "You destroy chance for peace, for all."

The Leader looked back at him. "At least not destroy offspring," he glanced at the Colonel, "mating her to him."

The Colonel's head snapped around to look back up the steps. Kera stood next to the armed Humanoid in the open hatch. "You're his daughter? This was all *set up*?"

The Leader laughed in the form of a growl. He stepped back and barked the order. "Kill them all."

The raiding party chose their targets. Small arms fire erupted from the surrounding jungle. Most of the rebels were blown apart by pulse weapons fire. They managed to get off a few random, un-aimed shots.

The Leader shouted to the Humanoid with Kera. "Kill him."

He shoved her away and took aim at the Chief Council. Kera's claws severed his head. The shot went wide and caught Colonel Hathaway a glancing blow to his upper left shoulder tearing the arm off. The Colonel went down. The last thing he felt was a searing, burning pain and then nothing.

The pulse weapon fired a bolt of superheated air. Fortunately for the Colonel the arteries were cauterized and blood loss was at a minimum. The massive amount of tissue damage had thrown him into shock and he lay unconscious on the ground.

The conspirators had underestimated the New Houston cloned security force. What these engineered beings lacked in personality they more than made up for with curiosity. Nothing that seemed out of the ordinary received less than one hundred percent of their attention.

Unfortunately Michael had not been involved at the beginning and in the minds of his security force the end justified the means. They had allowed the deaths of four innocent men in order to prevent a war that could have killed thousands. Once Michael was informed he understood the reasoning, but was very upset with their decision not to tell him.

After the transfer of equipment and bodies had been made, Michael and a security contingent stepped in and picked up everyone involved on the human side. Their fate would not be pleasant.

Every member of the population of New Houston had a unique identifier permanently implanted at birth. It took a little while, but once they knew who had died they tracked the bodies to the place where the ambush occurred almost arriving too late.

When these cloned humans stepped out of the jungle it was the first time they had ever been seen by the Humanoids. Their involvement with the ancient peace treaty had been done out of sight. Later there would be a lengthy conversation about them between the Chief Council and Terrance.

*   *   *

Kera never left the Colonel's side all the way in. The last words he'd spoken to her were accusing and she feared she'd lost him forever. She had to make him understand that even though their meeting had been planned what she felt for him was real and those feelings were manifested inside of her. She carried their child.

While the heads of state formally recognized each other Kera sat in a hospital room close to Fred. His vital signs were stable. He was being kept in a chemically induced coma. His body needed time to heal. Even as advanced as their medical technology was the arm could not be saved. It had been two days since the attack and Kera had never left his side.

When the Chief Council, and the rest of his group, had entered the city they were scanned to confirm they were not carrying anything in the form of a weapon. The scanning process looked completely through them. It was at that point Kera's pregnancy was discovered.

When Terrance found out who the father was everything changed. It had never even been considered that Humans and Humanoids would, or could, mate. Genetically it was possible the same as different breeds of certain animals could sire offspring. Kera had agreed to a complete examination on the promise that she would not be separated from the father of her child. Terrance was as good as his word.

Beth stepped into the open doorway. "I think they said your name is, Kera."

Kera nodded never looking away from the only thing that mattered to her now.

Beth stepped up behind her and placed her hands on her shoulders. "I'm Beth. I know you haven't eaten in two days."

"I don't require much."

"What about the life inside of you? You need to get something. Come with me. He's not in any danger."

Kera looked back at her. "You don't understand." She looked back at the Colonel. "I have to be here when he wakes. I have to tell him about the child. Maybe then he can forgive me."

"What good will it do if you wind up in the next room? Come on. We're not going far. He's being well looked after."

Kera touched her stomach. "Perhaps you are right."

"I know I am."

Kera stood up. Beth moved to the door. Kera took a couple of steps, looked back and then followed Beth out.

*   *   *

There was a small courtyard a short distance from the Colonel's room. Kera and Beth sat at a table across from each other. Each had a plate of food in front of them. Kera moved hers around with her finger.

Beth held up a piece in front of her face. "I had this yesterday. I'm not sure what it is."

Kera extended the claw on her left index finger, speared a piece and picked it up. "I know what it is. I just never knew anyone ate them."

"A boy or a girl?"

Kera tasted the morsel and then took the piece into her mouth. "A male."

Beth took a bite. "They told you this?"

"Males are larger they carry differently."

"You have other children?"

Kera looked at her for a moment. "Why do you want to know?"

"Sorry, I don't mean to pry. It's just I don't know anyone else who's pregnant. I want very much to have children. My hus... mate."

"I'm familiar with the human term, husband."

"Well he's not actually my husband. His wife was killed in an accident right after we left our home. We've been together ever since." She took another bite. "I love him very much. Do you understand the word love?"

"I do. And he loves you?"

"Yes, he does."

Kera speared another piece. "Then have children. No, I have no others."

As her hand neared her mouth Kera grimaced and grabbed her stomach. She stood up and the pain doubled her over.

Beth went to her. "What is it?"

Still in pain, "I don't know." She lifted her face. Her lips pulled back exposing her fangs. She fell back into the chair. "Help me, please."

First Kera and then the episode had attracted the attention of others. Beth looked at the nearest person. "Get us some help, hurry."

They ran for help while others gathered around them. Kera had laid her head on the table.

Beth had her arm around her. "Someone will be here soon."

Kera looked at her. "It's the baby."

*   *   *

Terrance and the Chief Council stood with Beth looking through a window into the intensive care unit where they had taken Kera. Several attendants moved around her.

The doctor stepped outside and addressed them. "You said this child was conceived only a few days ago?"

"She and Colonel Hathaway have only been together for a few days. She says it's his," answered Terrance.

Kera's father spoke up. "You created us, but don't know much about us."

Terrance rebutted. "My ancestors created you and we've had no real contact with you for a very long time."

The Chief Council looked at him. "Created others."

Terrance answered. "They don't reproduce. If we need another one, we clone another one."

The Doctor broke in. "Pardon me but we have a different problem here." He addressed Kera's father. "From what I'm told the normal fetus grows at an accelerated rate."

"Yes, compared to human."

"Your daughter's body is a host to, well the only way I can describe it is, an evolutionary war."

"A war" asked Beth?

"Yes. To put it simply, the part of the baby's DNA that stems from Kera wants to develop at its normal rate. The father's part, the more human part, wants to slow things down. Unless we can slow down part of it or speed up part of it the baby will tear itself apart at a cellular level and probably kill the mother as well. Of course there is another choice. We can terminate the pregnancy."

The Chief Council watched his child through the glass. "Choice hers."

Beth stepped in. "He's right it's a choice she has to make." She looked at the doctor. "If she wants to save the baby, I think we'll need help from her people." She looked at the Chief Council. "His medical staff understands part of this a lot better than anyone here."

The doctor spoke up. "Whatever you're going to do, do it quick. We only have a few days." With that he walked back in with his patient.

"I'll authorize anything that needs to happen," said Terrance.

The Chief Council nodded his agreement.

Beth moved toward the door. "Let's ask her."

*   *   *

Kera's answer was what Beth had expected, to save the child. Researchers from both worlds had reasons to see this child survive and all the stops were pulled.

Kera had asked Beth to watch over the Colonel for her. Early that afternoon Fred woke up. He had a problem focusing and he thought the person in the chair next to the bed was Kera. He asked, "Did the last several days mean anything or was it just diplomacy?"

Beth didn't want him to continue so she spoke up. "This is Beth not Kera."

He looked a Beth. "I guess I know the answer."

She got up and moved to his bedside. "I'm afraid you don't know anything. You especially have no idea how much that young woman cares for you." She reached for the chair and pulled it closer to the bed. Sitting down she said, "There are several things you *need* to know."

She started by telling him that everyone had made it safely into the city and that everyone involved with the attack had been captured or killed. Then she dropped the bombshell. "Did you know Kera is carrying your child?"

He flashed back to the last time he'd seen her and the way she was acting. He rolled up on his right side. "How is she? Is she okay?"

"Not too good I'm afraid. There's a problem with the pregnancy. You may lose them both."

A shutter went through him. Fate wouldn't do this to him twice. He pushed up and at this point he realized his left arm was

217

gone. With his right arm he continued up and swung his legs off the side of the bed.

Beth stood up. "What are you doing? You can't get out of bed."

"Find me some pants." He reached over with his right hand and felt of his left shoulder and said more to himself. "At this rate there's going to be nothing left."

The moment he raised up the telemetry feed to the monitors stopped. Alarms went off. In a few seconds someone was in the doorway.

Beth glanced at the door. "Get him some clothes."

*　　*　　*

While that played out in a building several blocks away, Aaron contacted the Georgana to fill them in.

After formal diplomatic relations had been established, almost immediately, there was talk of a joint mission to the Blue Ridge Mountain Group. The Humanoid Chief Council cleared the way for a group of Humans, accompanied by one of his Ministers, to travel to Anorphia, first as a show of good faith and second to sit down and discuss what would be required for such a mission. He had also ordered a medical team to leave immediately for New Houston. The Chief Council would stay in New Houston with his daughter.

All this was passed along to the ship's Captain as well as the unfolding drama with Colonel Hathaway and Kera.

Captain Kemp was very sorry to hear about the injury to the Colonel. He asked, "Under the circumstances, should command be passed over to the officer aboard the Georgana?"

Aaron said, "That's the Colonel's call. Move the submarine back to the anchorage in the channel and wait. At this point no one is authorized to board the ship. If they try, take it back out. If necessary, defend it."

The Captain acknowledged his orders. Afterward Aaron left for the hospital to find Beth.

*　　*　　*

Kera had drifted in and out of consciousness for two days. When the Colonel wasn't with her Beth was. Only once had Etac looked in on his child, more to tell them of the progress being made, than to visit. Aaron had also stopped by a couple of times. Most of his time was spent with Terrance and the Chief Council planning the mission.

The doctors and researchers from both worlds worked together and were close to completing an enzyme that should bond with the entire DNA helix and establish a common rate of development. The reason they were holding back was it might bridge the placenta barrier and attack the mother.

To solve that they created an artificial womb that would allow them to move the fetus.

It hadn't taken long for the Human members of the medical team to ignore the appearance of their Humanoid counterparts. It quickly became evident that some Humanoid research had developed procedures years in advance of their own.

Someone observed; had not all the time been lost, working together they might have advanced the world centuries beyond where it was today.

When the womb was ready. Kera was moved to a sterile operating room and she was prepared for surgery. Her body reflected the changes occurring inside of her. The Colonel had insisted on being with her.

Over the last few days she'd been vaguely aware of Fred's presence. She had glanced in his direction that morning. He'd taken her hand and she'd squeezed it.

The artificial world that would allow the unborn child to hopefully survive was moved in beside her. A team of doctors made up of both groups followed it in. Beth, Aaron, Terrance and Etac watched from above.

This move had to happen quickly. The child was losing its battle for life and was taking his mother with him. The baby was supplied oxygen from the embryonic fluid in his mother's womb. The umbilical supplied blood and nutrition. It was the oxygen

supply that was critical. The oxygen level in Kera's embryonic fluid had been raised thus giving them a few more seconds to complete the transfer. There wasn't time to synthesize the liquid world
the child would require. Pregnant females, of her own kind, had
donated the fluid that filled the artificial womb.

The moment was here. The incision was made. A Humanoid female had never given birth this way and it required someone
totally familiar with their reproductive system. The Humanoid doctors performing this procedure were absolutely precise. There was
no hesitation. In a matter of seconds the child was lifted from its
mother's body. The cord was cut and the unborn child was moved
over and immersed in the fluid that would supply its oxygen requirements for the next two months. The umbilical cord, still attached to the child, was spliced into the equipment that would
supply the rest of the child's needs.

Part of the team worked with the baby while the others
worked quickly to repair the damage to Kera. Her breathing became shallow. Her respiratory system was shutting down. They
were losing her. They were almost there. Alarms began to sound as
other vital systems began to show signs of distress. A ventilator
was put in place to help her breath.

The Colonel stepped forward, breaking the sterile field. He
knelt beside her. "Listen to me. I know you can hear me. You can't
leave me. I can't protect our child without you."

The numbers were falling. One of the doctors took his
shoulder and tried to pull him away. He shook him off, took her
hand and stood shouting, "Don't do this. You're stronger than we
are. I can't... I won't do this without you."

The heart monitor went flat with a solid tone that blotted
out every other sound in the room.

One of the doctors moved to try a defibulator. One of the
Humanoids stopped him saying it wouldn't work on her.

The doctor said, "I'm sorry, she's gone."

The Colonel looked at the one who spoke. "Please... help
her."

The doctor slowly shook his head.

Suddenly she squeezed his hand. He jerked around. The tone was gone. The monitor showed an erratic heartbeat. The ventilator kicked in. Her breathing was very shallow but it was there. They tried to pull the Colonel away. He wouldn't let go of her hand.

The Doctor who had spoken to him took him by the arm. "Let us help her."

The Colonel released her hand and stepped back. Everyone moved in to stabilize her.

One of the doctors glanced over at the Colonel, and then looked at the doctor standing next to him and said, "If anyone ever asked you, have you ever witnessed a miracle, you can tell 'em yes."

Beth was in tears. Aaron put his arm around her.

Etac made one comment. "Hard to kill." He then turned and left.

Beth cut her eyes at him. Her stare reflected her thought. Cold hearted bastard!

One day she would understand what he'd just done. What he'd said to her, a female, was reserved for warriors in battle. He could not have complimented her more.

Chapter twenty: Get ready. Get set...

Several days went by. Kera recovered quickly. The baby was the focal point of their life. She and the Colonel spent much of their time together with their child. The modified enzyme was doing its job. Cellular development had stabilized, but by human standards he was still maturing at ten times that of a normal human fetus and more than twice that of a Humanoid. Had they not removed him he would have killed his mother.

Time was needed to observe and understand this new evolutionary branch. Kera ovulated only once in an eighteen month cycle. For the moment there was no chance of another pregnancy.

If Terrance and his people had perfected anything it was the cloning process. That proved very beneficial to the Colonel. They had removed a few stem cells from him and at the moment a new left arm was developing in a jar, so to speak.

Even with the new appendage it was unlikely the Colonel would be continuing with the others. He now had the most unique family in the history of mankind and he wasn't about to leave them. A meeting was called and Corporal Hickman was invited to attend.

Terrance, Aaron and Colonel Hathaway were already there when Corporal Hickman arrived. Beth really wasn't part of this and had chosen to remain with Kera. A video link had been established with the Georgana. The Captain and Second Lieutenant Avery were present on two different screens. A decision had been made and the military command of the surface team was about to be passed.

The Corporal entered, walked to the table across from the Colonel, snapped to attention and saluted. "Corporal Hickman reporting as ordered sir."

Colonel Hathaway returned the salute. "At ease Corporal. Be seated." Corporal Hickman dropped his salute and sat down.

The Colonel glanced at Aaron and then at the two screens. "We are all in agreement?"

A unified "yes" was the answer.

The Colonel looked at the Corporal. "Due to the current situation and your performance in the field you are here by promoted to the rank of Captain and are granted all the privileges that accompany that position."

Corporal Hickman slowly stood up. "Sir?"

"And," the Colonel continued, "Are here by given command of all ground operations until so ordered to stand down."

The Corporal fell back into his chair. The Colonel looked at the Second Lieutenant. "I here by promote you to First Lieutenant and assign to you the position of Adjutant to the field commander."

The new Captain found his voice. He gestured to the Lieutenant. "Shouldn't he..."

Lieutenant Avery spoke up. "You have the field experience. You've seen it all, up close and personal, and I have no problem backing you up."

The Colonel looked at Terrance. "I assume you have an appropriate uniform and rank insignia?"

Terrance stood up. "Yes sir," then to Captain Hickman, "if you'll come with me."

Terrance stepped around the table. The newly promoted Captain stood, saluted the Colonel, did an about face and followed Terrance out.

Aaron said, "I think he'll do fine."

"I don't pass out field promotions if I think otherwise. Now, I have to go see a man about an arm."

With that they all left.

*   *   *

The Georgana re-anchored in the channel. The next four days were spent putting together the crew that would embark on the greatest adventure man had ever attempted; a journey to rediscover a world lost to them half a millennium ago.

The submarine was equipped with single side band communications equipment. The backup transceiver was taken ashore and installed. With this New Houston could maintain communications with the Georgana.

The next thing that had to happen was the recovery of the inflatables used to bring the landing party ashore. The damaged one would have to be repaired and they especially needed the one that carried the encampment supplies. It was one of only two large enough to carry some of the equipment they would require, ashore. A Humanoid recovery team accomplished this.

The Submarine could handle a crew of eighty-five. With the automated systems installed at Quanterra only ten were required to operate the ship. It was decided that an armed contingent of forty would be onboard, half of them humanoid and half of them human each with their own Commander. On the human side five were from the cloned population. Both teams would fall under the command of the ship's Captain. Scientists and researchers from both sides would fill thirty of the remaining spots. Terrance, Aaron and Beth handpicked twelve others. The Humanoids did the same. The five remaining places would be reserved for whomever they might recover at the Blue Ridge Mountain underwater site.

It took another week to resupply the ship. Beth spent part of the time catching up on her journal. Four transports were loaded into the forward hold. These would be used to travel across country when it became necessary.

Two days into that week the Humanoids came aboard. The inflatables were used to transfer them to the submarine. Because Humanoids and water don't mix, by the time they reached the boat most of them were throwing up over the side. Before allowing anyone onboard it was decided to run them around in the bay for a while to allow them to get their sea legs.

Their ability to adapt to this new environment happened quickly, after all it was what they were designed to do. A half an hour later they clamored aboard.

The Humanoid military commander was called Jton. All of them, even the non-military members, were physically intimidating. That was apparent by the reaction of the welcoming committee. The Humanoids sensed this and could have taken advantage of it if not for the specific orders of the Chief Council. Under no circumstances were they to become confrontational unless attacked and to follow Captain Kemp's orders as long as he remained in command.

They were given a tour of the sub and shown where they would be housed. Afterwards they all left the Georgana with the exception of Jton. He wanted to remain onboard to observe the crew and ask some questions. In a very short time he was actively involved in conversations that explained various systems and their functions. It became apparent to the Captain that these animalistic looking beings were very curious and highly intelligent. This raised concerns, which he would share with Aaron and the Colonel later.

The Captain contacted Aaron and made a request to come ashore to meet with him. It was granted as long as the ship remained secure. Command of the bridge was passed to his Executive Officer with specific orders to protect the boat at all cost. He then shared an inflatable with Jton and was ferried ashore.

Three and a half hours later he stepped into a room and met Terrance for the first time. Terrance greeted him and asked him to sit. He sat across from Terrance and Aaron and expressed his concerns.

"I watched this Humanoid Commander," he began, "he asked a lot of technical questions about the operation of the ship."

Terrance interrupted, "These people are incredibly curious about the environment they have to function in. It's the way they were designed. It's why they're able to adapt and survive."

"Yes," continued the Captain, "but his ability to grasp what he was being told to him was unnerving. He never asked to have anything repeated. Inside of an hour he was explaining things back to us. At this point he's fully capable of piloting the ship himself."

"Captain," said Aaron, "I agree, what you've said certainly requires some thought on our part."

Terrance stood. "Captain, we appreciate your concern. I'll have someone show you where you can get something to eat and a place to rest for the night."

The Captain stood. "I would appreciate the food, but I won't rest until I'm back aboard the Georgana."

"I completely understand. I'll arrange for transportation back."

With that Captain Kemp turned and left. When the door was shut Aaron asked, "What do you think? Is there a reason to worry?"

"We're dealing with a people we know very little about, but one thing I do know. They do what they say they'll do. If Etac has agreed to this joint venture and has instructed his men to cooperate that's exactly what they'll do."

"If that's all he's done."

"Well I'll put security on notice, but if nothing turns up, in four days we launch."

They started out. "I guess it won't hurt to run this past the Colonel," said Aaron.

*　　*　　*

Aaron found Colonel Hathaway and Kera in a room in the hospital set aside for families with newborns. The Colonel opened the door with his right hand. In two days he was set to receive his new left arm. Kera sat across the room holding a newborn wrapped in a blanket.

Aaron asked, "When did this happen?"

"He was removed from the artificial womb about two hours ago," answered the Colonel.

Aaron walked over. Kera moved the blanket back from the baby's face. His eyes were closed. He was light skinned and looked like any other human baby until he yawned. He had a full set of teeth with extended canines. He sensed someone different in the room and flared his nose. His eyes opened. The iris was pale blue with a slightly elongated pupil. He pulled an arm from under the blanket. His tinny nails were dark and came to a point.

The Colonel was beaming. "Isn't he great?"

"You have a name yet?" Aaron asked.

Kera answered. "Robert Seta Hathaway, but I still don't understand the need for three names."

Aaron watched the baby. "It helps us tell each other apart."

Kera brought the blanket back into place. "Your scent tells you apart."

Aaron grinned. "Well for those of us without your nose, it helps." He looked at the Colonel. "I need to speak to you for a second."

"What about?"

"A military thing," to Kera, "we'll take it outside. It was nice to meet you, Robert Seta Hathaway."

Once outside, Aaron related to the Colonel, Captain Kemp's concerns.

The Colonel voiced his opinion. "I haven't spoken to *anyone* about this, but if you want my opinion, I see no reason to re-think it. Go with what you know until something happens to change it. I've seen or heard nothing to make me believe it's anything, but what it seems."

"Okay then," he grinned a big grin, "a great looking kid."

The Colonel opened the door. Kera stood in the doorway with the baby.

"If you don't want me to hear something," she said, "you have to go farther away than that. You can believe what you want, but if my father wanted the submarine he'd already have it," to the Colonel, "I need your help. It's time to feed him and his teeth hurt."

The Colonel started into the room and looked back. "I know Etac well enough to believe what she says."

Closing the door Aaron walked away wondering what part the Colonel was going to play in feeding the baby?

*   *   *

The Georgana was being upgraded for its mission. Captain Kemp and Aaron toured the ship making sure all was in order. They stepped into the forward hold. Secured to the deck were four small vehicles. Aaron walked around them and looked them over but didn't question why they were there.

The Captain motioned him toward the hatch in the forward bulkhead. "Come here. I want you to see something."

Aaron followed him through the watertight hatch. The Captain switched on the light. Setting on the deck secured to the launch bay was one of the mules used to construct New Atlantis. Off to the right, hanging from an overhead crane, was one of the drones used to access New Atlantis years later.

The Captain asked, "You know what these are?"

Aaron stood for a moment with his mouth open and then said, "Are you kidding. That's a drone used to transfer personnel to New Atlantis and that's a mule. Just like the ones used to construct it. I've seen pictures of them"

"No," said the Captain, "Not like one. It *is* one."

"That can't be. All the mules were destroyed when the construction platform was destroyed."

"Not this one. It provided the basic design used to create the submersibles we use today. The men who occupied New Atlantis after it was finished used this one to ferry supplies down early on. It was left there. The Colonel and I decided it might come in handy and had it moved here. When we need to, we can flood this room and launch the mule or the drone through the bay."

Captain Kemp allowed Aaron to enter the mule and look around inside. Afterwards they inspected the drone and then left resealing the room.

*   *   *

The day arrived for the departure of the Georgana. The date recording system on the Georgana was set to that of Quanterra. That did not exactly match the calendar that New Houston operated by and the Humanoid system was different from both.

This moment in time needed to be recorded in a standard format that would forever pinpoint it in history. After looking at the calendars in use by all concerned it was decided that October the first, twenty-five seventy-three would be the starting point.

It also marked another milestone. It was a blending of cultures. It formed the first common thread between them. It would be left to historians to argue that the birth of Fred and Kera's child was the first.

When Terrance, Beth and Aaron arrived at the departure point on the beach most of the crew had already transferred over.

Etac, Colonel Hathaway and Kera had already arrived to see them off. Beth hugged Kera; The Colonel shook Aaron's hand with the hand attached to his newly acquired arm. He still had a problem with numbness in his fingers, but he was assured that his brain would eventually make the connection. Etac stood by and took it all in.

Aaron looked at the Colonel and asked. "Sorry you're not coming?"

The Colonel took Kera's hand. "Not a bit. I've got plenty to do here. Michael is taking over and completing Terrance's term in office and he and I are consulting on security issues. There seems to be some concern that the Drakmun demonstrated the ability to get around the shields on the vehicles."

Etac stepped in. "If become threat. Eliminate threat."

The Colonel continued. "Well that's one solution, but we're all descended from the same past."

"We're using an ancient form of communications," said Terrance. "Using single side band, and depending on atmospheric conditions, we should be able to stay in touch."

Beth looked toward the inflatable waiting to take them out. The pilot waved them over. "Looks like they're calling for us."

There was another exchange of goodbyes. Etac, the Colonel and Kera watched as Terrance, Aaron and Beth crossed the
beach, climbed aboard and the inflatable moved offshore.

Chapter twenty-one: Off to see the wizard

There was movement along the perimeter fence. Several Drakmun eased out of the jungle and approached the energy fence. Something had changed. They wore crude clothing made from animal skins and the remains of some of the uniforms taken off the bodies of Terrance's men.

They stood close to the fence. Several walked up and down the perimeter. Finally one of them touched it; a violent pop and the man was vaporized. The rest moved back. A moment later a dozen rushed from the jungle. They carried a felled tree. On impact the air exploded vaporizing the tree and everyone touching it.

Those remaining moved away, into the jungle. Their attempt to deplete the energy source and breach the fence had failed, this time.

The security system recorded the energy expenditure at the fence. It didn't reoccur and since large animals wandered into it from time to time no one checked surveillance.

* * *

Aaron and Beth retained their original cabin. It still contained the things they had left behind. The PA system announced a meeting with the Captain in his wardroom. Terrance, Beth, Aaron, Captain Hickman and Jton were invited.

Over five hundred years had passed since a meeting of this sort was held on the Georgana. This one was no less significant.

Everyone introduced themselves to Jton. He returned their greetings with a nod. Captain Kemp laid out his planned course and a timetable to get them there.

Aaron then changed the plans. "We need to set course for Quanterra."

The Captain looked Aaron in the eye. "Why would you want to do that? As I recall the last time they saw us they wanted to, how does it go, *blow us out of the water*." The Captain had been reading an ancient novel titled "Pride and Prejudice."

Beth picked it up. "I agree with Aaron. We've discovered something here that's very special. The world has suddenly become a great deal bigger. We have an obligation to at least pass this back to the millions that believe that they are alone at the bottom of the sea."

The Captain looked around the table. He saw no objection. "Very well, we'll set course for Quanterra, but we keep our distance until we're sure it's safe."

Aaron nodded his agreement and the meeting broke up. Jton and Captain Hickman walked off discussing tactics. Terrance accompanied the Captain to the bridge and Beth and Aaron retired to their cabin for some quality time together. Beth spent part of the time organizing her journals. She wasn't considering the historical significance these writings would one day have. She just wanted to be able to relive these moments in her life.

They were Twenty-five miles out when the Georgana submerged to make its approach to Quanterra. Right before, the Captain radioed back to the Colonel what they were about to do. The Colonel agreed with Beth that it was the right thing to do, but also suggested extreme caution.

The Humanoids sensed the gulf close in around them. For a moment the sounds of life in the sea were confusing to them. But true to their capacity to understand and adapt, the sounds of the sea would be recorded and remembered.

Aaron, Beth, Terrance and Jton stood next to the Captain. The Communications Officer was ready to initiate contact.

The Captain moved over behind the Communications Officer. "Send a request for a visual image."

The communications Officer brought it on line. The console in front of them had a split screen. On the left was the image of the Captain. On the right the words *Communications Link Requested,* under that a countdown clock counting back from twenty-five.

Everyone waited with great anticipation. It was about to time-out when the screen blinked and a man's face appeared.

The moments of silence seemed to last forever and then he said, "Captain Kemp I... We thought you were all dead."

Beth stepped in front of the Captain. "I'm happy to say we aren't"

The man on the screen seemed very excited. "Let me patch you through to Chairman Ramos."

Aaron stepped in. "Chairman Ramos? What about Chairman Kyler?"

Before making the transfer he commented. "There have been some changes. It's best you hear this from Chairman Ramos."

When the screen built into the wall lit up Chairman Ramos left the chair behind his desk and approached the two-way communications feed from the bridge of the Georgana. "It is you. We thought you were dead, that the sub had imploded after you left the dock."

Aaron stepped in. "And nobody bothered to look."

"You don't understand. You left from a place very few have access to. We were told that a team investigated the site and found nothing but wreckage. That the bodies were crushed beyond recovery."

"Who reported this," asked the Captain?

"The former Chairman made a general announcement to the population. Memorial services were held for all of you. You are all thought of as heroes."

"Where's Chairman Kyler? He obviously lied," asked Aaron?

Chairman Ramos backed up and leaned against his desk. "Aaron, your wife had a lot to do with the truth coming out."

Aaron was confused. "What did my wife have to do with any of this?"

The Chairman thought for a moment. "I don't know a good way to explain this so I'll just say it. Your wife's parents were clearing out some of her things from the damaged apartment and came across a voice recorder. On it were notes and commentary she had put together about events surrounding your departure. She had reason to believe Chairman Kyler and others were part of a conspiracy to stop you from actually leaving even if it meant destroying the sub and everyone on it. Because of the content they were justifiably concerned about turning it over to the authorities so they turned it over to the paper"

Aaron interrupted, "You're saying it wasn't an accident. That she was killed to keep her from finding something out."

"The Chairman was apparently assured by others that you would fail. That what you were being injected with would kill all of you. And if that failed they had a plan in place to destroy the submarine. Power and control can be an all-consuming thing. They were afraid that if you succeeded others would leave and one day Quanterra would cease to exist and with it their ability to rule."

"Somehow she found out," Aaron said, "Or she was about to."

The Chairman continued. "Or she was close enough to the truth that they couldn't take a chance."

Beth moved over next to Aaron and put her arm around him. "I'm so sorry."

"How many were involved," Aaron wanted to know?

"The Chairman and a few select others. They were arrested and charged with murder and conspiracy to commit murder. Not even the Chairman is above the laws of the city. They were convicted and executed. Aaron, if you want I'll make everything available to you, but justice *has* been served. The fact that all of you are still alive somehow makes for a better ending."

The Captain took back the conversation. "Well, there has been loss of life Colin Becker for one and several others."

The Chairman leaned away from his desk. "What did you find? Does life still exist on the surface?"

Terrance and Jton had been out of view. The Captain stepped back and invited them into the picture. "I'd like you to meet two friends from the top of the world."

Terrance stepped into view. "My name is Terrance Lieberman. I come from New Houston." Terrance motioned to Jton. "And this is Jton."

The Humanoid Commander stepped into the picture. The Chairman took a step back from the screen. "My goodness, you do have some interesting new friends. What are your plans? If you're planning to enter the city all of you will have to go into quarantine."

Aaron answered. "That's not our intension. We believe that others have survived and exist on the surface. We now know for a fact there were underground sites. We've also had to deal with the aftermath of hundreds of years of evolutionary change due to radioactive contamination. The world has become incredibly dangerous. Let me ask you this. Now that you know life *does* exist, and we've survived the trip, do you want to join us?"

"This conversation has been recorded. I intend to share it with the rest of Quanterra. Whatever we decide will be a decision made by all of us, the entire population."

"Well then," Aaron said. "There may still be samples of the serum left at the facility. It can be used to precondition your people for the surface. If not maybe we can find a way to help. I do hope you decide to become part of all this." He grinned and glanced at Jton. "And if you do, a small piece of advice. Before you land on the beach let us know you're coming. Jton's people are very *territorial*."

Jton nodded and showed his canines.

The Chairman smiled. "I'll remember that. It's great to know you *are* the heroes you were made out to be. If you'll pass the names of those you loss I'll see that the words *in memoriam* are removed from the other plaques."

The Captain signed off with, "I'll see to that. Hope to have you with us soon." The screen went blank.

The Chairman moved back around his desk and touched his interoffice communications link. "I need to arrange for a citywide broadcast. I want this on every view screen in every sector."

"What's this about?" Came the reply.

"It's about our future. It would seem we now have one."

* * *

The Georgana made a pass over Quanterra to give Terrance and Jton an idea of just how large the city was. Afterward a course was set for the Caribbean Sea. They would have to run on the surface most of the way to extend the battery life. They dare not let it go below one-quarter charge to ensure enough power to keep the internal systems functioning. At that point they would have to shut down propulsion to allow the fuel cells to recharge. Their maximum speed was thirty knots.

Without the electronic aids to navigation that existed in the distant past, pinpointing an exact location on the surface was going to be difficult at best. The onboard navigation computers were reprogrammed to use magnetic north as a reference point and reestablish the old longitude/latitude grid system. Where they were headed was off the eastern coast of an island named Puerto Rico close to a place called Culebra. The exact location was eighteen degrees nineteen minutes north and sixty-five degrees fourteen minutes west some two thousand miles away.

Beth and Aaron retired to their cabin to get some rest. They, along with Terrance, had an invitation to join the Captain and the other officers for an evening meal in the wardroom. The Humanoids and the cloned humans preferred their own company and had dietary requests that would not go well at a human dinner table.

* * *

Life in New Houston, as far as the general population was concerned, had settled back into its day-to-day routine with an occasional minor disruption caused by a visiting Humanoid.

The scientific community was totally caught up in the development of Kera's child. Not even the Humanoids had witnessed such and accelerated growth rate. Just in the week the Georgana had been gone Robert Seta Hathaway had gone from a newborn to a child of about three, in human years. Although a lot of the physical traits of his Humanoid mother were there one wasn't, the body hair. The hair on his body was reflective of his father.

His growth rate was only exceeded by his capacity to learn. One night Kera walked past Robert's room and noticed the light on. She looked inside. He was in the middle of his bed surrounded by books. He had taught himself to read.

When a desired result is obtained, it can't be quantified unless it can be repeated. The researchers wanted to repeat what had occurred between Kera and the Colonel. They realized the danger it would put the female in and decided to ask for volunteers from both sides to donate eggs and sperm so that another child could be conceived using the artificial womb.

At first they tried fertilizing a human egg with Humanoid sperm. The sperm attacked with such ferocity they destroyed the egg. It became clear that the egg had to come from a Humanoid female.

Next they went the other way. The results were the same in reverse. Within their lifetime human sperm were unable to penetrate the egg's membrane. They tried six times with six different donors with the same results.

They came to the only conclusion that made sense. Just through chance one human sperm had found a minute defect in the egg membrane and managed to fertilize Kera's egg. The odds of repeating that naturally could be one in a million. So they decided to give one human sperm a hand. They used a needle to inject one sperm into an egg. What happened was nothing short of amazing. The egg began to divide at such an accelerated rate that in a few moments the fetus began to take shape. A few moments later it literally exploded. They tried again and again with the same results.

The enzyme they had developed to stabilize fetal development had to be supplied by the blood passing through the umbilical. None of the fetuses survived long enough for that to happen.

The final realization was that what had happened between the Colonel and Kera was truly unique and could not be reproduced with anyone else and probably not even by the two of them. Whether or not their son could mate with either side was yet to be seen.

*   *   *

The Georgana entered the Straits of Florida and turned southeast along the coast of what used to be Cuba. Their destination lay one thousand miles ahead. It had taken almost a month to get this far. The power cells required longer than anticipated to recharge. During this process the sub remained dead in the water.

The crew had been confined to the inside of the submarine with an occasional trip up on deck to see the sun. The coastline in the distance to starboard became too inviting. After numerous requests to go ashore for just a little while, the Captain conceded and gave the order to slow and change course.

He cruised the coast until he found and area where the water depth would allow the submarine to get in close enough to use the inflatables to make a landing.

Everyone needed a break. Confined to the inside of the sub they had begun to wear on each other's nerves.

It was decided to use the two larger inflatables. Each would carry fifteen crewmen. Each group would include five armed military. Terrance, Aaron and Beth would ride in with the second group.

The sea was running one to two feet and the wave action to the beach was producing minimal breakers. The first inflatable pushed off and started ashore. It was decided to wait for the first to complete the landing before launching the second.

From the high ground above the beach the submarine, and the approaching craft, were being observed.

Terrance, Beth and Aaron stood on deck with the others and watched the inflatable grow smaller in the distance. Jton would be part of the escort on their boat.

The Captain observed the landing through the glasses on the external conning tower bridge. When he saw the inflatable carried up on the beach by the breakers and observed the occupants scramble onto the sand he looked down to the deck. "Looks like they made it okay. Load up and cast off the second one."

With that, the next shore party used the tethers to lower themselves into the second boat. When everyone was safely aboard they pushed off. The Coxswain brought the engine to life and swung the bow away from the sub.

The inflatable slapped its way ahead. A fine mist was being carried back across the open boat. Everyone watched the beach get closer and closer all of them anticipating the feel of solid ground under their feet again.

On the beach, two of the soldiers drove metal stakes into the ground to anchor the inflatable. Others watched the approach of the second landing craft.

One of the women needed a little privacy. Before they left they were instructed not to go anywhere alone. Being there were only two females they paired up and crossed just inside the tree line. As one loosened her clothes the attack came from three sides.

Four large burley males, with beards, long shaggy hair, and dressed in clothing made from homespun material, were on them before they could react. One did manage to scream before a closed fist took her to the ground. Two of them picked up the females and carried them into the trees. The other two continued toward the beach. These remnants of human kind stood over six feet tall, but the one single thing that stood out was their feet. They were big, wide and reflected a lifetime without shoes.

Everyone on the beach reacted to the outcry at the same time. In that same instant the tree line erupted. Dozens of screaming savages, swinging what looked like a rope with a large weight attached to both ends, poured onto the beach. The military opened fire taking down those in front. The ropes were released with deadly accuracy.

Those in the approaching inflatable heard the shots coming from the beach. They saw everyone on the beach retreat toward the surf and the bolo-like weapons take out all the armed members of the landing party. The four closest to the water made it into the surf. The others were run down and pinned to the sand.

The second boat was within range of their weapons, but before they could fire in defense of their friends the bow swung away.

Beth looked back at the one driving the boat. "What are you doing? We have to go after them."

The Coxswain pointed to his left. The beach curved away from them. Four large wooden boats had emerged from the curve and bore down on them. Ten oarsmen pulling in unison powered each boat. The forward momentum produced by the weight quickly closed the gap.

He wanted nothing to do with a rescue attempt and the Coxswain continued to swing the landing craft away. Beth was out of her seat and on him. He swung at her. His arm was caught mid swing. He was jerked away and thrown overboard.

Jton stood beside her. "Drive."

She took the helm, swung the boat back toward the beach and opened the throttle. Four members of the landing party were in the water being pursued by their attackers. Aaron pointed at the boats and shouted back to Beth. "Nose into them."

She nodded and swung the inflatable head-on into the small oncoming wooden fleet. The two military carrying pulse rifles understood what they were doing, each chose a target and opened fire. In a matter of moments the boats were transformed into funeral pyres. Living torches flung themselves into the sea.

The male who led the attack on the beach became enraged and crushed the skull of the man at his feet. The others, fueled by his rage, began killing the captives.

There was nothing they could do to save the shore party so the military opened fire on the attackers. The pulse weapons turned the beach into a firestorm.

The four in the water were losing the race. Those in pursuit were in their element and had quickly closed the gap. Jton opened fire with precision accuracy. His modified crossbow-like weapon fired a bolt of pure energy. With each shot a man died. In a matter of seconds it was over.

Everyone in the boat had moved to the gunwales. Beth maneuvered the craft in and the four survivors were pulled aboard.

She swung the inflatable back toward the Georgana. The Coxswain was still treading water waving to be picked up. As she backed off to drift in next to him a shot from Jton's bow took his head off. She jumped. The body rolled and sank from sight.

Jton stood next to her. She looked at him. He said, "That one coward." He looked at her, smiled his version of a smile and said, "You not."

She half smiled back, moved the throttle ahead and piloted the boat back toward the Georgana. In this life, death could come at any moment. Unfortunately she was getting used to it.

Chapter twenty-two: A lesson learned

Besides the lives, the most precious thing they lost that day was the inflatable. It was one of only two large enough to get the transports ashore. A radio account of what had happened was transmitted to New Houston. Two of the men killed on the beach were Humanoids. Their names were passed along to their people. It was a lesson learned well. From that point on, their objective was all that mattered. Terrance discussed matters of state with Michael and the sub continued southeast toward its rendezvous with the past.

Beth and Aaron had a private conversation with Colonel Hathaway and Kera. Before leaving Kera and Beth had discussed the length of Beth's hair. Kera couldn't understand why some human females wore it so long. Beth had since given up the vanity scarf. Her hair was showing signs of re-growth. The truth be known she liked the shorter look and it was a whole lot easier to keep.

After greetings passed between them the topic moved to Robert. At first he was aging at the rate of one human year every few days. It was feared that he would live out his entire life in less than six months. Then it changed. The rate of maturity slowed to half of that and in three days to a quarter of that. At this point he was a teenager.

Humanoids normally reached adulthood in about two years and then the aging processed slowed to what was normal for them. Robert was going to reach adulthood in about a tenth of that. His brain recorded and retained everything his five senses took in. He had already viewed almost half of the historical video records on file and he spent almost every other waking moment in the library.

As analytical as he was, socially he was warm and out-going. He was very attached to his parents and made friends easily. He already had twice the physical strength of an adult human male.

Colonel Hathaway had other news. "Quanterra floated a communications buoy. They've begun inoculating volunteers for a trip to the surface. They've also begun construction on a submersible that can carry over a hundred and fifty of those volunteers to shore. That little project will take almost two years to complete. What they want to know is if the Georgana becomes available can they enlist our help."

Aaron answered. "Tell them, of course."

Kera came back on. "When are you two going to get married?"

Beth asked. "Have you and Fred gotten married?"

"It was his idea," answered Kera. "Seems humans have to go through this ritual to demonstrate their willingness to be together. With my people the bonding is much more personal and takes place inside of us. Well, are you?"

Beth was a little embarrassed. She glanced at Aaron. "I haven't been asked."

"I don't know Kera," Aaron said. "She snores."

"What is *snores*?"

The Colonel rescued him. "Sorry, but we need to go. There's someplace we're expected to be. You two be very careful."

Aaron answered. "We'll reach the Blue Ridge Mountain underwater location in a few days. I'll call you before we go in."

"You do that. Take care." The Colonel killed the connection.

Aaron leaned over and kissed Beth. "I love you. I'm going to the bridge for a while."

"I love you too." She watched him leave. He apparently had no idea how much she wanted to answer that question.

*   *   *

A day after the beach encounter the weather turned nasty and the submarine submerged to give the crew a smoother ride.

When Jton's movement below deck brought him close to Beth he paid attention to her. He had recorded her scent and could locate her in any part of the ship. He liked being near her. He had developed respect for this human female. It wasn't so much that she was willing to take charge and do what was needed to save the lives of her crew. It was something that only his kind could recognize.

She had been totally fearless in her actions. It had nothing to do with what he saw. All animals, including humans, produce chemicals that radiate into the air when they're afraid. Other animals can pick up on this and become aggressive. Beth had become in fact totally fearless inside and out, and that deserved his respect.

Beth wasn't blind to these *coincidental* encounters. Had he been a normal human male she would have set him straight, but he wasn't. Jton was a genetically engineered super-human who, in keeping with the animalistic DNA enhancements, was completely honest about what he thought and with what he said. She respected what he was, and for reasons she couldn't put her finger on, felt totally safe and at ease when he was near by.

The Georgana finally passed beyond the sea being tossed up by the gale. It was time to resurface and give the fuel cells a chance to fully charge. The Captain gave the command, the ballast was blown and the sub rose to the surface.

They had lost eleven members of their crew making sixteen spaces available for whatever they found at the underwater site.

They were two days out when Terrance decided it was time to meet with everyone and fill them in on what had gone down at this site based on the video and audio record Janet had left behind.

Jton was the last to arrive in the wardroom. The only open chair was next to Beth. She looked at him as he took the seat. He took in a deep breath through his nose, held her scent for a moment and then let it out. Aaron hadn't noticed the ritual, but she had and purposely avoided making eye contact with him. There was no need in attracting attention to something she knew to be harmless.

Terrance began. "First of all we have no idea what we'll be walking into. If the complex has remained intact, and that's a big if, we still have to hope the docking system will allow the drone to connect to it. From what I know the essence, the memories, of these people were hard coded and stored. Even if the power has failed and the stored DNA is gone we should be able to recover the data and return it to New Houston on the Georgana after we drop everyone off."

Aaron and Beth both offered up a blank stare. Aaron spoke up. "Drop who off, where?"

"I assumed Colin had fully briefed both of you before he... I mean, what did you think the vehicles and the supplies in the forward hold were for?"

Beth answered that. "Plan B in case this turned out to be a waste of time a way to venture inland and then return to the ship."

Terrance looked at the Captain wanting some help. The Captain said," You dropped it, you pick it up."

"I see," Terrance continued. "There's another underground site inland on the Eastern coast. It's located in a place that was called Atlanta Georgia. After that there are two others up the coast. The Georgana will pick you up in three months off the coast of Virginia. Everyone on this boat volunteered for this mission. I can't believe the two who are supposed to lead it were never told."

Aaron looked at Beth and said, "What do you say? Adventure of a lifetime."

She looked at Jton and asked, "You coming?"

Jton looked back. "I go where you go."

She looked at Terrance. "We're in."

This time Aaron did notice something pass between Beth and the giant sitting next to her. If he didn't know better he'd think he was jealous.

"The other thing," Terrance continued, "there was a lot of discord in the final transmission Janet received. They never said exactly what the problem was and she never heard from them again. Bottom line, there may be nothing to find, but we won't know until we look. If we can at least recover the thoughts and memories of these people we'll have an intact record of the last days. Any questions?"

He looked from face to face. There was really nothing left to ask. "Okay, let's do it."

With that everyone one got up and moved toward the door. Beth followed Jton. Aaron was behind her. She reached up and touched Jton's back. She was only ushering him out but he looked back and smiled at her. Aaron's thoughts returned to the conversation they had with the Colonel and Kera. Maybe the question Kera posed needed to be asked.

*　*　*

The next two days were spent preparing for what was *about* to happen here. Aaron and Beth worked together outfitting the vehicles for the trip to the inland sites that would come next.

He watched her pick up this and put down that. She'd always had trouble deciding what to pack.

She caught him staring. "What?" She asked.

He watched for another second and then it just came out. "Do you want to get married?"

The words hung in the air for another second. She dropped what she had in her hand, ran to him, jumped into his arms and wrapped her legs around him. She moved her mouth close to his ear and said, "Yes." She leaned back. You're not kidding are you?"

He sat her back on her feet. "No. I know the timing isn't the best," he added.

"As soon as we get back then." He'd asked and she'd answered. That would be enough for now, she thought.

He had other ideas and pulled her toward him. "You know according to ancient maritime law the Captain of a vessel at sea has the authority to perform a wedding."

"You want to do this now?" She asked.

"Don't you," he answered.

"Yes. Do you think he knows how, or what to say?"

"Well I don't think it's so much what you say as what you mean."

She looked into his eyes for a moment. "I love you Aaron Colure with all my heart, and all my soul, and I want to spend the rest of my life with you."

Aaron smiled. "Let's go find the Captain."

Taking her hand, he led her out of the hold.

You would think the walls had ears the way news of this spread through the crew. What Beth and Aaron had intended for the Captain's cabin, found its way onto the mess deck surrounded by everyone who could squeeze his or her way in. Jton was not there for reasons known only to him.

Terrance stood with Aaron and one of the female crewmembers stood with Beth before Captain Kemp. Marriages, both civil and religious, were commonplace on Quanterra. However having no navy the ship's Captain was at a loss.

The Captain began. "What we are about to do here, on this ship, hasn't occurred in the last five hundred years. As Captain of this vessel I represent the rule of law. And in that capacity I'm going to preside over this event. I was informed this day of the desire of these two people to be joined together in a state of matrimony. They have expressed their love for one another in private and now wish to do so publicly before the members of this crew." He motioned to Beth and Aaron. "Would you both step forward and join hands."

Beth and Aaron stepped up. Aaron held out his hand and she took it.

The Captain continued. "I'm sure in past days there was a dialogue that addressed this occasion at sea, but on such short notice I have no idea what that was. I truly believe the feelings expressed by these two people, to each other, means more than anything I can say to them, so here goes." He looked at Aaron, "Do you love this woman? Are you willing to care for her and protect her and put her before all things as long as you live?"

"I do and I will."

He addressed Beth. "Betheny, Beth, Do you love this man? Are you willing to care for him and protect him and put him before all things as long as you live?"

"Yes, with all that's me."

The Captain placed his hands around their joined hands. "With the authority granted to me, as Captain of this vessel, I pronounce you man and wife from this moment and for as long as you both shall live." The Captain smiled. "I do recall what to say next. "You may kiss the bride."

Cheers went up from the crowd as Aaron took her in his arms and kissed her.

That evening they tried to place a call to the Colonel and Kera, but atmospheric conditions prevented it from going through.

That night they held each other and made love. This time it felt different for both of them. For him, she was an extension of his very soul. For her, he was the center of her universe. She wanted to love him, and care for him, and bear his children.

*   *   *

The Georgana settled in on the map coordinates provided in the video. In the distance an island loomed on the horizon. What bothered the Captain was, if they could see the island, then anything, or anyone, on the island could see them. It was decided not to venture a look at this time. Instead he would keep the lookouts, above the conning tower, manned around the clock. He wasn't going to get blind-sided again.

The Caribbean was crystal clear. The Georgana was outfitted with an underwater camera and light system. However centuries of sea bottom movement and generations of undersea life attaching itself to any protrusion, natural or otherwise, had masked all evidence of the site.

It was decided before they left New Houston that they would probably have to sound the bottom for the site. They retrofitted the sonar burst transmitter to fire a pulse similar to that used in their weapons system. It was much like the pulse systems mounted on the mules used to construct New Atlantis centuries ago. It was hoped that the returning signal would reveal any abnormalities below the sea bottom. If the site were still intact it should show up as a huge void beneath the sea floor. They would run track spacings fanning out a quarter mile in all directions from the central coordinates.

Their detection system worked better than they had hoped. Along the second track they found something very large. They traced the outer edges and found it to be a near perfect rectangle. Perfect, geometric, topographical shapes seldom occur in nature. This had to be it. Finding it solved the first problem. Finding a way in was a much bigger one.

Using the camera system they followed the edge. If you knew what you were looking for you could see the slightly raised sea floor that formed the roof of the complex.

Another meeting was held in the wardroom. Terrance, Aaron, Beth, the Ship's Captain, Captain Hickman, Jton and four other members of the Humanoid contingent were in attendance.

Terrance began. "I don't think there's any doubt we've located the site. Judging by what still shows and the amount of time that's passed I'd say it extended a ways above the sea floor.

Beth stepped in. "From what the cameras show I don't see a way in."

One of the Humanoids spoke up. "Punch hole."

We can't do that," Terrance answered. "We have to find the location of the airlock if we hope to get inside. If we attempt to breach the complex anywhere else we could flood the entire place and lose everything."

Captain Kemp asked, "Does this mean we're gonna have to dig it all up? Because that's gonna take a very long time."

Terrance continued. "You're right. That's not an option, but we are going to have to do *some* digging."

Terrance used a remote. A device in the middle of the table lit up and projected a three dimensional image of a large facility.

He continued, "Part of the research and development that led to the construction of the underground sites was done by Janet Crowley at the Houston site. She had nothing to do with the engineering or construction. She had everything to do with developing the policies, programs, and the philosophy, which enabled the people to maintain their sanity for hundreds of years in a very confined space. Because of that a lot of information about the other sites was stored where she would have access to it."

Everyone watched the three dimensional representation slowly turn in the air in front of them.

Terrance went on. "The one you see here is the Atlanta site." He touched the controls and another one appeared. "This is the Seattle site." Another appeared. "And this is the site outside of Denver." Several other images came and went.

Aaron spoke up. "I didn't see this site. How is this gonna help us?"

Terrance redisplayed the Atlanta site. "This site was never sent to her. None of these had airlocks, but they all had access to the surface. See the elevator shaft leading up." He began to cycle through the sites again. "Do you notice what they all have in common?"

It was Beth this time. "They're all located in a corner."

"Yes... We've always needed a little luck to pull this off. If we're lucky that airlock is located at one of the corners. All we have to do is dig it out."

"The mule," Aaron said, "You're gonna use the mule."

"Yes. We have a pilot," replied Captain Kemp. "We need someone to use the arms."

Until now Jton hadn't said a word. "I use."

Terrance smiled. "I was hoping you'd ask. Once we launch I'll run you through the controls and then you can practice until you're comfortable." Terrance looked at Aaron. "Mr. Colure the mule can carry three. Would you like to go along for the ride?"

Aaron didn't hesitate. "Yes, yes I would."

"Okay," Terrance turned to Captain Hickman, "Captain I need you to prepare a team to enter the complex. Bear in mind it's been sealed for a very long time. The air inside may not be breathable. We have rebreathers that will recycle the air in the mask. If we have to, we'll pump air down from the surface."

Jton spoke up. "Mine go too."

"Of course, said Captain Hickman. "I'll pick five of my men; you pick five of yours, but I'm in charge."

Jton nodded.

"Alright," Terrance said, "In the words of our ancient ancestors. Let's get this show on the road."

With that everyone got up and filed out. Aaron was thinking, history is about to be made and I'm going to *be* there.

It apparently never occurred to him that the moment the Georgana backed out of the dock on Quanterra he had already become part of the most important turning point in the history of mankind.

The batteries on the mule were charged before they left New Houston; however they required a little topping off. That would take the better part of an hour.

It was early afternoon before the hold was flooded; the lock was opened and for the first time in half a millennium the mule settled into the open sea.

Originally the atmospheric mix on the mule had contained an enzyme to raise the body's internal temperature. That, of course, would not be needed here. A simple oxygen/nitrogen mix would do.

It was early spring and the water temperature in the Caribbean was a chilly sixty-five degrees. Two hundred feet down the ambient air temperature in the mule required an extra layer of clothing at least for the more human members of the crew. Jton didn't seem to notice.

The pilot moved in, just off the northeastern corner. He held back to let Jton practice with the arms. Inside of ten minutes you would've thought he'd designed and built the damn things. The excavation began.

The work went slow. Care had to be taken not to damage the structure. Aaron had very little to do other than sit and watch so he recorded his impressions of everything going on.

Through history these recorded thoughts would be considered some of the most valuable pieces of audio ever preserved.

By the time it was obvious this corner was nothing more than a corner the sun was going down and the temperature was dropping in the mule. It was decided to abandon the site and start again in the morning.

That night Beth and Aaron lay beside each other in their cabin. Aaron was much too excited to sleep and Beth was trying to find a way to ask him something.

Finally she decided the best way to ask was just to ask. "I'd like to go on the mule tomorrow."

He rolled on his left side and pushed up with his elbow. The first thing that jumped into his head was Jton.

Before he could say anything she continued. "This is the most important archeological dig in the history of mankind. I have to be part of it... Please."

He watched her face, leaned down and kissed her. She kissed him back. He began to explore with his hands.

She giggled and said, "I still want to go."

He rolled on his back. "Okay, you win."

She smiled and said. "No, you win," and she climbed on top of him.

Chapter twenty-three: The time capsule

The next morning Aaron watched the mule circle on the surface and then slip below the gentle swells of the Caribbean. He smiled to himself. There was no doubt in his mind she knew the seat was hers if she asked. But he really liked her way of saying "thank you."

After all this time, the ViewScan system still worked. Beth knelt beside Jton and watched the monitor. The mule moved up on the northwestern corner.

When Beth climbed aboard Jton took in her scent. His hands moved with precision as the arms delicately removed layer after layer of deposits. After ten minutes she glanced up at him. He was watching her not the monitor. His hands never stopped. To say the least it was unnerving. For several long moments her eyes were fixed on his. She couldn't look away. Finally he broke the gaze and went back to the monitor.

Her breathing was short and quick and she could feel her heart beating inside her chest. She got up and moved to the back of the mule. His attention never moved from the monitor, but she could still feel his eyes. He had looked straight into her soul and a connection had solidified between them. It had nothing to do with the love she felt for Aaron. She couldn't explain it, but she knew it was there and she lost all track of time.

"Here," Jton's voice brought her back. "Airlock."

She was across the cabin in an instant. "You found it?"

There on the monitor was the distinct outline of a hatch. She looked up the ladder to the flight deck and shouted to the pilot. "Let me call it in."

The pilot, looking down at her, motioned her up. "Be my guest."

She climbed to the top of the ladder. He handed her the mike. She keyed it. "We've found it."

Aaron's voice came back across the speaker. "Great! We'll use forced air to clean it and hope the alloys they used have stood the test of time."

Returning to the sub; Beth joined Aaron and prepared to transfer to the site. The mule was fitted with a high-pressure jet air transfer system and re-launched.

Jton scrubbed every inch of the airlock's external hatch. The material used to construct the exposed part of the site was the same material used to construct New Atlantis. Seawater and pressure weren't a problem, but centuries of exposure to corrosive minerals, salts and the excretions from marine life might have solidified the moving parts.

Terrance, Beth, Aaron, Captain Kemp and all of the bridge crew gathered around a monitor on the bridge and watched the images being transmitted from the underwater cameras. If the locking mechanism for the airlock hatch was similar to the one used on New Atlantis it was both mechanical and magnetic.

"Depending on the state of contamination," Terrance said, "it might take the arm on the mule to release the mechanical lock. We'll use the control panel in the drone to release the magnetic lock. Hopefully there's still power on the site. If we break the mechanical seal and the magnetic lock isn't in place the airlock hatch might open to the sea. If that happens we'll flood the site." A decision had to be made.

The pros and cons of using the mule to break the seal were tossed around. In the end it was decided to launch the drone, seal with the airlock hatch and try to release the mechanical lock by hand. If it couldn't be moved the other option was always there. The mule would stand off and wait.

Terrance would stay on the sub. If something happened it would be his decision whether or not to continue the mission. Beth, Aaron, a half a dozen researchers including two clones and six military including Captain Hickman boarded the drone. Three of the military were Humanoids. Everyone was fitted with a skintight environmental suit and a re-breather.

They were seated down both sides of the drone. Aaron and Beth were seated together toward the back. He said, "This must have been what it felt like during the transfer to New Atlantis."

Beth took a deep breath and let it out slowly. "The difference being they knew they weren't coming back."

The bay was flooded. They felt the drone move. She took his hand. He squeezed it.

Under the submarine the launch bay doors pulled back. The drone was released from its mooring and drifted down into the Caribbean. Once it cleared the Georgana's hull the props propelled it toward the site.

The universal docking attachment on the drone protruded from the starboard side. It was located just ahead of the seating.

The Pilot's voice came over the speaker. "Five minutes. When the light above the lock turns green we have a seal."

Every eye was on the light. They felt the drone make contact. They could feel it adjusting its position. The drone shuttered and the light switched from red to green.

Captain Hickman stood along with the rest of his squad. He walked to the drone airlock. Beth and Aaron worked their way to the front. Captain Hickman released the seal on the hatch and swung it back. In front of him was the sealed hatch that led into the site.

It had been decided to release the mechanical lock first. The Captain took hold of the lever and pulled to the right. It didn't move. He placed both hands on the lever and pulled, but still it didn't move. One of the Humanoids stepped up and the Captain stepped aside. The Humanoid put both hands on the lever, braced himself and pulled. It budged slightly, but try as he would it did not move any farther. There wasn't enough room in the airlock for anyone to help.

The Captain stepped back to Aaron. "Looks like we're gonna have to do it the hard way."

There was the sound of an old, strained mechanical system grinding its way through a range of motion and then a loud clang as it stopped. Everyone stared at the airlock. One of the clones stood with his hand on the lever in the "open" position. At the very least, the Humanoids were impressed. The hatch remained closed that meant there was still enough power to maintain the magnetic seal.

The Clone stepped away. Aaron moved to the control panel that would release the magnetic lock. It normally required a coded card to activate the panel and a password to start the search sequence to find the code to release the lock. During the refit on Quanterra the engineers had by-passed the security system and fitted it with a simple on/off switch. The keypad code was changed to zero.

Aaron flipped the switch and the pad lit up. He glanced around at everyone, looked back at the pad, took a deep breath and pressed zero.

A ten number readout began cycling through numbers for each of the digit locations. As the correct number was located it was locked in. Everyone watched as the last number was entered.

There was the sound of a mechanism within the hatch changing position, the seal was broken and the hatch door swung open a couple of inches. A rush of air entered the drone.

There was no light showing through the crack. Aaron pushed the door back. After a foot or so overhead lighting leading away from the hatch snapped on. After five hundred years the relays in the hatch still worked. That meant that other things might still work.

Terrance and the others broke into cheers when the word was passed back to them.

What they were about to enter was nothing less than another time capsule. A world that had remained untouched by the outside for centuries. Everyone stepped through the hatch and into the past.

They checked their communications and then resealed the hatch. The hatch in the drone was closed just in case the airlock seal failed. They would have to be let out when they wanted to leave. The control panel on the inside had not been jury-rigged. At this point they were locked in with no escape. Leading away from them was a passageway.

Next, to boost the communications signal, they set up an amplifier carried by one of the soldiers. They needed to be able to talk with the Georgana.

Aaron tested it. "Terrance how do you copy?"

"Loud and clear," came the answer.

The lighted passage extended almost the entire length of the complex. These time travelers slowly made their way down the hallway. On the right side were several sealed doors that required a key card to enter. At the far end stood an open elevator. Nothing was labeled or tagged. The walls and ceiling were gun metal gray. Existing in a sealed, dust free environment had preserved everything down to the paint on the walls.

Everyone stood in front of the elevator. Aaron started to step in. Captain Hickman stopped him. He held up his palm. "Wait, Let me check it out."

Aaron stopped. The Captain eased up to the opening. As he broke the plain of the doorway, lights came on inside and a green arrow, pointing down, flashed above the door.

The elevator car was fifteen feet deep and ten feet across, inside. Captain Hickman stepped in and walked around.

Aaron looked at Beth. "Ladies first or in this case second."

She stepped in. The others followed. The last man was redirected by Captain Hickman to remain in the passageway.

"Remain here," the Captain said. "Keep an eye on the front door."

There were no floor numbers, just an up arrow and a down arrow.

Beth commented. "I guess it only stops once."

Aaron pushed the down arrow. A mechanical trip closed somewhere, and with a slight jerk the elevator descended into the sea floor.

A readout above the door changed quickly. It became evident the numbers represented feet and they were sinking fast.

Beth asked. "Anyone wondering why all this stuff still works?"

Aaron said what the others were thinking. "Scheduled maintenance?"

The changing numbers began to slow down. The readout was approaching two hundred. Between one hundred and ninety and two hundred they had slowed to one every couple of seconds and then the elevator jerked to a stop. They had arrived.

The door slid open and Beth got her answer. A four-foot tall, wheeled maintenance robot greeted them, literally.

In a human female voice it said, "Welcome to the Blue Ridge Mountain research facility. How may I help you?"

Aaron looked at Beth, smiled and said, "I wonder how long it's waited to say that?"

"Five hundred and four years, two hundred days, eighteen hours, forty-two minutes and twelve seconds approximately," came the answer. Everyone laughed.

Captain Hickman got back to business. "I need an atmospheric check."

"One hundred percent nitrogen," replied the robot.

One of the clones stepped up with an air-sampling device in his hand. He made some adjustments, checked the readouts and said, "It's right. Pure nitrogen."

Aaron looked at him. "Nitrogen?"

The robot said, "Wait."

"The lack of oxygen," said Beth, "could explain this level of preservation."

A slight breeze entered the elevator. The clone took another reading. "Oxygen reading at twenty percent. No detectable issues."

One of the researchers commented. "It's the undetectable ones I'm worried about."

The Captain looked around and said, "Only one way to find out."

With that he broke the seal between his suit and his mask. After a small rush of air he removed the headpiece. Even he was reluctant to take that first breath. A few seconds later he blew out what was in his lungs and inhaled through his nose. Everyone watched.

Somebody asked, "Well?"

"Lubricant," he said. "I think it's our little friend."

Everyone followed his lead and removed their headpieces.

Aaron stepped toward the little robot. It held its ground.

It asked, "First you must answer the security question. Who was the first person to enter New Atlantis?"

Aaron answered, "Christopher Wincrest."

The small robot deployed a weapon. "Incorrect. Who was the first person to enter New Atlantis?"

One of the military brought his pulse rifle to bear on the robot. A single round from the robot's weapon killed the man instantly. Blood splattered the inside of the elevator and everyone in it.

Several others started to respond, but stopped when Aaron raised his hand. "Stop, it's programmed to defend itself. We're boxed in. Next time it might take us all out." Aaron keyed his com-link back to the Georgana. "Terrance, you there?"

"Yes, what's wrong?"

"We've encountered a small problem. I need the answer to a question. Who was the first person to enter New Atlantis?"

The silence was deafening. Terrance's voice came across. "Commander Edward Willingham."

The little robot secured its weapon and rolled back from the elevator. "Welcome, you may enter."

Everyone eased their way out of the elevator. Beth looked back at the body. "What do we do about him?"

Captain Hickman motioned to one of his men. "Take the elevator back up. Place him on the drone. Tell 'em to carry him back to the Georgana. Have him placed in the reefer. We'll take him back to be buried."

The man stepped into the elevator careful to avoid the body and the blood and pushed the up arrow. The door shut.

One of the soldiers next to Aaron said, "Let me take that little bugger out." He began to handle his weapon.

Aaron placed his hand on the pulse rifle. "No, that robot may be the only way to bring this place back on line."

"Well, when we don't need it anymore, it's mine." The soldier walked away.

The robot seemed to sense something and kept the soldier in its field of view until he rejoined the others.

Beth asked, "How do we find whatever they called a control center?"

A clone standing within earshot looked their way. "Why don't we just ask? The robot seems to have a fairly sophisticated AI."

Aaron thought for a second and then said. "We're friends again, right? Why not."

Captain Hickman walked up. "I think we'll break up into three squads and search this place from top to bottom."

Aaron started toward the robot then glanced back at the Captain. "Good idea, but we better ask permission first."

The Captain watched as Aaron approached the robot. "We need to find the control center. Can you help us?"

The robot turned toward a hallway leading off to the right. "Follow me."

The robot pulled away. Everyone began to run to keep up. It sensed this and slowed down to allow everyone to catch up.

The hallway had no rooms that opened onto it. At the end it turned to the right and opened up into another elevator lobby. Where everything up to now had been purely utilitarian in appearance this lobby was a drastic change. The walls were dark maple with polished brass accents. The elevator doors, three of them, were dark onyx set in brass frames.

Beth summed it up for all of them. "Wowwww."

The robot had a wireless interface with the elevators and opened the middle set of doors. It stood back and allowed the others to enter. The inside walls were marble with wood trim. The robot followed them in. There was a control panel that indicated the complex had six levels. The button marked with a two lit up, the doors closed and the descent began.

The ride down took less than thirty seconds. No one said anything, but everyone watched the robot. The elevator stopped and the doors opened to total darkness. The robot rolled out. A few moments later overhead lighting began to brighten the room.

Aaron stepped to the doors. "Let's see what we have." He stepped out followed by everyone else.

The décor reflected its purpose. Not as bleak and colorless as the first halls but not as warm as the second elevator lobby. The room was round. Twenty feet in from the wall was a glass enclosed circular control center. It occupied the entire center portion of the room. Through the glass segmented wall you could see a number of workstations located around the perimeter. On an elevated area in the center sat three chairs surrounded by consoles.

Beth asked, "Now that we've found it what do we do with it?"

"Nothing, if we can't find a way in," said Aaron. He looked at the Captain and pointed. "Go that way and see if you can find an entrance."

Captain Hickman waved and he and two of his men started around one side while Aaron and Beth went the other way. Everyone else, including the robot, waited.

A minute later the Captain shouted. "Got it."

Everyone headed that way. In a few moments they stood outside an arched entrance. The glass sliding doors had a card activation slot.

The Captain looked at the slot and turned to Aaron. "What do you want us to do?" He raised his weapon. "It's glass. We can take the doors down if we need to."

The robot's voice came from behind them. "Not required. The security protocols were suspended when I granted you access to the site."

The robot moved forward. Everyone stepped aside. It approached the doors; the locking system tripped and the doors slid open. The robot entered the control center followed by everyone else.

Aaron keyed his com-link. "Terrance, you still there?"

"Your signal is weak," came the answer. "But I can still make you out. Where are you?"

"We're on the second sublevel inside the control center. We've loss a member of the squad. The drone is returning with him to the Georgana."

"What happened?"

Aaron looked at the robot. "When I see you."

"The drone is docking now," said Terrance. "We've recovered the mule. Jton and I will be coming over. Wait where you are until I get there."

Aaron spoke into his com-link. "Take the elevator at the end of the hall."

The robot started for the entrance. "I'll go get them."

"Just wait inside the lock," said Aaron, "The robot will meet you."

"What robot?"

"I'll fill you in when you get here. You won't need the environmental suits. We could all use a change of clothes." Aaron released the transmit button on his com-link.

Terrance answered. "See you soon."

Beth was up on the platform looking over the consoles. The clones and the Humanoids were comparing notes. The others were using the available seating to get off their feet.

The Captain walked up to Aaron. "This place is very interesting, but why are we here?"

"The underground sites, New Atlantis, all of it originated here. If we can revive some of the people, what they know will be invaluable."

"You mean some of the people that built this place are still here?"

"In a sense. Their memories are stored here along with samples of their DNA. With the robots help I hope to clone some of them and then transfer their memories back."

"I don't know," said the Captain. "Sounds like trouble waiting to happen."

"That's why you're here. To handle trouble if it happens."

Forty-five minutes later the robot escorted Terrance, Jton and several others, with the requested clothing, into the control center. Beth, being a married female, took hers and left for the elevator to change. Aaron followed, but she waved him back. Aaron and the others changed in the control center.

Chapter twenty-four: Help from the past

While all that was going on the robot had moved to one of the workstations. For all its access to the site, this was the one room it had been denied access to until now. The console lit up. Windows opened up on the screen and data began to scroll down the display. A moment later a digitized rendering of Jake Taylor's face appeared on the screen.

"Ally, it's been a long time," said Jake. "I assume we have visitors."

"The first in over five hundred years," she said.

"Five hundred... Have any of them survived?"

"Yours and four others."

Jake's face took on a concerned look. "I sense something else, what happened?"

"My security protocols caused me to kill one of these people when they tried to enter the site. I fear for my safety."

"Bring them to me."

Ally backed away, turned and moved toward the others.

Beth walked up just as Aaron finished pulling on his boots. "What do you think of all this," she asked Terrance?

"Pretty impressive. Aaron just filled me in on what happened. Maybe we should shut down the robot."

"Please don't," came Ally's voice from behind them. They all turned as she rolled up. "There's someone who wishes to speak with you. Please follow me." She turned and started back toward the console. They all looked at one another and then followed her.

As they entered Jake's field of vision from the monitor he greeted them. "Welcome, it's been a very long time."

Terrance recognized him. "Jake Taylor!"

"I'm sorry, I'm at a loss."

"My name is Terrance Lieberman."

"Lieberman?"

"Yes, I'm descended from Daniel Lieberman."

"Janet Crowley's son-in-law," said Jake.

Aaron broke in. "Excuse us but I'm Aaron Colure and this is my wife Beth."

Terrance picked it up. "Sorry, this is Jake Taylor the man who headed up the team that made our two worlds possible."

"I would like all of you to meet Ally," Jake said, "My wife."

Ally spoke up. "I'm very sorry for the loss of your team member."

Everyone looked at the robot.

"Please don't blame her for the death." Jake continued, "Until the protocols were bypassed she had no control over what happened. It was a programmed response."

"Let me get this straight," said Beth. "Your wife exists inside this machine?"

"Just like me, her memories, her knowledge, maybe even her soul, has been hard coded into its flash memory. We needed someone to look after everything. That steel contraption she exists in is the only thing that's kept this place alive, in a manner of speaking, but not for much longer. The power source has been stretched to its limit."

The Captain and several others walked up. "Who are you talking to," he asked?

'Our host," answered Terrance. Then to Jake, "If everything's been hard coded we can safely move it to another location."

"The cooling system is failing. When that happens a two kiloton melt down will crush this entire complex."

Terrance asked, "How long?"

265

"No way to know at this point. A week, a month, tomorrow, besides there's only five of us left to save."

"What do you mean," asked Beth.

Ally answered. "In the beginning there were fifty-one of us. At first we thought we would have to sacrifice one in order to save the rest. Someone had to be here to complete the last transfer with no way to save themselves. Trying to choose that person ended in violence, and we almost lost it all. Then we came up with me, or it, or whatever you want to call this thing I'm in. Part of the failsafe system in place requires the introduction of the person's living DNA to override the security protocol that will erase the flash memory when those modules are removed from storage."

"Terrance asked, "Why would you even do that?"

"Paranoia was running pretty high. We didn't know how well the counter attack had worked. We didn't want anyone to find this site and extract the location of New Atlantis or any of the other sites. The DNA requirement wasn't noted anywhere. In the end it was left to Ally to protect all of this for whatever amount of time. No one had any idea that it would take this long."

The Captain broke in. "Why do we need all of this? We know the location of the other underground sites. I think we need to leave. If this place goes up and we're still here everything we've done so far will amount to nothing."

Jake answered him. "He's right. All I ask is that you take Ally with you."

Ally rolled her way to the console. "No! She said to Jake. "The only thing that's kept me going is the thought of being back with you some day." She deployed her weapon. "I won't go without you."

By now everyone had gathered around the console. They all stepped away from her.

Aaron asked Ally, "How long will it take to extract Jake's memory core?"

"An hour, we have to go to level three to get the DNA key. It's in cryo storage. It'll take a little while to thaw to the point where we can use it. Then we go to level four to access the mainframe. I can't do it by myself. I can't get up the stairs to access the core storage rack."

Aaron turned to Terrance. "Get everybody back on the drone. I'll go with her..."

Beth grabbed him and pulled him aside. "No, all they need is a set of hands. Anyone can do this."

"I can't trust this to anyone else. Besides nothing's gonna happen. Like he said it could be weeks."

She was scared to death and it showed in her voice, "Or minutes, please don't do this."

"Listen to me. We need these people..."

"They're not people," she said. "Just zero's and ones encoded on a piece of silicon."

"They were there at the beginning. They know things we'll never know. If nothing else they'll remind us of where we came from, and where we wound up. We have to learn from our mistakes, and we can't afford to make the mistake of throwing all of this away."

Beth wiped tears from her eyes. She knew he was right. "You move your ass." They rejoined the others. She looked at Ally. "If anything happens to him I'll turn you into a pile of scrap metal." She started for the entrance. "Come on let's get the hell outta here."

Jton moved to catch up with her. Terrance waved the others out and then looked at Aaron. "You're right. We need these people but we need you too. Hurry..."

Ally looked at the screen. "We'll get you out."

Jake replied, "I love you."

The screen went blank. Ally swung around and headed for the entrance. Aaron ran after her.

By the time Aaron and Ally reached the elevators the center one was closing. She activated the one on the left. The doors opened and she and Aaron entered. She lit up the number three. The doors closed and the elevator started down.

Aaron said, "I know what it means to lose someone you love. My first wife was killed because of all of this."

"She's wrong. We're a lot more than just circuitry. At the moment I'm scared to death."

The doors opened and he followed Ally out. She took a left down the hall and stopped at a door marked cryo lab number three. It started to open and then the lights flickered and it stopped about half way. Ally didn't hesitate she drove straight through bending it out of the way. Aaron followed her in.

She went to a glass door. This time it opened all the way. Inside was what she was looking for. Several rows of small glass cylinders sat in individual compartments. Most of them were dark. Five still showed a light. The frosting on the glass indicated they were still frozen.

Aaron asked. "This is all that's left?"

"Yes, the others have failed"

"Pull them all. If they've survived this long I can't let them die now."

She opened each compartment and removed what looked like a metal syringe from each. She placed them on a tray, picked it up and headed out. He followed her.

Beth and the others were nearing the air lock when the entire place shuttered. She stopped and looked back toward the elevator. "I have to go back."

Jton took her by the arm. "What honor do him if both die."

She looked up at him and then shouted at the empty elevator. "Hurry, damn you."

The airlock had been opened and the others had entered the drone. She didn't move.

Jton looked back at the open elevator and then down at her. "Go, I get." He stepped away.

She took him by the arm. He looked back. "Thank you." She let him go and watched until he entered the elevator. After another moment she entered the drone.

Aaron and Ally stood before a raised platform. Along that platform were the modules that contained what remained of the lives of fifty human beings. Each was numbered to match its corresponding DNA sample. Each had a red light glowing above it. Now it was a waiting game.

"Seeing him again was almost like seeing a ghost," said Ally. "I had to dispose of the bodies after the transfers were complete. They were incinerated and the ashes were dispersed into the sea. It was very hard."

Ally monitored the temperature of the samples. Her sensors would tell her when they were fluid enough to be injected. The lights flashed again and the room shook.

Aaron nervously looked around. "How much longer?"

"Almost," came her answer. "We'll need something to move them on."

Against the wall across the room was a metal cart. Aaron went for it. By the time he was back with it she handed him the tray.

He climbed the stairs to the platform and began looking for the numbers to match the keys.

She called out. "That one is Jake."

He checked the number and inserted the key. He pressed the button on the end with his thumb and the content was forced in. A moment later the light turned green and the module popped out about and inch. He pulled it out, sat it down and went looking for the next. In a few minutes he had five containers to hand down to her. She placed them on the cart. As he leaned over the railing to hand her the last one the room shook again. He lost his footing and fell landing across the cart on his left side. You could hear the ribs crack.

Ally tried to help him up. He was in a great deal of pain, but managed to get to his feet with her help. She pushed the cart toward the door. Aaron managed two steps before going to his knees. He began to cough and blood from a pierced lung dripped from his mouth. At that moment Jton entered the room.

He walked to Aaron put one arm behind his back, the other behind his knees and easily picked him up. Ally had stopped.

Jton hurried past her toward the door. Ally quickly followed him from the room pushing the cart.

Beth had waited as long as she could. She went through the airlock into the hall just as the elevator doors opened. Her heart sank when she saw Jton with Aaron in his arms. She screamed "Help," and ran to meet them.

She reached Jton and her hand went to her mouth. Ally stopped at the entrance to the airlock, turned and watched as Terrance and others ran past her.

Aaron's mouth and chin were bloody. The front of his shirt was soaked. She couldn't say anything. Her heart was in her throat.

Aaron smiled at her. "I always was a little clumsy."

She was crying. "Please, don't talk."

"No..." He coughed up a little more blood. "I have to say something. You have to promise me something."

She took his hand and kissed it.

"Promise me something." His voice was soft and trailing off.

Her world was dying before her. Everyone else was standing with her.

"Promise me you'll finish what we've started." His voice got stronger. "Promise me, damn it." He coughed again.

That startled her into a response. "I promise."

He smiled, glanced up at Jton. "Take care of her, big guy. I think she likes you."

With his body cavity filling with blood his heart stopped. The light left his eyes and he died.

Beth slumped to the floor, sat and cried into her hands. Jton passed Aaron off to two others, leaned down, picked her up and carried her into the drone.

Ally's metal body had no way of expressing the utter sense of despair she felt with the loss of this one human life.

Chapter twenty-five: A brave new world

The drone broke its connection with the site and headed back to the Georgana. Captain Kemp was informed of Aaron's death. He in turn informed the rest of the crew. When the drone was recovered a small honor guard was in place to receive the body.

The Georgana submerged and headed away from the site at best possible speed. Forty minutes later the nuclear power plant beneath the site went critical and then went up. Four hundred feet below the surface the sub was still buffeted by the wave that passed overhead.

It was decided to suspend the mission and return to New Houston. Time was needed to heal.

*   *   *

Word was passed to Quanterra about the death of Aaron Colure. After returning Aaron's body the Georgana returned to Quanterra, docked in the bay it had departed from, took on fifty new adventurers from the city under the sea and returned to the Texas coast.

Aaron was laid to rest in a very private ceremony. Two months later a memorial service was held. Colonel Hathaway, Kera and their son Robert, stood with Beth and Jton and some two thousand others to pay their respects.

Clones, one female named Ally, one male named Jake and the four others saved by Aaron attended, but stood apart from Aaron's family and close friends.

The DNA encoded into the memory modules and the robot, was used to recreate exactly, those ancient ancestors.

Robert had matured into an adult in record time. Then the process all but stopped. The aging process was now even slower than that of a normal human being. His capacity to learn was only exceeded by his physical being. He had shown resistance to almost all known disease and his healing capacity was phenomenal. These traits would eventually allow him to fulfill his destiny. Researchers were anxious to have him mate. He informed them that would happen in his own good time.

Beth would keep her promise. She and Jton would put together another expedition. The Georgana dropped them off on the eastern coast and with Jake's help they located the Atlanta site. What they found had long since passed into oblivion when the power plant below it had gone critical.

Over the next three months they would locate two more. The first one contained a small pocket of survivors happy to have been found. Their ancestors had long since shut down the reactor.

The second proved to be much more hostile. The reactor had failed, but instead of imploding it had just leaked radiation and over time had mutated the inhabitants. It cost the lives of several of their party.

This was the world they lived in. It would take humanity another thousand years to pull itself together to once again rule planet Earth hopefully with more respect for it, and themselves, than was shown the first time around.

* * *

As for now, two years later, Quanterra would launch the SM Aaron Colure. The vessel was four hundred feet long and reached four stories into the air. It would carry a crew of thirty along with two hundred passengers and several tons of cargo. Its power source was hydrogen power cells. Its fuel supply as limitless as the oceans it would traverse. A method of deploying the blister to the outer skin would enable the submersible to resist the water pressure, and just about anything else while submerged.

When on the surface exposure to the air dissolved the blister allowing the vessel to function there. Beth was invited to christen the ship. She was happy to do so.

Many other vessels would be constructed through the centuries, but the Aaron Colure would always represent the heart and soul of those first brave men and women to venture back to the surface. The vessel would remain commissioned for one hundred and twenty-one years. In that time it would be largely responsible for bringing the two worlds together. Beth thought it was a fitting monument to the memory of her husband.

After the christening she and Jton returned to New Houston. In the waning light of day they stood together in front of two carved headstones. One was for Colin Becker and the other for Aaron Colure. History will remember both of these men as heroes who were largely responsible for the rebirth of humanity.

She kept her hair clipped short. Her clothing closely resembled that worn by Jton. Her jacket-like top was sleeveless. Weapons were slung across their backs. He carried his crossbow and she carried a pulse rifle. Attached to her right thigh was a nine-inch knife and scabbard. Her exposure to the sun had turned her skin a golden brown. She had a knife scar that started at the top of her left shoulder and ran down the outside of her arm to just above her elbow. Her body was sculptured and lean.

She stepped forward and knelt in front of Aaron's marker. Tears welled up in her eyes. She slowly ran her fingers across his name.

More to herself she said, "I love you. I will always love you."

Tears ran down her cheeks. She wiped them away with her other hand. After a moment she stood, stepped back, turned and stepped up to Jton. He pulled her to him. She placed her arms around him, buried her face in his chest and quietly sobbed.

He let her cry for a few moments and then said, "Need go."

She stepped back, again wiped her face with both hands, stepped around him and walked away. He turned and walked off beside her.

They stayed together for the next fifteen years until he reached the end of his life cycle. Together they faced many adventures. They became legends and legend has it she bore him a daughter. Historians say that was impossible. Then again, isn't that what legends are made of. But that's another story.

THE END

4912092R0

Made in the USA
Charleston, SC
04 April 2010